Mystery
on
Meadowsweet
Grove

BOOKS BY CLARE CHASE

Mystery
on
Meadowsweet
Grove

CLARE CHASE

bookouture

Published by Bookouture in 2024

An imprint of Storyfire Ltd.
Carmelite House
50 Victoria Embankment
London EC4Y 0DZ

www.bookouture.com

ISBN: 978-1-83525-220-8
eBook ISBN: 978-1-83525-219-2

To Lizzie, with thanks for everything that you do and the community you've built

PROLOGUE

A SATURDAY IN JUNE

It was a perfect early summer's day and Saxford St Peter was milling with people. Almost everyone was involved in the village's inaugural open-gardens contest. They were buzzing with nerves or excitement and either waiting for the judges or dashing round the village to size up the competition.

A man on the corner of Dark Lane was tweaking anxiously at a rose, trying to alter its position so it would be seen to best advantage. Out on Heath Lane, a woman spotted some bindweed she'd swear had grown overnight. Oh, the tension! She almost wished the event wasn't taking place. She'd spent hours on it that she couldn't spare, but everyone else was taking part. They'd think she was standoffish if she didn't join in.

As the woman yanked up the bindweed, she felt faintly resentful of Cleo Marbeck, who'd organised the event. Cleo was a born leader, with her jewellery shops, multiple properties and way of steering the village in whatever direction she chose.

It wasn't everyone who could announce a new event and have the locals rallying around. And yet Cleo wasn't universally liked. She was an odd combination – bags of charisma, plenty of backbone, but ruthless in business according to gossip. And of course, there was the scandal. An old, old rumour and baseless perhaps, but who knew, really? A lot of people said there was no smoke without fire, and with a death involved—

Her thoughts were interrupted by the sight of her husband, stepping through the French windows with the judges just behind him. The woman stuffed the bindweed into her pocket and felt slightly sick.

In another part of the village, people were funnelling into Cleo's garden. The woman at the head of the queue was surprised not to find her waiting for them. When you visualised her, you imagined her striding forwards, smiling, confident, immaculately dressed with a sparkle in her eye, especially amongst male company. A lot of the lighter gossip was about her love life. The heavier stuff was way more serious. It made you wonder.

Cleo had done well with her own garden of course, just as she did with everything. The colours were magnificent: hot-pink salvias and saturated-purple lavender. Bumblebees landed on bloom after bloom.

'Cleo's one of life's winners, isn't she?' the woman said to her daughter, but the words died on her lips.

What was that, ahead of them, near the pond?

Legs, stretched out on the gravel. And an outstretched arm. Limp.

Her breath caught in her throat, her chest tight as a drum.

She walked forward without wanting to. Until she met Cleo Marbeck's blank gaze, directed towards the glorious blue sky.

Cleo's tailored top was dark around her chest and shoulders and her hair was damp. Close by, a weathered statue of a water nymph lay on its side, and from the back of Cleo's head came a trickle of blood.

1

A WEEK EARLIER

Eve Mallow was enjoying her walk up Meadowsweet Grove. It was one of her favourite lanes in Saxford St Peter; she'd aired her dachshund Gus along it many times. When she'd first moved to the village, she'd hesitated, because it felt private. There were only five houses on the road, tucked in amongst the lush green foliage, and no parking. At this time of year, the lane was smothered with flowers: honeysuckle, creeping St John's wort and guelder rose. The lane was narrow, so you were never far from one of the cottages. It would be a dream for children playing hide-and-seek, with places to duck between the plants and side passageways begging to be explored.

A couple of months after she'd moved, Eve had realised it wasn't a dead end after all. If you walked far enough you found a footpath, to the right of The Briars, where Cleo Marbeck lived. The path took you to Parson's Walk and on towards the village green. It made it a perfectly legitimate dog-walking loop. Eve had tried to analyse why she'd felt shifty going there when she'd thought it was a cul-de-sac. She wouldn't normally. When she'd asked her friend Viv about it, she'd discovered that Cleo owned four of the five houses on the road. The three she didn't occupy were rented to personal contacts and the village regarded the grove as hers. Perhaps that was what Eve had picked up on.

Eve passed the one house Cleo didn't own: Shell Cottage, a tidy whitewashed place with a red-tiled roof. It must feel odd to be an independent bastion in Cleo's mini empire.

A moment later, she and Gus reached Cleo's house, right at the end of the road, as though the grove was its driveway and existed to frame the property. The Briars was Edwardian, painted Suffolk pink, and larger than the other homes, though they were older.

The front door was ajar, and Eve could hear voices beyond. She wasn't the first, then. That made a change. She'd love to switch off the habit of arriving early but attempting a more laid-back approach made her twitch. She pushed the door wider and entered the hall, to be greeted by Cleo herself.

She was around Eve's age – somewhere in her fifties – and glamorous, the picture of rude health, her hazel eyes sparkling. The ruby and gold necklace she wore went with her profession. She sold the most sought-after vintage jewellery in Suffolk from her three stores. People came from miles around to buy her goods and she was about to expand further, sending a new recruit, Abby Porter, down to London to open an outlet. Eve imagined the Suffolk success was down to Cleo personally. She had drive and charisma. There were odd whispers about her: that she broke up marriages and wasn't a hundred per cent honest, but there was something compelling about her too. Abby would have to work wonders to replicate Cleo's success, but she had the required experience – she'd come home to Suffolk from Paris, where she'd worked in a top boutique.

'Eve! Excellent! Come and help yourself to a drink.' Cleo shepherded her over the tiled floor, past the steep stairs and into a spacious living room at the back of the house. They found Moira, the village storekeeper, there, peering at the message in a card on the mantelpiece. She leaped back hastily, and Eve suppressed a smile. They had come for a planning meeting for the open-gardens event, but Moira would be in it for the food and gossip.

She was blushing, and Eve took pity on her as she lifted a glass from the drinks table. It was time to distract their host. 'That's a lovely drawing.' She pointed at a framed picture on the wall above a bookcase. The subject was a thatched cottage, a bower to one side, the artist's name in the corner.

'It is, isn't it?' Cleo touched the frame lightly. 'A friend of mine drew it from a photo as we sat chatting. I used to love watching her work – so focused – and when I admired the picture, she gave it to me.' She looked emotional, but blinked quickly and the glistening was gone. 'I never imagined how significant it would prove. Funny how small, chance happenings can alter the course of one's life.' She turned to stare out of the window and swallowed. It was almost as though she'd forgotten Eve and Moira were there.

Moira caught Eve's eye, cocked her head and raised her eyebrows dramatically.

Embarrassingly unsubtle. But Eve was curious too, of course. As an obituary writer, discovering people's histories was hard-wired in her. She wished she could ask more, but at that moment there was a knock at the door and Cleo dashed to answer it. 'Come in, come in!' She was back on form. 'Don't stand on ceremony.'

'It's no wonder she looked so emotional, Eve,' Moira said breathlessly, before Cleo returned. 'That drawing was done by Honor Hamilton, who died at the bottom of the stairs in this very house. And I can tell you—'

'I'm sure you can, Moira, but perhaps now is not the moment.'

Moira's mouth opened again but she was interrupted by Viv, who bounded into the room and screeched to a halt next to them. 'What's all this? Gossip?' Her hair, a vibrant green this season, gleamed in the sunlight slanting through the window.

Eve shook her head. Viv was incapable of lowering her volume and Cleo was eyeing them from the doorway.

'Not at all, Viv,' Moira said quickly. 'We were just talking about our duties for the event.' Moira was keeping notes on jobs, so that she could boss everyone around. She'd already taken a big, important-looking folder out of her bag and put it on a beautifully polished coffee table. The whole room was elegant, all the proportions just right, with lovely period furniture.

'It's a bit intimidating, isn't it, the air of calm?' Viv was following Eve's gaze. 'For me at least. You'd be fine with it of course. But I mean, no clutter! What's that all about?'

Dark-haired and elegant Abby Porter appeared to Viv's right and raised an eyebrow. She'd come on board to help monitor the open-gardens' finances. 'It's all a front.' There was an edge to her voice. 'You need to consider what goes on behind closed doors.' She moved across the room and opened the understairs cupboard.

Cleo was laughing. 'I'll get you for this, Abby!' She chuckled fondly as she served another committee member a drink, but Abby wasn't even smiling. When Eve had seen them together previously, they'd looked like bosom buddies. They were full of excitement about Abby launching the London store, of course. Now, Abby's face was white and tight-lipped. She stood back so they could see the cupboard.

It was stuffed with papers, boxes and general junk. Eve itched for a couple of hours and some solitude. She could have it all sorted.

'How did you discover her secret?' Viv's voice was full of awe.

Eve noticed how tightly Abby clutched her drink. 'She sent me to find a vase once, but I got the wrong cupboard.'

'Amazing!' Viv sounded delighted. 'And how are things going with the plans for the London store?'

Abby didn't reply. There was definitely trouble afoot.

'I wanted to ask you more about it last time, only everyone kept going on about the open gardens.' Viv seemed oblivious. 'How did you hear about the job? Did Cleo advertise it in Paris?'

'It wasn't quite like that.' Abby's voice was tight, barely controlled. 'Getting the role came about by chance. We connected when we realised we were being two-timed by the same man.'

Awkward. But that didn't explain her behaviour now. The two-timing must be old news.

Abby bit a nail. 'My relationship with Sean was long-distance by that stage – we both grew up here, but then the job in France came up. When Cleo and I realised what was going on, we ditched him.' Her voice slowed. 'Cleo treated me like a sister and she was excited when she discovered my profession. She asked if I'd launch the London store and I leaped at the chance. I ditched my Paris job and moved into the cottage our ex had moved out of, here on the grove. I should have dumped him years earlier. He always had a wandering eye.'

It seemed as though they'd triumphed over a cheating swine, but Abby didn't sound jubilant.

She fell silent and Eve explained about her own divorce to take the pressure off. She hated talking about it, but something was needed.

At last, a straggling committee member arrived and Cleo called order. Jobs were assigned, from working out rotas so people could take it in turns to explore the event, to collecting outstanding entry fees. 'I'll pop round the village to take some photos for advance publicity this week, and you're down to categorise the entries, Abby.' There were different classes according to garden size. Cleo's eyes were on her beautiful notebook, thick and heavy in her hands, decorated with bluebirds and honeysuckle, but at last she looked up.

Abby was staring at her, a tic going in her cheek. Cleo started to speak again, but she lost her thread each time their eyes met, Eve noticed.

When she'd finished, she crossed the room to talk to Abby, taking her hand, but Abby yanked it away.

Eve heard snatches of their conversation.

'What on earth is it?' Cleo's frown was deep.

Abby's hand was up to her cheek. She muttered something inaudible.

Eve caught Cleo's impatient reply. 'I don't believe it! Someone's been talking when they shouldn't have!'

'That's hardly the point!' Abby's voice rose and cracked with emotion. 'You know what you said before I moved in! This was massive for me! Massive!'

Cleo's tone hardened. 'Nothing's final until a contract's signed. You're savvy enough to know that. I need to tackle this before the whole village is talking about it.'

'That's the least that you deserve!'

They seemed to have forgotten their audience. Viv mouthed, *Awks.*

Cleo snatched Abby's hand again, more firmly this time. Eve had to strain to hear her words. 'In the end I could never give you the role. You know how well I knew Sean.' Her eyes were fixed on Abby's. 'He told me, Abby. Do you understand? I know what you're capable of!'

Abby jerked away again, so hard she crashed into the drinks table. A couple of glasses tumbled and elderflower cordial poured onto the carpet. Abby swung towards the door in the now-silent room. Eve caught her expression: fury and upset. Disbelief. In the doorway, she paused and turned.

'I gave up everything for you, Cleo. I had a wonderful life in Paris. But I suppose I can guess who you've chosen to head up the London store instead of me!'

She wheeled towards Richie Hamilton, a young man in his late twenties who'd been put in charge of selling raffle tickets.

Eve had heard people talking about Richie in Monty's, the teashop Viv owned, where Eve worked part-time to supplement her freelance journalist's income. Richie was discussed because of his appearance. He was one of the most objectively beautiful people Eve had ever seen. Like a classical statue, with exquisite bone structure. He was made flesh and blood by a mop of dark hair, bronzed skin and delicately shaped lips. He looked utterly confused at Abby's outburst.

Abby left then, slamming the door so hard that Cleo's antique vases rattled on her display shelves.

2

Cleo Marbeck stared after Abby for a moment, chewing her lip, but then turned to the committee members with a wry smile. 'I'm sorry about that, ladies and gentlemen. I owe you an explanation, but most of all Richie.'

She turned to him.

'Richie, darling, that was *not* how I wanted to offer you the London job! Someone must have gossiped before I had the chance to handle the situation like a professional.' She frowned. 'I'm sorry about the histrionics. We must talk about Abby and I'll explain. I can guarantee I haven't been unfair. But please say you'll take it! You've been excellent as my second-in-command here in Suffolk. You'll make the new store as iconic as the ones here.'

Richie's dark liquid eyes were wide, his lips parted.

'I'll support you every step of the way,' Cleo went on. 'Teach you everything I know.'

Eve wondered what that might mean. Cleo had built her fortune quickly. Eve tried not to listen to village gossip but it was impossible to blot it out completely. Some implied Cleo cut corners, some said a lot worse than that. Cleo always laughed and said they were jealous.

'Say you'll do it.' Cleo fixed Richie with her brandy-eyed gaze, a twinkle in her eye despite everything. 'It's your big chance. You've had some bad luck but it wasn't deserved. Now's the time to be selfish – grow into what you could be. I'm offering a good manager's wage and accommodation, of course. In a nice part of London.'

Richie blinked. 'Yes. Yes, I'll do it. Thank you, Cleo. But Abby—'

'Don't worry about her. She'll get over it. In the meantime, hooray!' Cleo's radiant smile lit the room. 'Never mind the elderflower! This calls for champagne!'

Cleo left for the kitchen as the rest of them turned to each other in silence. Eve could see Moira was desperate to dissect what had happened but it was awkward in front of Richie. Instead, they muttered their congratulations.

Cleo returned and they stood there, sipping their champagne stiffly. Eve wondered what the atmosphere would be like in Meadowsweet Grove. With Richie and Abby both occupying cottages owned by Cleo, things could get seriously tense. Though maybe Abby would leave, after what had happened.

She wondered what Abby had done. *I know what you're capable of!* Cleo had said.

At last, the meeting wound up and Eve, Viv and Moira walked home together.

Viv began to air her feelings when they were still worryingly close to The Briars. 'Poor Richie. Talk about an awkward situation. Everyone in Saxford thought Abby Porter was the firm choice for the job. It seemed like a natural next step for her.'

No wonder she'd been knocked for six. 'What's she been doing since she returned to England?'

Viv pulled a face. 'Working in the womenswear section of Parker's while the details of the London premises were finalised.'

It was the local department store. Not staid exactly, but unlikely to feature in Vogue any time soon.

Moira sighed. 'It's hardly the same as Paris.'

Eve felt the enormity of the situation. 'I suppose Abby should have insisted on a contract up front.'

Viv scoffed. 'She shouldn't have had to. There's a thing called common decency.'

Eve agreed, though in Abby's place she'd have got one signed and sealed before she'd boarded the Eurostar. She'd seen the murkier side of human nature after all the interviews she'd done.

They were cutting through Parson's Walk now, but still Eve glanced over her shoulder before she spoke. 'I wonder how Abby discovered she was out of the running. Cleo strikes me as a clever woman with a strong sense of self-preservation. I doubt she'd discuss the matter casually. Perhaps her staff aren't as discreet as she is.'

'Some people do like to gossip, Eve.' Moira shook her head. 'I find it shocking.'

Viv caught Eve's eye and Eve tried not to laugh.

'It's interesting that Richie said yes on the spot,' she said, when she'd recovered herself. She would have asked for time to think. It was a big decision.

'Why wouldn't he?' Viv replied. 'His previous business ventures went south. Now Cleo's offering him a dream ticket, all expenses paid.'

'And of course,' Moira said, 'dear Richie must feel a deep obligation to Cleo. After his mother died, she let his grandmother rent their house for next to nothing. He's had a secure upbringing, thanks to her.' She lowered her voice. 'Though some people do say she acted out of guilt. And it could be a troubled conscience that's led her to hire Richie now.'

Viv was shaking her head.

'No, but it's like you said, Viv, Richie's other ventures failed!'

Moira's eyes were bright. 'And it was Cleo who lost out. She loaned him the money for each of his enterprises. Choosing him to manage her London shop does seem a little odd.'

'What are you talking about?' Eve had come to Saxford from London four and a half years earlier; there were still gaps in her knowledge.

'Well, Eve,' Moira said, 'I'm afraid we did have some idea a long time ago that Cleo felt the need to... atone, shall we say.'

Viv rolled her eyes. 'But we changed our minds, didn't we?' She turned to Eve. 'The previous vicar put a stop to the gossip. He said it was poisonous and there was no evidence and everyone respected him enough to shut up.'

'We realised he was right,' Moira said, piously. 'But the trouble was, Cleo *was* heard having such a very violent argument with Richie's mother, just hours before she died. I was about to tell you her story just before the meeting, Eve. She drew that picture you were admiring. Cleo made their relationship sound so cosy, but in fact it was tempestuous. Fond one minute, antagonistic the next. Then one day, word went round that Richie's mother had discovered something terrible about Cleo. Cleo tried to get round her, plying her with drink. And the next thing we knew, Richie's mother was dead. Found at the bottom of the stairs in The Briars as I told you! So you see—'

Viv stepped in front of Moira so Eve's view of the storekeeper was blocked. 'Don't pay any attention, Eve. Cleo didn't own The Briars at the time.' She flicked a look at Moira. 'That family who were friends with the Oxleys lived there, don't you remember? They had to leave when the dad got that job in Germany. The place was empty.'

Moira's face poked round from behind Viv's shoulder again. 'That is true, Eve. Though it's said Cleo bought The Briars at a knock-down price, because no one wanted a place associated with tragedy.'

Viv took a deep breath and tried again. 'I can't remember the details, but Cleo had an alibi. She was nowhere near The Briars. As the vicar pointed out. Repeatedly. The coroner ruled the death was an accident.'

Moira shook her head. 'You're quite right, Viv. And of course, I shouldn't be talking out of turn. It's more your business than it is mine.'

Eve glanced at Viv. What did Moira mean by that?

But the storekeeper rushed on. 'And it's true about the alibi.' She paused, frowning. 'Though people pointed out that she might have had an accomplice. And guilt *would* explain her actions ever since.'

3

When they were alone again, Eve asked Viv what Moira had meant by the death being Viv's business, but Viv shook her head. 'I'll explain this evening at the pub.'

The only time she ever held back like that was when she needed to keep a brave face. She was about to re-enter the fray at Monty's. Not the moment for unbridled emotion. Eve gave her shoulder a squeeze and let her go.

She'd have to wait until their meet-up. They'd been planning to talk weddings. Viv's son Jonah was due to be married shortly and his fiancée Stevie was coming to stay with her in the run-up. Eve was glad she'd be around to monitor preparations. There was still a lot to do and, Viv being Viv, the plans were chaotic.

Eve was fetching her and Viv's drinks at the bar that evening when she discovered the answer to her question.

A man in a navy T-shirt was perched on a stool with his back to her, chatting to a friend. As Eve waited to be served, she heard him mention Cleo and Abby.

News of the row was bound to spread, of course. Moira had probably told everyone she'd bumped into.

The man in navy whistled. 'Anyway, sounds like there was quite a to-do. Of course, we talked about it at home. Mum still thinks Cleo was mixed up in Honor Hamilton's death so she's not surprised she's done the dirty on Abby Porter. Speaking of Honor, did you know her niece is due in Saxford any day now? It's her wedding in a couple of weeks.'

'What wedding?'

'To the son of the woman who runs the teashop. Mum thinks there'll be a standoff between the bride and Cleo. Or if there isn't then there should be. She can't see how anyone related to Honor can let the matter lie. She says she'll give the niece what for if she doesn't challenge Cleo. Reckons it's her duty.'

The other guy chuckled. 'Your mum, honestly. I wouldn't cross her!'

'Right.' Mr Navy T-shirt laughed too. 'Of course, there's no proof, but—'

Heck. A chill settled over Eve as one of the casual bar staff took her order.

Back at the table, she put a glass of Merlot in front of Viv, then sat down with her Shiraz. 'Viv, is Stevie Richie's cousin? Was the dead woman her aunt?' She'd known Stevie had been born in Saxford but her mother had moved to Glasgow, hence her plan to stay with Viv before the wedding.

Viv grimaced. 'I was going to tell you about it tonight, now Honor's death has cropped up. I don't mention it normally. The last thing Stevie needs is a tragic label hanging round her neck. I know what that's like.'

Viv's husband had died when her three children were young. She'd told Eve before how everyone had been more awkward with her afterwards.

'I understand.'

Viv's brow furrowed. 'How did you find out?'

Eve's heart sank. She was forced to explain what she'd heard at the bar.

Viv put her head in her hands. 'This is the kind of thing I was worried about. Stevie's meant to be in Saxford for a joyous reason. I want her and Jonah to have an idyllic wedding.' Her eyes met Eve's. 'It'll be ruined if people keep going on about what happened. I called her about it after the meeting, as a matter of fact. I thought I should warn her the gossip's kicked off again. She's determined to make a fresh start with Cleo but toxic talk like this will make it impossible.'

It was a miserable situation. 'Maybe we can help somehow.'

Viv nodded. 'That's why I wanted to talk to you about it. I want to do something concrete.'

'I can't see us calling order like the old vicar did. Though we could ask Jim to help.' The current incumbent was enormously well liked by believers and non-believers alike.

'Let's do that.' Viv bit her lip. 'But even if it damps things down, the rumours always resurface.'

'We'd need to unearth the truth to really stop the cycle.'

'I know. What about if we try to get it? I can't bear the thought of people dividing into huddles at the wedding, spewing bile. I want it to be perfect.'

Eve could understand that. She'd hate anything to mar her own son's upcoming celebrations. But proving a negative was a tall order. 'You want us to dig into Honor's death and somehow demonstrate that no one pushed her?'

Viv sipped her drink. 'Or work out who did.' She held up a hand before Eve could speak. 'I know, I know. It was investigated at the time and I was the one saying the conspiracy theories were rubbish. But the rumour stuck for so long, even my mum started to wonder if there was something in it. Cleo had an alibi – she can't be guilty personally – but the history is murky. It would help Richie, Stevie and Stevie's mum if we got the truth.'

Eve could see that. The death had probably been accidental,

but there was bound to be more to find out. There always was. The way Cleo talked about the picture Honor drew had been intense. *I never imagined how significant it would prove. Funny how small, chance happenings can alter the course of one's life.*

Why on earth had the drawing had such an impact? And why had Cleo appointed Richie in Abby's stead if his previous business ventures had been a flop? Was it really guilt?

'What do you think?' Viv leaned forward. 'Can we do it? Will you try to find out more? Please?'

The task might be a poisoned chalice but what Viv said was true: Honor's death was still affecting people. 'All right. I doubt it'll lead anywhere, but I'll do some research – quietly.'

It would be interesting to talk about it with her fiancé, Robin. As Saxford St Peter's gardener, he was lying low at home. The villagers had been pestering him ever since the open-gardens event was announced. Some wanted extra sessions and two had even offered him bribes to nobble the competition. He was down to act as an expert advisor to the judges, so he was determined to distance himself. At least people knew he was a former police detective now, dedicated to upholding law and order. He'd had to change his name and profession after outing corrupt colleagues down in London. Years later, the gang was behind bars and he was free to open up about his past. His expertise would be useful.

Eve ran her eyes over the pub's clientele. If any of the open-gardens committee came in, they were bound to talk about Cleo and the past, after Richie's sudden promotion. Eve would need to keep her eyes and ears open.

'Tell me everything you know. Let's start with Stevie.'

Viv's chest rose and fell. 'Honor was her mother's sister and Stevie wasn't a fan of Cleo, growing up. It's a fact that Cleo upset Honor and got her drunk before she died. She might never have fallen if it hadn't been for that.' She sighed. 'Stevie's mum had a breakdown after the death too. Stevie was just a young child at the time; it must have been very hard. They'd moved to another part of Suffolk by that stage, and I think her mum felt guilty that she hadn't kept a closer eye on Honor. Their parents had emigrated to Spain, so she didn't have much support.'

Eve grimaced. 'Rough all round.'

Viv nodded. 'All the same, Stevie does want to move on. She's determined to come to the open gardens, despite it being Cleo's gig. And she pushed to hold the wedding here because it's Jonah's home and she was brought up in Suffolk too. Her mum's another matter though – she'd have preferred them to tie the knot in Glasgow. Cleo's still persona non grata in her book.'

The thought of the villagers triggering a stand-off between Stevie and her mum was awful. Eve took a deep breath. 'Right, thanks. And what about Richie? He's accepted Cleo's job offer, but if half the village blames her for his mum's death – I'd expect him to have mixed feelings.'

'You'd think, wouldn't you?' Viv agreed. 'But he was brought up by his dad's mum, and she didn't think much of Honor either.'

How sad. But of course, Eve knew nothing of Honor's character. Perhaps she'd been difficult. 'Why was that?'

Viv sighed. 'I only know bits. Honor cleaned for my mum and dad for a while, and Mum said she was vulnerable. An innocent who'd married the wrong man, far too young. She was only nineteen or something when they got hitched. And before they knew it, they had Richie to look after too. Richie's dad tired of her. He might have worn a sharp suit and had a good salary but he wasn't kind or romantic. Mum said he treated her like a brainless skivvy. He left her shortly before she died.'

'He sounds awful.'

Viv nodded. 'And as I said, her family weren't in the village to help. Honor only had her mother-in-law, Joyce, and she was a controlling woman. I imagine she influenced Richie as he grew up.'

'Honor must have been desperately lonely.'

'Absolutely. Mum said it made her even more vulnerable. She took to latching on to anyone who was kind and charming with a strong character. That was where Cleo came in. Honor cleaned for her too and they seemed to form a close bond. Cleo was ten years older and sure of herself. Full of plans and energy. Mum said Honor was like a leaf, blowing in the wind.'

'And given their closeness, Honor could have found out something damning about Cleo?'

Viv sipped her wine. 'I'd say so.'

The picture Honor had drawn in Cleo's kitchen showed how informal their relationship had become. It was intriguing. When a sophisticate like Cleo befriended someone like Honor, it was usually because they wanted something. Eve had come across that dynamic when interviewing for obituaries. The more powerful partner might get a buzz from steering the weaker person's life, but it could be more than that. 'All this must be years ago.'

Viv nodded. 'Twenty-five by my reckoning.'

'Yet the gossip still flares up.' Saxford left Eve agog at times. She wouldn't go back to living in London, but a village had its downsides.

Viv shrugged. 'All those long memories. It's not constantly under discussion, of course. But every so often it comes to the fore. It kicked off big time eighteen months ago when Richie's granny died.' That had passed Eve by. 'Cleo spent a lot of time with her at the hospice. Saxford's usual suspects decided she was confessing to the part she'd played in Honor's death.'

Honestly! 'That doesn't even make sense. You told me Richie's granny didn't like Honor. Why would Cleo feel the need to unburden to *her*?'

Viv turned her palms upwards and shrugged. 'You're preaching to the converted. But the hardcore gossips were loath to abandon their theory and Cleo and Joyce weren't close.'

'So her presence at the end *was* odd.'

Viv nodded. 'It's something to get our teeth into and we need that. There's not much time to restore harmony before the wedding.'

It was true, the clock was ticking. On the upside, some of the key players who'd been at The Briars had appeared in the pub now. Cleo was clearly still celebrating, with Richie in tow. She was telling everyone what a success he'd be but Eve thought he looked nervous. Every so often, Cleo clutched Richie's hand and raised it in the air in triumph.

Abby had come in too, accompanied by a woman with tortoiseshell glasses. Abby's eyes had flicked towards Cleo as she'd entered the bar. Eve was sure she'd have run back out again if the other woman hadn't dragged her to a far-away table.

Eve leaned towards Viv and gave a subtle nod in the pair's direction. 'Do you know the woman with the tortoiseshell glasses?'

Viv nodded. 'Lara Oxley. She lives on Meadowsweet Grove in the one house not owned by Cleo.' She looked thoughtful. 'She and Abby must have made friends. Lara's the chief stylist at the salon at Parker's, so they work at the same place.'

Her beautifully cut bob fitted her profession. It swung this way and that as she turned her head.

'I'd give a lot to know what they're saying.' They were bound to talk about Cleo after the row earlier.

Eve needed an excuse to approach them, and in a moment, she spotted it. Beyond the pair, Gus and the pub schnauzer Hetty were receiving attention from a couple who'd come in for dinner. It would only be polite to check they weren't being inconvenienced.

She whispered her plan to Viv, then strolled towards the dogs, not moving too quickly.

'The way she's treated you is unbelievable,' Lara was saying, as Eve neared their table.

She moved beyond them, then snatched another glance.

Abby's head was in her hands. 'I should have been more wary. When something seems too good to be true it usually is. I can't think why I didn't—'

Eve missed the rest.

'Cleo meant you to think you'd got it!' Lara's voice was fierce and loud. 'You're eminently well qualified, whereas Richie's way too young. It's positively unfair to push him into the new role. I'm going to talk to her about it.'

Eve greeted the friendly dog lovers, but between pleasantries, she focused on the other conversation, shifting a little, so she could see what went on.

Lara was half standing but Abby had grabbed her arm. 'Please no!'

Lara looked taken aback. 'She shouldn't get away with this! So far all you've done for revenge is shout at her and show the open-gardens committee her grotty understairs cupboard!'

They must be close. Abby had clearly told Lara exactly what had happened.

The woman who was tickling Gus's tummy asked about Hetty and Eve gave a brief reply as Abby spoke again.

'I don't want you to talk to her, Lara!' She sounded angry. Scared. Eve guessed she was worried Cleo might reveal her secret: what she was 'capable of'. Whatever it was, it must be serious.

Eve asked the dog people another question, then guiltily tuned their answer out as Lara flumped back in her chair. 'All right then, I won't. But I don't think I can bear to stick around while Cleo lords it over everyone. I'll go away for a day or two as soon as I've done your open-gardens bit.'

'Thanks for offering to take that on. It's just categorising the entries like I said, but I can't be involved now. It's too awkward, but I know you loathe Cleo too.'

Lara shook her head. 'I'm doing it for you, not her. I'm not entering, but I'll be around on the day, just to keep an eye on things.'

Eve didn't think she could stretch the dog chat much further. 'I'll let you get on with your meal,' she said to the couple. 'It was lovely to meet you.'

She made her way back to her table, with the dogs in tow. By the time she was seated again, Lara was staring at Cleo. It seemed almost extraordinary that Cleo didn't sense it, her look was so full of venom.

4

First thing the following morning, Eve looked for news coverage of Honor's fatal fall. There was a contemporary report online and some articles relating to the inquest.

The facts left Eve feeling even more uneasy. Honor had been found at the bottom of the stairs at The Briars, which was up for sale at the time. It was the estate agent and a client who'd discovered her, and that client had been none other than Cleo Marbeck. Had the scene come as an horrific shock, or had an accomplice told her what to expect? Either way, it was chilling.

The row between Cleo and Honor beforehand was mentioned. Several witnesses said the quarrel had been fierce. Someone who'd seen them emerge from Cleo's house described Honor as 'red-eyed and flushed, as though she was still upset'. They said Cleo had been 'smiling, with an arm around Honor's shoulder'. That could have been comforting or controlling.

Another witness overheard a snippet of their conversation. Cleo had said, 'So we're agreed then, you'll say nothing, do as I say, and work for me.' They said Cleo had sounded threatening and Honor hadn't replied.

In her evidence, Cleo said they'd quarrelled over Richie,

then aged four. She claimed she'd told Honor she wasn't looking after him properly. She said she'd offered her extra work, running errands for her firm, to help with finances and get Richie some proper childcare. When she'd said, 'you'll say nothing', she was asking her not to spread it around in case the job offer looked like favouritism. The 'do as I say', had been in reference to the advice she'd given her. Cleo had been a critical friend. She'd felt she had to be. The explanation sounded contrived to Eve.

A neighbour who'd dropped in on Cleo shortly after that conversation had noticed there were two glasses on the coffee table and a half-empty bottle of brandy. The whole place smelled of spirits. Cleo didn't deny she and Honor had had a drink. It had felt like the right thing to do. The girl had been upset. Yes, she realised it was a little contradictory, as Honor would shortly be going home to her young son and Cleo had been concerned for his welfare.

It sounded odd to Eve, but Cleo was unconventional. All the same, it wasn't surprising that there'd been rumours. Perhaps Honor really had known something damaging about Cleo.

The post-mortem showed Honor had drunk a lot. The pathologist said he wasn't surprised she'd fallen downstairs with that much alcohol inside her.

The time of death was precise, thanks to Honor's Mickey Mouse watch, which had smashed and stopped when she fell. A Mickey Mouse watch... Heck, Honor had only been twenty-three, still with sentimental childhood possessions. Eve closed her eyes. Thought of her twins. Felt the pain. What must Honor's nearest and dearest have gone through? Though her husband had already left her by the time she'd died, of course. After Richie had lost his mum, he'd been brought up by his paternal grandmother, who hadn't liked Honor. And Cleo had spent a lot of time with the grandmother just before her death, sparking yet more rumours.

The next bit of the news report covered Cleo's alibi and that was especially interesting. She'd been given it by Lara Oxley, the owner of Shell Cottage. They'd bumped into each other along the River Sax, out of town, at the crucial time.

Lara hated Cleo now, clearly. It would be useful to check what had triggered the animosity. If it predated Honor's death the alibi would seem even more solid; Lara would hardly lie for an enemy. But of course, Cleo could still have conspired in Honor's death.

Later that day, Eve asked Jim Thackeray, the vicar, for help in damping down the rumours about Honor, but despite his best efforts, by Wednesday morning they continued to fly. Or at least they did in the queue at the village store, when Eve dropped in for milk.

Beyond the gossip and the scant news reporting, Eve had picked up what she could, but oft-repeated legends drowned out new information. She needed to approach the matter differently. Immerse herself in Cleo's world.

She'd seen her the day before when she'd come to talk to Robin about the open-gardens event, but there hadn't been much time to chat. Cleo had swept off immediately afterwards to take publicity photos.

But Robin was due to garden at The Briars today, so Eve arranged to meet him afterwards in Meadowsweet Grove. It would give her an excuse to spy out the land. She'd go early and try to bump into one of Cleo's neighbours.

She went to keep the appointment, taking Gus and a picnic basket. She and Robin were going on to the beach by Watcher's Wood, south along the coast. There were trees close to the shore there; it was an idyllic shady spot, tucked away in comparison to the beach at Saxford.

Eve arrived at the entrance to the grove and hovered out of

sight, waiting for someone to appear. It wasn't hard to stay hidden. The lane was thick with greenery, and alive with birdsong too, the scent of honeysuckle hanging in the air. She'd been there around half an hour when she spotted Abby Porter.

She was scuttling up the lane towards Lara Oxley's cottage, a bunch of keys in her hand. She flinched when Eve caught her eye. It must be horrible dealing with the villagers after the scene with Cleo. Eve explained she was there to meet Robin.

'I'm just going to feed Lara's cat.' Abby bit her lip.

'I heard she was going away. She doesn't think much of the open-gardens event?'

Abby turned away slightly. 'No. Though she's got green fingers.'

'She's not so keen on Cleo?' Eve watched Abby's eyes.

She let out a long breath. 'No.'

Eve hoped Abby would talk. She surely didn't feel any loyalty at this stage. 'They're different types?'

Abby nodded. 'Cleo's pushy. She wants to buy Lara's cottage and Lara's fed up with her asking. She went into overdrive trying to get it a few months before I moved in, then again a couple of months before Perry came. She's like someone playing Monopoly. She was offering big bucks.'

Eve wondered how much. 'Who's Perry?'

'Perry Bancroft. He's writing the biography of Marbeck's.' Abby's jaw tightened as she mentioned Cleo's firm. 'I thought I'd feature in it. We had an interview booked in.' Lara's keys were digging into her hand, her fist was clenched so tight. 'If I was Lara, I'd leap at the chance to move away.' Abby paused, her eyes on the middle distance. 'But I can understand not wanting to take Cleo's money.' She shook her head. 'I should have listened to Lara. She told me I was wrong to trust her.'

This was important. Eve wanted to date the tensions between Lara and Cleo. 'Lara knows her of old then, I guess.'

Abby nodded.

'I wonder what put her off Cleo.' Eve let the silence ride.

At last, Abby sighed. 'I do too. It goes way back. I've always suspected it has something to do with Lara's brother.'

Eve frowned. 'I haven't met him.'

'And you won't, I'm afraid.' Abby cast her eyes down. 'It's a sad story. Shell Cottage belonged to Lara's parents. She and her brother were brought up here. The dad was in the army. Killed in action. From when Lara was fifteen it was just her, her mum and her brother.' She shook her head. 'The brother joined the army too, but he was home on leave when he died.'

Just when he should have been safe. It was heart-breaking. 'What happened?'

'He slid on black ice and landed his car in the River Sax. He was west of here on lonely roads. The water was freezing and he hit his head. He had no chance.' She shuddered. 'He was only twenty-four. Awful. And whenever his name comes up, or someone refers to the accident, Lara ends up talking about Cleo. There's such bitterness in her voice.' Abby closed her eyes for a second. 'It's the memories that keep Lara at Shell Cottage, of course.'

'I can understand that.' Eve half wondered if she'd opt for a fresh start in Lara's place, but it would be a wrench. And if she'd made up her mind to stay, she'd certainly resent anyone trying to push her out. 'Did Cleo and Lara's brother know each other then?'

But Abby shook her head. 'Not that I'm aware of, so it's odd. Cleo hadn't moved to the grove when he died.'

That was even more curious. Eve needed to get to the bottom of it and check the date of the brother's death too. If Abby was right, it had triggered Lara's hatred of Cleo. And if that had happened before Honor's death, it was unlikely that Lara had lied for her.

They said their goodbyes and Eve followed Gus further along the lane, as he explored a narrow gap between some shrubs. The pair of them were hidden as he sniffed around some roots but Eve could see into the grove. She caught movement: Cleo, peering towards Shell Cottage. There was something furtive about her look. Eve crept closer to the entrance of her hiding place and watched. Cleo paused for a moment, frowned, then walked on again. What was she up to? Was she going to talk to Abby?

Eve looked left and saw Cleo glance over her shoulder then disappear from sight. She crouched down to face Gus and put a finger to her lips. He knew that sign. His expressive eyes conveyed stoical suffering.

They emerged into the lane and Eve crept left, back towards Shell Cottage. She was just in time to see Cleo craning to see into the shadowy house, then stepping inside. She wasn't after Abby, if Eve was any judge. She was creeping into Lara's house in secret. Sizing it up, maybe, in the hope of adding it to her collection. Eve didn't imagine Lara had given her permission, under the circumstances. She wondered if Abby would catch Cleo at it and what she'd say. For a second, she debated alerting her, but it wasn't her battle and Cleo couldn't do much harm by looking. All the same, it told her something: Cleo was unscrupulous when it came to getting what she wanted.

5

Eve turned away from Shell Cottage and walked towards The Briars. It was time to get moving; Robin would be waiting. She called to him as she opened Cleo's side gate and he dashed over to her, holding her tight as she laughed at the mud on his cheek. He smeared some on her nose. He made her feel like she was twenty again: the goosebumps, the giddy happiness, the excitement. She couldn't regret her marriage to Ian, despite him being a two-timing worm: without Ian she wouldn't have the twins, the most beloved of offspring. But all sorrow over the divorce was gone. Way before Robin, she'd realised she was better off without her ex-husband.

They had a lovely picnic on the beach, paddling in the shallows, eating and drinking. Robin never forgot to pay Gus attention too, the mark of a decent human. They threw a ball for the dachshund countless times and his ears turned inside out as he bounded along. The beach was picturesque, with a boat moored in an inlet, and birds wheeling overhead. At last, it was time to leave. They dusted the sand off their clothes, and Robin took her hand.

'Ready to go and fetch my gloves?'

'Definitely.' She'd asked him to leave them at The Briars as an excuse to go back again. The more visits she made, the more chance she had of gathering information subtly. They ought to get a few words with Cleo out of the visit.

It was still light as they strolled up Meadowsweet Grove. Eve and Robin held hands and Eve listened to the gulls overhead. She was in an idyllic bubble, but outside it, Meadowsweet Grove's troubles were massing. New adventures were opening up for Richie Hamilton but against the backdrop of the loss of his mother and the row Honor had had with Cleo before she died. And then there was Cleo's desire to own every home in the grove. Did she want to control the people, as well as their houses?

Robin knocked on the door of The Briars but there was no reply.

'She might be round the back.' Eve thought she could hear voices.

They walked to the side gate, but before they had the chance to knock, Eve caught some of the conversation beyond it.

'Thank you.' A man's voice. Stilted. Cracking with emotion.

A light laugh. Cleo. 'What on earth for?'

There was a short pause. 'Well, for Perry. For getting him here to work for you.' There was silence again for a moment. 'He hasn't spoken to me yet, but having him back in Saxford's a major step forward.'

Cleo laughed again. 'My dear Max, it's not all about you, you know. *I* wanted him here.'

'Well, of course, to write the biography. He's a talented boy.'

Robin was stock-still next to her. Eve was holding her breath.

'He's not a boy any longer, Max, and it's high time you acknowledged it.' Cleo sounded exasperated. 'Even as a child he was more self-possessed than you gave him credit for. Unless you secretly realised it.'

Her words felt full of hidden meaning.

'I'm not sure what you're getting at.' Max sounded as mystified as Eve felt.

'Really?'

The man called Max muttered something. He sounded irri-
table too. 'Either way, I'm glad he's here writing about Marbeck's
and living in the grove. Cleo, can we talk properly now please?
You know that's why I'm here.'

Cleo groaned. 'Not this again, Max. I've told you.' She
sounded infinitely weary.

'I've wanted this for a long time. And I think if you agreed to
marry me, Perry would come to accept us. Reconcile himself to
what happened when he was a child. See that we're serious
about each other.'

'Is that really what you think? Perry's not a soft touch, Max. I
don't believe you know him at all.'

'He must be coming round. He'd never have accepted your
contract otherwise.'

'Oh, I'm not so sure about that. I've given him an excellent
package and I suspect there's more at play.' Then she changed
tack. 'Besides, you seriously think I'd marry you to improve your
relationship with your son? Good grief, Max!'

'It's just one reason. The overriding one is that I adore you. I
always have and I always will.'

'Yet all those years you were married you refused to leave
your wife. If you'd been honest with her, history might have
played out differently.'

'Do you think I don't know that! It was a mistake.'

'A mistake that went on for ten years! You only decided you'd
like to settle down with me when she left you!'

'I don't understand.' The man called Max sounded desperate. Eve could tell he was on a hiding to nothing and doubted he
deserved any better. 'You say you love me!'

'When did I last say that?'

There was a long pause. Eve could see Viv in her mind's eye, mouthing *Awks*.

'I did love you, once. But you're not my one and only now, and you know it! Why should you be? I wasn't yours for years.'

'You're just punishing me!'

'Yes, and it's wildly enjoyable. But if you think I need you, you're wrong. You lost your power over me a long time ago. I won't make sacrifices for you. Take it or leave it. You're just light entertainment now, and often not even that.'

There was a huge crash. Eve's eyes met Robin's and they moved as one towards the gate, Robin calling to Cleo as he went.

'Cleo? Are you round the back there? Sorry, it's Robin. I left my gloves behind.'

By the time they opened the gate, Cleo was alone, but Eve saw movement on the far side of the house.

She smiled at them. 'I'm afraid I dropped my decanter, or I'd offer you both a drink.'

She refused to let them help clear up and it obviously wasn't the moment for the casual chat Eve had planned. Robin got his gloves, they said goodbye and left.

'An interesting end to the evening,' Robin said, once they'd left Meadowsweet Grove.

'You said it. I'm not sure if I'm more worried about the past or the present. You've been in Saxford longer than me. Do you know anything about the man Cleo was talking to?'

'He's Max Bancroft, and he owns a letting company,' Robin said. 'Mostly holiday cottages. I believe he helped Cleo set up her business – premises or a cash investment or both. His son Perry was brought up here, but he's lived in London all his adult life.'

Eve looked Perry up on her phone. 'He must be quite sought-after. He's been commissioned to write books on rock stars and royals.' A people-watcher, just like her. 'Cleo was lucky to get him. Do you know anything about her affair with Perry's dad? I thought her lovers were transient.'

'Not in this case. The relationship is at the root of Max's estrangement from Perry, from what I understand. It started before Cleo bought The Briars and launched her property empire, when Max was still married. It's an open secret these days.'

'You think Perry knew back then, and was upset for his mother?'

Robin nodded. 'The story goes that Max and Cleo managed to keep the relationship secret from her for a long time, but Perry saw them together when he was quite young.'

'Poor child. I suppose he kept quiet to protect his mum.'

Robin nodded. 'That's the word on the street. When she finally found out she was devastated. She moved out with Perry but she died within a couple of years – meningitis, I think.'

Poor Perry. What a horrendous situation. 'I can see how he must hate his dad. And Cleo too, probably. It's weird that he agreed to work for her.'

Robin's expression was sober. 'I agree. And so does Cleo by the sound of it.'

Eve replayed her words. Cleo had implied he wasn't just here for the generous package she'd offered. So what was Perry Bancroft doing in Saxford?

6

The following day, Eve got a text from Viv to say that Stevie had arrived safely. Eve was due to meet her for the first time the following evening. For now, she'd leave them to get sorted. She hoped that would include Stevie taking control of the wedding admin. Viv had given her and her son Jonah the impression that everything was in hand, which was stretching the truth.

Viv had a to-do list, which was a cause for celebration. On the downside, she'd written it on the back of a receipt from the cash and carry. Eve kept seeing it floating around the kitchen at Monty's and had twice picked it up off the floor. She'd been surreptitiously photographing it every so often before it got lost all together. She took a deep breath. Not her business... in theory. She should use up her energy helping to organise her own son's wedding, which was soon after Jonah and Stevie's, and her own, booked before the year was out.

She switched focus to an obituary she was finalising, then searched for details of Lara Oxley's brother's death online. Entering 'Oxley', 'drowning', and 'ice' was enough to bring it up on Google. It was so sad, reading the article, but it looked like a straightforward though tragic accident. No one else had been involved when Freddy Oxley had skidded off the road and there'd been no fault with the Mini he'd been driving, so there was no question of someone having tampered with it. Eve noted the date. Shortly before Honor had fallen to her death. If Abby's hunch was right, Lara's hatred for Cleo predated the alibi she'd given her. It made it feel more solid, but it was as she'd thought before – Cleo could still have connived with someone over Honor's death.

When the time came for Gus's evening airing, she chose the Meadowsweet Grove loop. Robin came too, and they let Gus sniff each gatepost and shrub to his heart's content. The longer they loitered, the more likely they were to see something.

They were close to The Briars when Eve spotted Abby Porter.

She was standing amongst some greenery near her garden gate. The moonlight picked out her features and there were tears streaming down her face. Her eyes were fixed on The Briars and Eve sensed she'd have approached the house if they hadn't appeared.

Even if Eve hadn't been on a mission to understand Cleo, she couldn't have ignored the situation. She could feel Abby's distress – the intensity of it. As she got closer, Eve was struck by her expression. She wasn't just upset, she looked stunned. She was still staring at Cleo's place as though she'd never seen it before.

'Abby, are you okay?' Stupid question. She clearly wasn't. She'd jumped at Eve's words, as though she hadn't even noticed she was there. Robin stood back in the shadows with Gus. He wouldn't want to crowd her.

Abby put a hand over her face. She was clutching an envelope, with her name and a Paris address written on the front. She closed her eyes for a moment and Eve saw her swallow. 'I-I thought I'd have a sort out because I want to move out soon.' Her voice was croaky, still full of tears. 'And I found a letter. Sean must have intended to send it to me, only he never managed it. You remember I told you Cleo rented him my cottage before I had it?'

Eve nodded. Sean. The two-timing boyfriend who'd told Cleo Abby's secret.

'I feel terrible now. I was deleting his emails and texts unread. I suppose he thought I might relent and read a proper letter.' She took an unsteady breath. 'It explains some things.'

'Maybe you can talk to him about it.'

But Abby closed her eyes again and shook her head. 'He died just before he was due to leave the grove. A heart attack. I suppose that's why he never sent the letter.'

Eve reached out then and gave her a hug. It felt a little forward but also impossible not to. 'I'm so very sorry. It must have been a huge shock, finding the letter. I hope in time it helps heal some wounds.'

Abby nodded. She looked again at The Briars, then up at the moon and at last she turned back towards her cottage. But as Eve and Robin went on their way, Eve glimpsed her hesitate and twist towards The Briars again.

Perhaps she would go and tackle Cleo, if not tonight, then soon. She clearly wished she could turn back time. It wasn't surprising she was so upset, but she'd looked stupefied too. As though the letter made a fundamental difference, and that didn't make sense. Sean had been two-timing her with Cleo, which would make the women equally wronged. Even if Sean claimed Cleo had done all the running, Eve doubted Abby would give him a free pass. Eve certainly wouldn't. So what the heck had Sean written?

As for Cleo, it brought home her complicated love life. She'd clearly had Max and Sean on the go at the same time, and maybe there were others too. She'd told Max he wasn't her 'one and only' any more.

As Eve, Robin and Gus made their way along the grove, the

silence felt full of the thoughts she wanted to share. As soon as they were home, she'd let them out. For now, she considered each of the houses and their occupants as she walked past. Abby to their left, who'd been dragged over to England from Paris for a job which was no longer hers, all thanks to a damaging secret Cleo knew. And opposite her, Perry, who'd come to Suffolk to work for Cleo, despite her affair with his dad. Then Shell Cottage, also on their left, home to Lara, whose hatred of Cleo seemed bound up with the tragic death of her brother. And opposite her, Richie, a young man who rented his house from a woman who might have conspired to kill his mother.

It was deeply unsettling.

As they reached the end of the short lane, Eve looked back over her shoulder to see if she could still see Abby.

Instead, she saw someone else, standing in the glow of the only streetlamp, staring at The Briars. She touched Robin's arm and nodded in the figure's direction.

It was only when they'd left the grove that Robin asked her about it.

The thought made Eve anxious. 'I might be mistaken. She wasn't terribly well lit and we were a couple of houses away. Besides, so far I've only seen her in photographs. But I *think* it was Stevie, Jonah's fiancée.'

Stevie, who wanted to put the past behind her, apparently. But who'd come to stand and stare at The Briars on her very first night in Saxford.

7

The next day, Eve worked at Monty's and updated Viv on developments, such as they were. Then in the evening, she met Stevie for the first time at the Cross Keys. Robin had stayed at home again to avoid villagers requesting last-minute landscaping. Roll on next week...

The sight of Stevie next to Viv made Eve teary. It almost banished the memory of her staring at The Briars, but Eve was sure it had been her now. Perhaps it wasn't unnatural. She'd want to face up to past emotions – get them out of the way.

Viv was looking at her future daughter-in-law with such fondness, and Stevie looked radiant, her deep chestnut curls glossy, eyes shining and cheeks rosy. She laughed readily and was talking proudly about the sought-after patisserie masterclass Jonah was about to attend in France. It was competitive; the tutor, a world-renowned chef, only took those he thought had true promise. As Stevie spoke, Viv looked increasingly emotional. Suddenly, Eve felt she could forgive the fifteen 'something-blue' items Viv had amassed on the table in Monty's office. She might have to draw the line at the 'borrowed', 'old' and 'new' things in the corner of the kitchen though. There were limits.

The wedding was two weeks away, but sometimes it felt like months.

When Viv went to the loo, Stevie leaned towards Eve and said: 'I do hope Viv's been all right.' Worry creased her lively face. 'I heard her crying after I'd gone to bed last night. I think it was over Oliver.'

Eve's heart contracted. Viv must feel the loss of her husband especially sharply right now. Eve hadn't known Viv when he'd died. She could only imagine her grief, and the huge challenge of bringing up the boys and running the teashop.

Heck, Eve probably looked emotional now too. That wouldn't help Stevie. She took a deep breath. 'Even if the wedding brings back memories, your and Jonah's marriage has given her the utmost joy, Stevie. Truly. I'll talk to her about Oliver in case she wants to offload.' Maybe Eve would yield over the borrowed, old and new too, under the circumstances.

She went back to Viv's house after the pub and managed to talk to her while Stevie took a bath. They shut the sitting room door, Viv had a good cry and there were lots of hugs and memories.

'Thanks.' Viv blew her nose. 'Isn't Stevie the nicest person you could think of for Jonah? I hope to goodness they have long, happy lives.'

Eve squeezed her hand. 'Most people do. It's rotten that Oliver was so unlucky. As for Stevie, she's a treasure.'

Viv sighed. 'I'm glad we're looking into the Honor business, you know. I think she's more affected by it than she lets on.'

Having seen her in Meadowsweet Grove, Eve thought so too.

Later that evening at Elizabeth's Cottage, Eve lay in bed next to Robin.

'What's your gut instinct about Honor's death?' He turned to her. 'The rumour-mongers could easily be fuelled by vitriol, considering Cleo's current entanglements.'

But Eve thought of Cleo's words as she'd looked at Honor's drawing. *I never imagined how significant it would prove. Funny how small, chance happenings can alter the course of one's life.* She'd looked as though she was about to cry. 'I think Honor looms as large in Cleo's memory as she does in the collective one. And not just because of the scandal. I believe there was more to their relationship than anyone knows yet. But Cleo could still have conspired to kill her. She's ruthless, Robin. You only have to look at the way she's treated Abby to see that.'

Robin slung an arm around her. 'Open gardens tomorrow. Maybe you'll find out more then.'

'I hope so.'

Eve tried to settle her mind enough to sleep, but thoughts of Cleo and her difficult relationships spun in her head. The quarrel with Max Bancroft had been unnerving. She was sure it would have turned violent if she and Robin hadn't burst in when they did. Cleo felt she'd been taken for granted, but there was more to it than that. Stuff to do with Max's son Perry and his biography of Marbeck's. Eve couldn't make sense of it, except that Cleo thought Max was blinkered where his son was concerned.

Eve ran through the occupants of Meadowsweet Grove again. Abby and her secret, Lara and her dead brother, Richie and his mother's fall, Perry and his dad's affair. Four people with unhappy connections to Cleo, living on her doorstep.

It was discomforting and intriguing, but none of it shed light on Honor's death.

At last, Eve slept, but she didn't sleep well. At three in the morning she dreamed of thudding feet, down in Haunted Lane. A sign of danger, according to village legend. On waking, she listened hard. Nothing... but downstairs, Gus was whining.

8

It was glorious weather the following day for the open-gardens event. Eve drank a cup of strong black coffee after her rough night and tried to put her nightmare out of her head.

She met Viv and Stevie as planned in the morning. It was lovely not to be competing, thanks to Robin advising the judging panel. He wouldn't do any of the scoring, but Eve had argued his involvement would make entering unethical. She adored their garden and hated the idea of anyone peering at it with a critical eye. Viv had entered, but with Monty's garden, not her own. It meant the teashop staff could keep an eye on visitors.

Eve felt a twinge of anxiety. She was in charge of Monty's admin and ran a tight ship, but two of their regular servers, Tammy and Lars, had gone travelling. Their replacements each had... issues. At least Allie was an old hand now.

Eve, Viv and Stevie were taken up with a beautiful display of old garden roses on Love Lane and before long the talk was of the flowers for Stevie and Jonah's wedding.

Moira was in a state of nervous excitement when they reached her place. 'Dear Robin has just called with the judging committee. Of course, they have to play their cards very close to their chest, but I could see my display got a reaction.'

Eve could understand why. Moira had installed some extra garden ornaments as soon as she'd heard about the event. She had a sizeable stone elephant on her lawn that looked as though it was being strangled by some jasmine. The enormous parrot surrounded by very English-looking meadow crane's bill was an unexpected feature too. Gus was circling the display warily, a suspicious look in his eye.

'It's very striking.'

'Stunning.' Viv's smile told Eve she might convulse with laughter at any moment.

Eve glanced anxiously at Moira, but she'd been distracted by Stevie, who was exclaiming over some enchanter's nightshade in a woody corner. Moira looked disconcerted. Eve suspected the nightshade hadn't been part of the grand plan.

'It's not poisonous, is it, Eve?' Moira hissed anxiously.

Eve shook her head. 'Not especially. It's part of the willowherb family – not related to the deadly sort.'

Moira let out a long breath. 'Thank goodness. I can't think what the judges would say if someone fell ill.'

Her sense of priorities was deeply worrying.

At that moment, Moira's husband arrived, and her face lit up. 'Ah, here's Paul now to mind the garden.' Eve could understand Moira staying until the judges had been. Paul wasn't a people person. 'My niece is looking after the shop today,' she went on, bustling towards the house, 'so I'll come with you and look at what everyone else has done.'

Viv caught Eve's eye and mouthed, *Oh joy.*

A little later, they passed the turning down Dark Lane and approached Parson's Walk on the left, where they fell in with a crowd of villagers.

Moira was a little ahead of them, talking to a friend.

'Who's that?' Eve whispered to Viv, indicating a serious-looking man with a neat beard. Somewhere in his thirties, she guessed. She'd seen him in the Cross Keys a few times recently, yet she didn't think he was local.

'Perry Bancroft. You know, the writer who's doing the book about Marbeck's.' Viv frowned. 'You wouldn't think the firm was well known enough to warrant its own history yet, would you? But that's Cleo for you. She probably chatted up the publisher.'

'*Please* keep your voice down.' Eve must have spoken too sharply; Gus was standing to attention.

Viv lowered the volume a fraction. 'Perry's dad, Max, lives here on Parson's Walk.'

Ah. Max the lover.

'This is his place,' Viv said, nodding at the house before them. It looked very much like The Briars.

Perry Bancroft looked blank at the sight of his father's house and walked past without a backward glance. At the doorway, a man stared after him, his hand half raised, lips parted. But in the end, he didn't call out.

It had to be Max. Eve felt a tiny pang for him, despite everything. The idea of being cut off from her twins was too painful to contemplate. But his actions had caused the heartache. He'd fallen out of love with his wife and *in* love with someone else. Okay. It happened. But did he have to keep up the betrayal for years, in front of his son? He'd wanted to have his cake and eat it. What a weasel.

Max's eyes were still on the lane as he moved back to let the next batch of visitors in, including Eve and her party.

He was handsome like his son but clean-shaven. His hair was greying about the temples, his expressive eyebrows still dark. He moved to the back of the hall, ready to escort them through, but he didn't get that far.

It was Stevie who stopped him in his tracks. Eve was

standing next to her and sensed her whole body stiffen. She looked at her quickly. Was she ill? The colour had drained from her cheeks and she was staring straight ahead, unblinking. Viv and Eve moved in, Viv taking her arm. Gus whined.

'Stevie?'

She gasped, put her hands over her eyes and let out a piercing scream which was greeted by a volley of barking from Gus.

Max Bancroft dashed towards them; they were still standing near his front door. Stevie kept her eyes covered and turned towards a row of coats as though she wanted somewhere to hide. Her cheeks had gone from white to bright red.

The villagers who'd already moved to Max's back room returned to the hall and crowded in behind him, whispering and staring at Stevie.

It was horrible. Like she was an exhibit. Eve had no idea what had happened but scrutiny would be the last thing she needed. She turned to Max. 'Do you mind if we go into your front room for a moment?'

Max looked ashen. 'Of course.' He didn't stop to ask what was wrong and Eve was glad of that, though it struck her as odd.

She opened the first door off the irregular-shaped hall which led into a small sitting room. A moment later she'd ushered Viv and the now tearful Stevie inside, Gus scampering anxiously around their ankles. Thank goodness Moira had been ahead of them. Her presence wouldn't have helped. Several of the villagers tried to follow them in but she closed the door firmly, knocking Gwen Harris's toe slightly. It had to be said, it served her right.

They got Stevie to sit down on a small blue sofa. Viv perched next to her and held her hand while Gus stared at her as though she was a firework that might go off.

'Just take some time,' Eve said.

'But also tell us urgently what happened,' Viv added.

Eve sighed, but of course, she was deeply curious too.

Stevie's head was in her hands again. 'It's so embarrassing. I had the most horrible... I don't know what. Vision? Flashback?' She looked at them both at last. 'A dead body. Auntie Honor at the bottom of the stairs.'

9

Viv gasped and gripped Stevie's hand more tightly. 'Here? You remember seeing Honor's body here?'

Stevie looked at them with damp brown eyes. 'I don't know. I suppose so. But it could be a false memory.'

'Do you remember visiting this house as a child?'

Stevie shook her head.

Eve knew from her research that she'd only been four when Honor died. Most people's conscious memories didn't stretch back that far. But Stevie was shaking. Eve didn't think such a violent reaction could be based on nothing. 'But wait,' she said, after a moment. 'This house and The Briars are built to the same layout. Identical irregular halls with smaller front rooms and the larger living rooms at the back. Could you be remembering that house, not this one?'

Viv nodded slowly. 'Of course. You're right. Did you visit The Briars as a child, Stevie? It was unoccupied when Honor was found.' She patted Stevie's hand.

'I don't remember.' Stevie frowned, her eyes tearing up again. 'I'll have to ask my mum. It'll be hard though. Mum still finds it difficult to talk about Honor. She hates it that she wasn't in the village when life got difficult.'

The thought of a young Stevie discovering her aunt's body anywhere was shocking. They were close to The Briars now. By rights it would be one of the next gardens they visited, but it would be an ordeal.

'We don't have to go to Cleo's place if you'd rather not,' Viv said. Perhaps she was thinking the same thing.

But Stevie shook her head. 'I want to. It looks as though there's something buried in my memory. Seeing the place where Auntie Honor died might release it.' She was brave, that was for sure. 'In any case, I barely know Cleo. I should find out more. I've spent a long time thinking of her as this malignant force, but Richie likes her, and his loss was far greater than mine. I can't even remember what Honor was like.'

Gus put his head against Stevie's leg and she patted him as Viv took a deep breath. 'Okay.'

Stevie insisted on visiting Max's garden before they left too, though Eve noticed her shake as she passed the bottom of the stairs. Outside, they found her scream was still the topic of conversation. The villagers turned to her as one, but it was Moira who asked what had happened. It figured.

Stevie looked uncomfortable but she didn't duck the ques-tion. 'A buried memory, we think. Not actually of this house but of The Briars. It's the same design apparently.'

Moira nodded knowledgeably. 'I'd noticed that.'

'I think I must have seen Honor's body after she fell. I suppose I'd wandered off and got inside the empty house. Today I had a vision of her lying at the bottom of the stairs.'

She looked a little sick again and Eve silently berated Moira for asking. The villagers surged forward with expressions of sympathy, all except Max Bancroft, who watched from a distance. His expression got Eve's full attention. He looked scared.

If Cleo had wanted an accomplice to get rid of Honor, her long-time lover would be an ideal candidate. It was a horrible thought, and not good that Stevie's story had got out. It would be all over the village by evening. Of course, there was no evidence that Honor's death had been anything more than a tragic accident. And it was perfectly true that The Briars and Max's place were built to the same design. But Eve had a nasty feeling there was more to come out. If so, it could be in more than one person's interests to keep Stevie quiet.

By the time they reached Meadowsweet Grove, via the pathway that linked it with Parson's Walk, Stevie and Viv had more colour. That was good news. As they approached the doorway to The Briars, Eve saw Stevie tense, but she didn't pause.

Cleo met them as they crossed the living room to reach the garden. 'I've just heard what happened at Max's place.' She looked as pale as Stevie had earlier. Beyond her, Eve could see Moira. How had she got there ahead of them? But of course, if there was gossip to spread, she could put on a good turn of speed. 'Here.' Cleo shepherded them towards a drinks table. 'Let me get you some lemonade. Or elderflower cordial? You need a sweet drink after something like that.'

'I'd like a cordial, thank you,' Stevie said, 'but I'm quite all right.' All the same, she clutched her drink tightly when Cleo gave it to her.

Cleo asked if Stevie remembered visiting her house or Max's before. Eve couldn't help wondering if she was checking how much Stevie knew.

Speculation about Honor's death would be rife all over again. Eve reviewed the basic facts. The only way Cleo could have been involved was if there'd been a conspiracy. That would imply forward planning, but if you wanted someone dead then pushing them down a flight of stairs wasn't a reliable way to achieve it. That said, the flights concerned were unusually steep, with unforgiving tiles at the bottom.

All Cleo's focus was on Stevie. 'I was so sorry when your mother had her breakdown.' She didn't express regret over Honor's death. Perhaps she felt it would be like admitting her guilt. 'You'll have heard that your aunt and I quarrelled before she died, but I was very fond of her. The gossip was motivated by malice, I promise you. Some people don't like my approach to life.' She grimaced.

That might be true, but Cleo could still have been involved.

'Stevie, there's something I'd like you to have.' Cleo walked towards the picture Eve had admired when she'd visited the house a week earlier. 'Your Auntie Honor drew this for me. Richie already has lots of her sketches. This one should come to you.'

Spots of colour tinged Stevie's cheeks. 'But it was a present; you should keep it.'

'No, really. I insist. Don't take it now. It'll be inconvenient to carry. I'll drop it off at Viv's later. I must add it to my to-do list.' She picked up the pretty notebook Eve had admired before, with the bluebirds and honeysuckle on the cover.

As Eve, Viv and Stevie made for the outside, Eve heard one of the villagers hiss: 'It's that guilty conscience at work again!'

They did a circuit of the garden, weaving between the shrubs where they made awkward small talk about a stone statue and the pond.

Stevie looked uncomfortable.

'We shouldn't have come,' Viv said.

'It's not that, it's the drawing.' She sighed. 'How will I explain it to Mum if I've accepted gifts from Cleo? She's trying to be kind, of course. To build bridges. But having to meet her halfway makes me feel like a traitor. I know it's wrong. She argued with Auntie Honor and they got drunk together. That might have led to her fall, but it wasn't deliberate. I need to forgive Cleo, but I don't think Mum ever will. She hangs on to it.'

Viv rubbed Stevie's arm. 'You and your mum aren't under any obligation. We're all only human.'

But at last, Stevie shook her head. 'To hell with it. I'll accept the drawing. If I don't make a stand this village war will last forever. I'll explain it to Mum.'

Eve thought of the man in the navy T-shirt at the pub, and hoped no one would challenge Stevie over her decision. It would be deeply unfair.

On the other side of the garden, Max's son Perry was looking at a bank of verbena, waving in the breeze. Once again, Eve wondered what he was doing, working for Cleo. He must feel conflicted about her, just as Stevie did. And for him it was different. Stevie saw Honor's death as a tragic accident, whereas there was nothing accidental about Cleo's affair with Max.

10

Eve hadn't realised how on edge she was until she, Viv and Stevie returned to Cleo Marbeck's sitting room. There was a crash which made her jump violently. Turning to look, she saw a beautiful mahogany box on the floor, its lid flung to one side.

Nearby, one of the villagers was rubbing her hip. She must have collided with the side table next to her and sent the box flying. She looked around, twitched her shoulders irritably and sighed. 'There are too many people in a small space. I hope I haven't broken anything.'

Next to the box on the floor was an unusual necklace – jade in a gold setting.

'It must have been inside the box.' One of the other locals bent to pick it up.

Another woman nodded. 'Yes, and I'd like to know what it's doing here.'

'It doesn't belong to Cleo?'

There was a look of relish in the other woman's eye as she shook her head. 'No. It's Lara Oxley's. I've seen her wear it. So pretty, with the tiny turtle doves.'

In moments, someone was calling Lara through the open

window. She dashed into the room a minute later, blinking as the neighbour showed her the necklace.

Cleo appeared half a second after that. 'What's going on?' She was smiling as usual.

The neighbour turned to her. 'That box got knocked off the table.' She pointed. 'The necklace was inside.'

Lara's eyes were fiery as they met Cleo's. 'What the blazes are you doing with my mother's jewellery?'

Cleo looked incredulous. 'I have no idea what it's doing there. I haven't looked in that box for months, I—'

'You've been in my house!' Lara's eyes flashed. 'You must have! Not just inside but upstairs!'

'There has to be another explanation!' Cleo looked uncomfortable now. 'Didn't Abby go in to feed your cat? Perhaps someone followed her.'

Eve wondered if she should speak up, but in a roomful of people it felt wrong. She'd have to talk to Cleo and Lara alone, later.

'Perhaps *you* did!' Lara countered. 'We'll have to ask Abby. I can imagine you wanting to look inside. To size it up. And then I suppose you couldn't keep your hands off one of my most precious belongings. How could you?'

Cleo looked at her, open mouthed. 'This is a conspiracy. It's persecution!' There were tiny flashes of pink on her cheeks.

'Oh, far from it!' Lara dug out her mobile. 'This fits! You're cruel, without a shred of conscience! I'm calling the police now. We'll let them sort it out.' She dialled.

Moira was looking on, of course. She seemed enthralled, but Eve had had enough. As Lara's call connected, she turned to Viv and Stevie. 'Maybe the gardens on Dark Lane will be more soothing.' As they walked, Eve thought back to Cleo sneaking into Lara Oxley's house. She *could* have stolen the necklace. But it might have been planted too. Abby had reason to get back at Cleo. What if she realised she'd followed her into Shell Cottage and hoped someone else had seen her too? She could have crept into The Briars and sneaked the necklace into the box. Except she couldn't guarantee someone would knock it off the table.

At the top of the lane, Stevie decided to go back to Viv's place for some time out. Viv was determined to go with her but Stevie insisted she was all right on her own.

'I hope I've done the right thing, letting her go,' Viv said as they continued their tour.

Eve patted her arm. 'I can imagine wanting time with my thoughts in her place.' Not everyone was as extrovert as Viv.

An hour later, they'd explored several more gardens. They were passing the end of Meadowsweet Grove again, ready to make for the village green and Monty's, when they saw people running up the grove towards The Briars.

'Blimey,' Viv said. 'What's up now? Shall we ignore it? It must be nearly lunchtime.'

But Eve could see a villager gesticulating. Then Jim Thackeray, the vicar, appeared from one of the cottages and hastened up the grove too. Robin and the chair of the WI were just behind him. Eve had a bad feeling about the whole thing. 'I think maybe I should find out what's going on.' She turned to Viv. 'If the police have turned up and there's a row over the necklace, I should probably stay in case I need to make a statement – I'd have to tell them what I saw. You carry on.'

Viv sighed. 'All right. I'd like to get back to Stevie.' She'd been twitching ever since she'd gone home. 'I'll meet you in Monty's for a full debrief.'

Eve nodded. There were Tilly and Emily, the new waitresses, to consider too. Allie might be losing patience, but for now, all Eve wanted to do was chase after Robin and find out what the heck was going on. She dashed up the lane towards The Briars. There was no police car outside, but she could hear that Jim was on the phone to them.

Why the second call?

And then she heard his words. 'No. Someone rang the local police this afternoon about another matter. A possible theft. But this is a death. Yes, as I said, it's the householder. Cleo Marbeck. It looks as though someone knocked her out, then drowned her in her pond.'

11

Jim Thackeray disconnected his call to the police and looked at Eve from under his bushy white eyebrows, his eyes troubled.

'Cleo's dead?' It didn't seem possible. They'd been talking to her so recently.

He nodded. 'A family found her. Sylvia and Daphne were there too.'

'Oh no, how dreadful.' The couple were her neighbours on Haunted Lane. They were part of what made it home now, as valued as the roof over her head.

'They were too shocked to call, so I said I'd do it.' Jim shook his head. 'The police say they'll be here shortly. Robin's clearing the area.'

It made sense for him to do it, though Detective Inspector Palmer on the local force wouldn't like his involvement. He and Robin had clashed before.

'Didn't any officers come earlier, after Lara Oxley reported the theft?'

He shook his head. 'I'm afraid not. They might have prevented this if they had. The person I spoke to had a record of the call but a possible theft between neighbours wasn't "high priority", apparently.'

It was tragic that they'd never made it. Poor, poor Cleo. Her past raised a lot of questions, but the way things had ended for her left Eve feeling wretched. 'Thanks for trying to stop the rumours about Cleo.'

Jim sighed and shook his head. 'I didn't succeed, and I can't help wondering if this is related. People can be cruel, but my predecessor said it was worse just after Honor's death. Like a witch hunt. He did what he could to shut the rumours down. He thought it was the right thing for her and the villagers.'

Eve wondered if Jim had ever questioned Cleo's innocence. Either way, it seemed almost impossible that current and historical events weren't related. Stevie had reminded everyone of Honor's death, and in no time, Cleo was dead too.

The rest of the open-garden event was cancelled, of course. The police wanted to see everyone who'd visited The Briars. They set up an incident room in the church hall, which was close to Parson's Walk and the cut-through to Meadowsweet Grove. Robin texted to say he'd see her there. Eve popped Gus home, then called to collect Viv and Stevie before joining the other villagers in the hall.

Stevie reached the queue to talk to the police first. Her back was straight, but she was visibly shaking. Detective Inspector Palmer appeared with Sylvia and Daphne.

'Fancy having to endure him on top of finding poor Cleo,' Viv said.

She was right. Eve wouldn't wish Palmer on anyone. She knew him of old after feeding the police information she'd gathered when writing the obituaries of murder victims. It was inevitable that she'd pick up evidence. She tended to speak to the exact same people as the authorities, and they were less guarded with a civilian. You'd think Palmer would be grateful, but no. 'Maybe we'll get to talk to someone better.' DS Greg Boles, perhaps. She'd text him about Lara's necklace and what she'd seen if he wasn't here. He was excellent, and also happened to be married to Robin's cousin, so she knew him personally. She kept the connection secret, though. Greg found Palmer as trying as she did and discussed cases with Robin when his frustration boiled over. It would be a sacking offence if Palmer found out.

Robin arrived at that moment and came over. 'Are you okay?' he asked Eve, and hugged her.

'I can't believe she's dead. We were with her an hour or so beforehand. There was an argument. Something about a stolen necklace.'

'I heard. A neighbour who called the police?'

Eve nodded. 'How the heck did someone manage to kill her? The houses were crawling with visitors.'

'They must have been extremely angry or desperate. I'd guess things came to a head when the pair of them were alone, or the killer hid and waited for their moment.'

'There's a lot of cover in Cleo's garden.'

Robin nodded. 'The circumstances have given the killer two advantages. The entire village was scattered to the four winds. It'll be hard to place everyone. And when it comes to trace evidence, half of Saxford must have been in Cleo's garden today. You've only got to look at the numbers here.'

It was true. The chatter in the hall was so loud Eve could hardly hear him.

He went to join the back of their queue. They could talk properly at home. Eve couldn't wait to retreat to Elizabeth's Cottage, shut the door and come to terms with what had happened.

Stevie had reached the front of their queue now. They watched as she was taken behind the scenes, her hand up to her cheek. *Heck.* It looked as though she'd got Palmer. Probably because of the buried memory.

Viv bit her lip and for once lowered her voice, though the hubbub made it unnecessary. 'I don't like this. I mean, of course I don't, but for Stevie specifically. *We* know she'd never attack Cleo, but Honor was her aunt.'

It was a nasty thought. Stevie had been trying to put it all behind her, but accepting Cleo's olive branch had been hard. And if anyone else had seen her staring at The Briars they might mention it.

Eve took a deep breath and focused. 'There will be plenty of other suspects.' She thought of all she knew and what she should say when she was interviewed. What a terrible, tragic mess: both Cleo's death, and the unanswered questions about a troubled young woman who'd lost her life long ago.

Eve had a crawling sensation under her skin: an anxious fidgety feeling. There was work to be done. Truth to uncover so the village could rest easy again and Stevie could have her dream wedding. They needed facts, not more toxic rumours. If only she'd worked faster before Cleo died.

'Viv, I've got another worry about Stevie. It goes without saying, but keep an eye on her, won't you? If Honor *was* killed, her buried memories are a threat to the murderer.'

Viv paled. 'I'll watch her like a mother hen.' She turned to Eve. 'I'd never forgive myself if anything happened to her. What can we do?'

'She'll have to tell the police what she knows but if she remembers more, we need her to be careful who she confides in. If there was a killer and she finally remembers them, then the moment she passes the information on, she's protected. But if her recollections come in dribs and drabs, it might be dangerous.'

Viv clasped Eve's arm. 'Even if she tells the police, it could get out.'

It wasn't ideal. Eve gave her a quick hug. 'They need to know, though. We can ask Greg Boles to get someone to look out for her.'

Viv closed her eyes and took a deep breath. 'We need to dig all the harder to find out the truth. I won't be able to sleep until the police have arrested someone.'

'We'll do our utmost.' Eve's stomach knotted as she thought of the threat.

At last, Eve was called. She got DC Olivia Dawkins. Just as good as Greg. The only downside was that she was too professional to give away details of the case. But Greg would check in with Robin. Eve would get the lowdown.

She faced Dawkins across a desk and gave her account of the morning, then Dawkins asked if she knew of anyone who might have wanted to harm Cleo.

Eve was going to have to go for it. Tell the detective constable everything and trust her to treat the information sensitively. 'You know what it's like in a village,' she said at last.

'Wheels within wheels?' Dawkins's pen was poised. 'Anything you've seen could be valuable. Just tell me what you know.'

12

Eve reached Elizabeth's Cottage by late lunchtime, ahead of Robin. Gus dashed to the door to greet her, a bundle of enthusiastic wire-haired dachshund warmth, tail wagging.

She bent to give him a cuddle. When something awful happened, Gus was a major source of comfort. She went to the kitchen to refresh his water, then sat at the table with her laptop. She hadn't eaten, but she wasn't hungry. Images of Cleo kept flashing in her mind – from her celebrating joyously with Richie after he'd accepted her job offer, to her apparent shock when Lara's mother's necklace was found in her sitting room.

She took a deep breath and tried to shake the images from her head.

First things first, if she was going to look into Cleo's death, it would be a heck of a lot easier if she was writing her obituary. The excuse to quiz people was invaluable. Besides, she *wanted* to write it. She was already fascinated, and outraged by the horror of what had happened. She was in a good position to make sense of any clues too, after watching Cleo and her contacts for the last week.

But where to pitch the obituary? That was the question. She

considered her press contacts. Cleo wasn't a big enough name for her standard outlet – *Icon* – but she bet she could get *Suffolk Monthly* interested. She sent a text to a contact at the local glossy then emailed a follow-up pitch.

She'd just finished when Robin texted to say he'd arranged to snatch a quick word with Greg. He ought to have news soon. Eve decided to invite the gang round for drinks that evening. That meant getting messages to Viv, her brother Simon, Sylvia and Daphne. Simon came with a wife, Polly, but she didn't usually show up, despite Eve's invitations. Viv found it hard to hide her relief at each non-appearance. Polly was oppressively perfect, youthful and conventional. She regarded sleuthing as a matter strictly for the police.

Sylvia and Daphne would want to be involved though, after being present when Cleo's body was found. She knew Robin wouldn't mind sharing information. Every member of the gang could be trusted, and they were a well-connected lot. They'd need all hands on deck if they were going to keep Stevie safe and free from Palmer's attentions.

She texted Simon, Sylvia and Daphne, but went to deliver Viv's invitation in person. It would be good to check on Stevie – see if she'd remembered anything more.

Viv greeted her like a long-lost friend, though they'd only parted an hour earlier. She was baking in Monty's kitchen, so they could talk openly. In the teashop, Eve had passed a harassed-looking Allie, her beady eye moving from one new waitress to another. Eve was slightly concerned that their combined training efforts hadn't yet had the desired effect.

'Have you had lunch?' Viv looked at her as though she was her mother. 'Have a scone, right now. We can't deal with this on empty stomachs.'

Eve took one and Viv did too.

'I'm so worried, Eve.' Viv was whispering, which was almost unheard of. 'Stevie's called Jonah. It's the first day of his course and she didn't want to worry him, but I insisted. I was hoping for a word, but he had to dash. She's gone to call her mum now – she's between shifts apparently.' Eve remembered she was a nurse in Glasgow. 'Stevie's hoping she'll know how she might have come to see Honor's body.'

Viv brightened marginally when Eve asked her to come and pool resources later.

'I thought we could meet at half past six,' Eve said. 'We should have news by then.'

'It'll feel good to be doing something.'

Stevie appeared. She still looked pale, her eyes clouded with worry. 'The police have asked to speak to me again tomorrow, but I've already told them everything.' She shuddered. 'They must know I had cause to resent Cleo and someone's told them I was outside The Briars, the night I arrived.' It was just as Eve had feared. 'DI Palmer asked me what I was doing there. When I told him I was facing up to the past he underlined something in his notebook.'

He would, the oaf.

Viv pulled Stevie into a floury hug. 'Take no notice of that prize prune Palmer. No one in their right mind would think you had anything to do with it. Besides, no one would kill over a rumour.'

'The worst was when he asked me about the flashback,' Stevie went on. 'I had to relive it all again. I couldn't think of any details that would confirm which house I was remembering, so Palmer thinks it's The Briars, because that's where Honor was found. I'm worried he thinks I blame Cleo for her death and the flashback pushed me over the edge.' She gave them a wry look. 'Someone saw me looking at the statue of the water nymph in her garden. That was the weapon used to knock her down.'

Hardly the most compelling evidence. Eve felt angry at the informant, whoever they were.

Viv pulled Stevie into a hug again. Eve had a hunch Stevie

wished she'd let her go, but to her credit, she didn't say so. And Viv definitely needed it. Over Stevie's shoulder, her eyes met Eve's, wide with alarm.

'Viv says you've been talking to your mum,' Eve said, when Stevie emerged from the embrace. They needed to home in on the facts to resolve this.

Stevie nodded. 'She's going to ask for emergency leave, though I've told her not to worry. The hospital is short-staffed; they won't want to let her go. And I'd rather see her when all this is over.' She pressed clenched fists to her eyes. 'I want to be chatting about the wedding, not Honor's death and Cleo's murder.'

Eve got that.

'She cried when I told her about the buried memory,' Stevie went on. 'I keep wondering if Auntie Honor was still alive when I found her. Maybe if I'd understood more, I could have saved her. Made someone call an ambulance. I wish I could remember.' She swallowed. 'Mum says I used to come back to Saxford to visit a friend who lived on Parson's Walk and I was here the day Honor died. The friend's mum had picked me up from nursery school.' Eve wasn't surprised to hear the shake in her voice. 'Perhaps I could have escaped their garden and managed to get into The Briars.'

'Maybe you followed Honor in,' Viv said. 'Do you remember seeing her alive?'

Stevie shook her head. 'I have the impression of walking into a place that was very still and deserted.'

'How would Honor have got in? To The Briars or Max's place?'

'She had keys. Auntie Honor cleaned for the people who lived at The Briars before they moved out.' Stevie twisted one of her chestnut curls around a finger. 'Afterwards, the estate agent asked her to pop in to dust from time to time. She did for Max Bancroft and his wife too.'

Eve pulled out her notebook to record the details. 'Do you know who else she worked for?'

Stevie frowned. 'I asked Mum. She mentioned Cleo. But not Abby or Lara's families. Several other villagers employed her, of course. Half of Saxford, Mum said. But no one else with a particular connection to Cleo, she doesn't think.'

If Honor had worked for Max Bancroft, they'd probably chatted. He could have picked up on it if she'd become a danger to him or Cleo. Maybe she'd threatened to reveal their affair.

'Do you remember what it was like at your friend's place?' Eve asked. 'Could you have slipped out?'

Stevie nodded slowly. 'I hadn't thought of it in years but it's coming back to me. You could push through their back hedge. I can remember the smell. Conifers, I think. And beyond it, there was a footpath which ran parallel with Parson's Walk and the cut-through to Meadowsweet Grove. It was very overgrown and spanned the backs of the houses, from the churchyard to a side passage by The Briars. We weren't supposed to use it. My friend's mum, Rose, was strict about that. But if she put the tent up in the garden, she couldn't see what went on beyond it. We used to dare each other to go down the path, past next-door-but-one's garden. There was a woman there who used to chase us, banging a saucepan with a wooden spoon.'

She would have been an excellent deterrent in Eve's eyes. Each to their own. 'Wouldn't you have told Rose you'd seen Honor?'

Stevie frowned. 'I'm not sure. I was so young, you see, and I'd have known I'd get into terrible trouble for leaving, let alone going into someone else's house. When I had the flashback, the fact that Honor was dead – and even that it was Honor – felt like a horrific revelation. I suspect I was meshing the memory with what I know now. And like I said, she might not even have been dead at that point.' She closed her eyes.

13

When Eve popped back to Elizabeth's Cottage, Robin hadn't returned yet and there were still precious hours before the gang meet-up.

As she walked Gus round the village green, she prioritised immediate actions. It seemed highly likely that Cleo's death was related to Honor's. It made understanding the earlier mystery crucial and it was time to spy out the land.

She needed a view of the rear of Parson's Walk, to see how easily four-year-old Stevie could have reached Max's house or The Briars. And how she could have got in, too. She could have followed Honor, as Viv had suggested, but Eve doubted it. Honor's keys had probably been for the front doors, whereas it looked probable that Stevie had gone in round the back. And besides, Stevie's sense that she'd entered an empty house didn't fit with Honor being alive when she'd arrived.

Eve needed to think through the possibilities. If Honor had been pushed and died at Max's place, how had he moved her body without being seen? Eve couldn't imagine him manhandling her into a car, even if it had been after dark. The lane was intimate, the houses closely packed – even more so than on

Meadowsweet Grove. But Max was a large man. Him carrying her along an overgrown pathway was plausible.

What she needed was the view from the bird hide on the marsh meadow beyond Parson's Walk. It would be a perfect lookout tower, though dogs were banned.

'Sorry, buddy.' She bent to stroke her dachshund before walking him home. 'This will be a solo mission.' She dropped him off and snatched up her binoculars. Nice and compact. Not too self-advertising.

Minutes later, she crossed the village green and St Peter's churchyard, exiting through a weathered wooden gate to access the meadow. It felt as though she was leaving the village. Ahead of her was nothing but wide skies, the mid-afternoon sun mellow, the estuary snaking its way past. She could smell the brackish water and hear the anxious parental calls of a group of avocets.

Eve followed the boardwalk to the hide, treading over the wooden planks. The approach was on the far side of the lookout from the village, so she hoped she wouldn't be seen. She was banking on being alone up there too. After such an horrific event in the village, she didn't imagine many people would be birdwatching.

At last, she reached the door to the hide and let herself in. It *was* empty, shaded and breezy, smelling of wood and creaking underfoot. The viewing panels faced the wrong way of course, but Eve could open the door a crack and look down in the direction she needed.

She took up her binoculars. Spread out below her, running from the village green to her left, to Meadowsweet Grove on her right, was Parson's Walk. Where the walk met the grove, there was a narrow cut-through, allowing pedestrians to traverse between the two. Parson's Walk was at right angles to the grove and Eve was facing the back gardens on its west side. Between her and them, she could just see the passageway Stevie had mentioned, running from the churchyard by the village green, all the way to The Briars and Meadowsweet Grove. The rear of The Briars and its back garden were visible too, thanks to its position at the head of the grove. Eve could also see Abby and Lara's houses, on the grove's north side.

Relying on her memories of the garden tour earlier, Eve picked out Max's place on Parson's Walk. Its rear was brick built, with French windows and a solid back door. If he'd just killed Honor, she couldn't imagine him leaving either of them open. Especially not if he knew about the children who explored the pathway just beyond the hedge that enclosed his garden. Eve wondered what she'd been hoping for. Her grandmother had had a large cat flap that her dogs and cats had both used. If Max had had something like that, Stevie could have got in, but he didn't.

Eve turned to train her binoculars on the rear of The Briars. The place was crawling with scientific support officers, dressed in white overalls. The back of the house differed from Max's. Perhaps one of them had been remodelled at some stage. Cleo had two sets of French windows. Of course, if Honor had been stumbling round The Briars after too much to drink, and had died by accident, she might have opened the back doors. The house was empty after all. She'd only herself to please. Stevie could have pottered in then. Eve needed to get a more detailed account of the scene when her body was discovered.

She sighed and followed Stevie's pathway with her binoculars. It was beyond a hedge that separated it from the marsh meadow, so she couldn't see down into it. At the Meadowsweet Grove end it was hard to discern it at all. There were trees that masked its approach to The Briars. Eve tried Google Earth but it was still hard to see. She wondered what Robin would say if she announced she planned to explore the route after dark. It could be useful and she'd prefer not to be seen. She wouldn't go alone though; she didn't have a death wish.

She exited the hide and was about halfway through her descent when her attention was caught by a bright flash – like light bouncing off a mirror.

Heck. She was pretty sure it had come from an upper-floor window at Max Bancroft's place.

When Eve was all the way down, close to the edge of the meadow and behind the cover of a tree, she trained her binoculars on his window.

There he was. Eve held her breath. He was standing perfectly still with a pair of binoculars, just like her. Currently, he was facing The Briars, but earlier when she'd seen the flash, he must have had them pointed in her direction.

As Eve walked back towards Elizabeth's Cottage, she wondered how much Max had seen. The thought made her glance over her shoulder more than once.

Against his involvement was the unlikeliness of Stevie getting into his house and the difficulty he'd have had moving Honor's body. In favour was the extreme reaction Stevie had had in his hallway, and his look of fear after her flashback.

If Max had killed Honor, he could have been in cahoots with Cleo, or have done it for his own reasons. Maybe he'd seduced her and she'd threatened to tell. Or she could have known about his affair with Cleo, as Eve had thought earlier. After all, Honor and Cleo had spent a lot of time together.

It took Eve back to the rumour that Cleo had been pressing Honor to keep a secret, just before she died.

Back at home, Eve checked her emails. *Suffolk Monthly* had already come back to accept her pitch for Cleo's obituary. That was good news. After that, she turned her mind to Cleo's death and who might be responsible.

She was writing her notes when a text came in. She'd anticipated an update from Robin, but in fact it was Ella Tyndall whose name flashed on the screen.

Ella was a teacher at the village primary school and a keen local historian. She wanted to know if Eve could meet her for a quick drink at the Cross Keys. Right now.

What was going on?

Eve checked her watch. She just had time before the gang were due. She replied to agree, and found Ella outside the pub. She was shifting from foot to foot, her jaw tense. 'Thanks for coming. Shall we go in?'

It had to be to do with Cleo's death. 'Of course.' They entered the crowded bar. The place was full of locals, and reporters too. They stood out, asking pushy questions and making calls in corners, earning a scowl from the pub cook, Jo Falconer, who'd appeared behind the bar, a tea towel over one arm.

Once they'd managed to get served, Ella looked around, her eyes anxious, then suggested they go to the garden. It was crowded there too. Everyone would want to share their horror over what had happened.

Ella found a perch on a low wall, well away from the other customers.

Eve leaned forward. 'What is it, Ella? Are you okay?'

The woman sighed. 'I wasn't sure whether to say anything.' She glanced over her shoulder again. 'It's about the flashback Stevie had. I guessed you and Viv would be worried about it. And that you might look into the death, if you're interviewing for Cleo's obituary.'

Eve nodded. Most of the villagers knew she'd given the police information in the past. 'I'll certainly keep my ear to the ground.'

Ella lowered her voice further. 'It's just a story I heard once when I was researching Saxford's history. It might not even be true.'

'Go on.' Eve sipped her drink.

'A person I spoke to said there was once a tunnel that led from an outbuilding at Max Bancroft's place to The Briars. It ends up inside the house, according to the rumour. The man who built both places lived in Max's and had a lover at Cleo's. He was married, and used the tunnel for secret assignations, or so they say.'

Wow. If Max had moved Honor's body, that would have made his job a lot easier.

'I can tell the police, of course,' Ella said, 'though I doubt they'll be able to do anything, even if someone proves it exists. Either way, I wanted to let you know.'

'Thanks, Ella.' Eve felt goosebumps rise on her arms.

14

Back at Elizabeth's Cottage, Robin was home. Eve put out drinks and nuts, ready for the gang, and told him what Ella had said.

'I've got lots to pass on too. D'you want a preview?'

Eve was dying to know but it made sense to wait until everyone was assembled. They arrived moments later. Viv was first. She looked anxious and breathless and had Stevie in tow.

Eve poured them drinks, then did a second round when Sylvia and Daphne appeared with Simon hard on their heels.

She hugged her neighbours. 'How are you? It must have been awful to find Cleo's body.'

They looked pale. 'We've come through worse.' Sylvia took the gin and tonic Eve had poured and thanked her.

'I can't think when,' Daphne said, and did the same.

Sylvia sighed. 'More personal loss, I meant. It's not as though we were close to Cleo. She was hard-nosed. Willing to ride roughshod over convention. But I liked her energy. She took life by the throat.'

Daphne sighed. 'She certainly caused trouble though. Her affair with Max tore a family apart.' She turned to Eve. 'I worked with his wife, you know. A lovely woman who ran a gallery in

Blyworth. They took a lot of my work.' Daphne was a potter. 'She was utterly devastated when she found out about Cleo and Max. The awful thing was, I'd heard a rumour about the affair. But what on earth does one say?'

'An impossible situation.' Eve doubted she'd have waded in either.

When they were all seated, she filled them in on everything she'd discovered so far.

'A tunnel?' Simon said. 'It's like something from a children's book.'

'Ha!' Sylvia took some nuts. 'There's nothing childlike about a married man building a secret route to reach his lover. Still less about another married man using it to move a body.'

'No, I know.' Simon looked defensive. 'But still.'

'We don't know the tunnel's definitely there yet,' Eve pointed out, 'but it's an interesting possibility.'

Viv was perched on the edge of one of Eve's couches, her shoulders hunched. 'If it does exist, then how come it's not common knowledge?'

'I was wondering that.' Eve leaned forward. 'Maybe the householders blocked it off and it passed into history. If it's truly there, then I guess Max discovered it at some point and investigated. He'd have known The Briars was empty, so it would be safe to transport poor Honor there, so long as he avoided estate-agent viewings.'

Viv nodded. 'What about you, Robin? What have you heard? You don't mind Stevie listening in?'

'Not at all.' Though he looked uncomfortable. 'But this has to be between us. Greg would get the sack if Palmer knew he was leaking information.'

'Absolutely understood.' Viv did the scout's honour salute.

Robin gave her a wry smile. 'I'm so glad you're more trustworthy than you look.'

Sylvia snorted. 'Low bar.'

Robin opened his notebook. 'The time of death was between eleven and twelve this morning.'

It was so utterly reckless. Robin was right: they must have been desperate.

Daphne shuddered. 'It's awful to think of Cleo lying there as people wandered round her garden.'

Robin nodded. 'Though she might have died just before she was found. With no sightings during the window, it's impossible to say.'

'What about alibis?' Eve said.

Robin rubbed his brow. 'None of the key players has one. The timing's too imprecise.'

'If only the police had come after Lara Oxley called they might have been there themselves. It seems so odd that Cleo would steal that necklace.' Eve couldn't fathom it. 'It would be terminal for her business if she was found out.'

Robin turned to her. 'I agree, but you saw her sneak into Shell Cottage. She must have had a purpose.'

Eve still couldn't see it being theft.

'What about suspects?' Viv's voice quavered slightly.

'Abby Porter's on the list, for obvious reasons. Everyone can see she might want revenge.'

But Eve thought a motive linked to Honor's death was more likely. She didn't say so though, for fear of putting Stevie in the spotlight.

But Stevie took a deep breath, her eyes clear as she spoke. 'And me. It's all right, you can say it. I could tell when they asked me to talk to them again tomorrow. And not to leave Saxford.'

Robin sighed. No wonder he'd looked worried by her presence. 'We all know you wanted to build bridges with Cleo.'

'I wish I hadn't been seen staring at her house.' Stevie clutched at her hair. 'And the inspector's making a lot of me admiring Cleo's statue.'

'I'm sure half the village noted it,' Robin said.

Eve took out her notebook. The only way to help was to solve the mystery. 'So, we've got two possibilities: that Cleo's death relates to Honor's and was triggered by Stevie's flashback.' She gave her an apologetic look. 'Or that one of Cleo's current entanglements led to the attack.' To Eve's mind, the first was considerably more likely than the second. The way the death had followed the flashback so fast was too much of a coincidence.

'Max is high up my list of suspects,' she went on. 'He looked terrified after the flashback. If we find anything to support him moving Honor's body, he has to be a top focus. Assuming he and Cleo conspired to kill her, they could have panicked after Stevie's memory surfaced, and argued over what to do next.' What if Max had suggested they silence Stevie and Cleo had refused? What if Jonah arrived back in England to find her dead? Eve took a deep breath and tried to stop the horrifying thoughts.

She focused on action instead, casting Robin a sidelong glance. 'I'd like to see if we can find Ella's tunnel after dark.'

He grimaced. 'I had a feeling that was coming. The trouble with being an ex-cop is that you're very aware of offences like trespass and breaking and entering. But I agree, we need to know. The police won't have enough evidence to request a warrant.'

Eve felt her shoulders relax. 'Thanks.'

'And what about Richie?' It was Stevie who'd spoken. 'It's all right. I know he's as much of a suspect as I am.'

It was a relief to be able to talk freely. 'I think it all depends on whether the flashback made him question Cleo. I'm sure she was genuinely fond of him; she might have found it hard to lie convincingly. If she admitted to a part in his mother's death it would have been utterly devastating. How well do you know him, Stevie? He seems the sort to feel things deeply.'

She nodded. 'I've been to visit since I arrived, but we didn't see much of each other, growing up.' She blushed. 'I should have spent more time with him last time I came to Saxford, but I met Jonah, who was visiting too, and well, we fell for each other, and I got distracted. But I agree. From what Mum says, he sounds quite like Honor. Everything touches him.'

Eve would set up a meeting with Richie as a priority. 'I need to ask him about his mum and Cleo to gauge his feelings.'

'What do the police think?' Sylvia asked.

Robin sighed. 'They asked Max about the flashback of course, but there's nothing that's specific to his house. He's denied all knowledge and as far as they're concerned, Honor's death was an accident, so they're not pushing.' He glanced around the group. 'Unfortunately, it was Palmer's uncle who led the original investigation. Greg says he bristles at any suggestion that something was missed.

'And to be fair, we can't prove that it was. They're willing to believe that someone killed Cleo to avenge Honor's death, but based on village rumours, not fact.'

'And that's where I come in,' Stevie said.

Robin grimaced. 'They have no evidence; it's all speculation. As for Richie, he's further down the suspect list in Palmer's eyes. Even if the flashback made him wonder about a conspiracy between Cleo and Max, Palmer argues he would have taken the job and money Cleo offered before killing her.'

'Which shows what a cold fish he is.' Eve despaired of him. 'From what I've seen, I doubt that would have held Richie back. He minds about things. Look how anxious he was about Abby when Cleo ditched her in his favour.'

'And even if he was the hard-nosed sort,' Robin said, 'what Cleo was offering was a nice package, but not a fortune. The pay for the role's guaranteed for four years but it has to come from profits after that. There's money to cover accommodation for four years too. The provisions are all laid out in her will.'

'That was fast work,' Sylvia said.

'She updated the paperwork a few weeks back, in fact, well

before her forced public announcement. And Abby never featured – not even in the earlier version.'

Eve thought of Richie, heading off to establish the new branch of Marbeck's, and felt a twist of anxiety. Everyone said he'd failed more than once at his own business ventures. And now he had no Cleo to guide him.

'Where does the rest of the estate go? To Cleo's family?' Eve hadn't had time to research them yet.

Robin glanced at his notebook. 'Not the most immediate lot here in Suffolk. She's named some distant cousin in Canada who's a high-flyer, just like she was. Norah Campbell.'

'I guess she won't be very hands on when it comes to running the company.' The bequest made Eve wonder about Cleo's relations with her immediate family. She hoped they'd agree to an interview. She'd want to talk to someone from Marbeck's for the obituary too. She'd be more thorough than her fee warranted. She couldn't make a decent job of it otherwise, or have any hope of finding Cleo's killer.

'So, on to the motives that don't relate to Honor.' Eve knew they needed to keep them in mind.

Robin nodded. 'Max is on that list as well as the other. The police are interested in his affair with Cleo, but he's not a chief suspect. They know they fought on Wednesday, thanks to our evidence, but if Max killed from passion, they want to know why he waited until today.'

The row could still be relevant though. Cleo's rejection might have made it easier for him to kill her over their history.

Eve went back to her notes. 'Apart from him, it's possible Abby killed to keep her damaging secret if she thought Cleo might pass it on. She was already furious at losing the job, so lashing out sounds plausible. It would be a heck of a risk, though. I need to find out if the secret was worth killing for.'

'Sounds tricky,' Viv said.

'It's connected with her ex, Sean. Or at least he knew about it. I'll dig into his past and see if I can talk to his surviving friends or relatives.

'Then there's Lara. I want to know why she hated Cleo and if anything recent might have led her to act on it. The theft of the necklace made her angry, but that doesn't feel like enough. She wanted Cleo prosecuted, not dead and past caring. Abby thinks the tensions date back to when Lara's brother died.

'I also want to know why Perry accepted Cleo's job offer when there's bad blood between them. I'll need to talk to him.'

She turned to Robin. 'But I still feel Honor's fall is probably at the root of all this. Do you think Greg would let me read the files on her death?'

He winced. 'You don't ask for much, but I can see what he says.'

'And what can we do?' Simon asked.

'Keep your eyes peeled, for a start. Let's use our WhatsApp group to send updates.'

'I think a visit to the bird hide might be in order,' Sylvia put in. 'Daphne bought me new binoculars for Christmas.'

'Maybe not alone though,' Eve said. 'It was unnerving, the feeling that Max had spotted me there.'

'We'll go together.' Daphne's eyes were serious, though Sylvia laughed.

Simon sat forward in his chair. 'So, we're looking for someone who was overcome with emotion.'

'I think so,' said Robin. 'Anger, hatred or fear. Self-preservation's a powerful motivator.' He turned to Stevie. 'Whatever happens, take great care. Measure every word you say to people in the village. Never let any additional memories slip out unless it's to one of us or the police.'

Eve leaned forward. 'And we'll do everything humanly possible to find out who did this so you can rest easy again.' They couldn't work fast enough.

15

'I can't believe I agreed to this.' It was dark and Eve and Robin were skirting the edge of the marsh meadow beyond the houses on Parson's Walk. The bird hide was off to their right.

'I'm quite surprised too,' Eve whispered back. 'But it feels like the only way if the police aren't pursuing Max Bancroft for Honor's death. And maybe it's better if he feels that the threat has gone away. I couldn't bear it if anything happened to Stevie.'

He took her hand. 'I understand. All the same, I hope I don't have to swap our honeymoon suite for a prison cell.'

They were looking for somewhere to push through to the pathway Stevie had sneaked down, twenty-five years earlier. They were less likely to be seen that way than if they walked its length.

After that, their plans were fluid. It all depended on what they found. The thought of exploring Max's property to find the tunnel was tying Eve's stomach in knots. But Ella had said it opened into some kind of outhouse at his end. It was less threatening than breaking into his home.

Every step they took sounded loud in the quiet night, with dry twigs cracking under their feet. Eve wished the moon wasn't so bright and full; they were practically floodlit. At last, they found a place where the vegetation was less dense.

Robin turned and squeezed her hand. 'Ready?'

She nodded and they pushed their way through. Now they were in a narrow tree- and shrub-lined walkway that smelled of conifer, laurel and earth. Eve imagined being Stevie, wandering along the path alone, a tiny little scrap of a thing, going on an adventure.

'I'll need to peer through the trees to see if we're behind the right house.'

She pushed her face into the foliage, the citrusy smell of pine engulfing her. She'd dressed all in black. At least she shouldn't stand out, and she was only peeking, not trespassing yet. Unfortunately, she was already breathing fast enough to make her dizzy.

'Not this one,' she whispered, pulling back. 'But I think he's right next door.' Her mental image of the row was clear.

'Okay.'

They moved a short way along the path and Eve checked again. There it was, the rear with the French windows. And to Eve's right, a brick-built garden store. It had been masked by hedges when she'd looked from the bird hide.

The house itself was in darkness. They'd waited until one in the morning. Eve hoped Max was in bed.

Robin swapped places with her. 'I can't see any cameras,' he murmured, pulling back again. 'There's a movement sensor under the outside light but we shouldn't trigger it if we stick to the end of the garden.'

Eve tried to steady her breathing. 'Any ideas what to say if we're caught?'

'I suggest we avoid that.'

'Hmm.'

They'd already agreed that Eve would keep watch while Robin tried to break into the outhouse. He was more expert in that area. As he skirted the building, heading for the door, Eve flattened herself to one side, amongst the shadows, and channelled her attention to keep them safe. All the while she knew Robin would be exposed in the moonlight. At least he shouldn't be recognisable. He'd dressed for the occasion like her, with only a small part of his face showing.

She heard rather than saw him get the outhouse door open and worked her way around the building, her eyes still on the house. They were going to swap at this point, on the principle that if push came to shove, Robin would be better at seeing off an attack. He happened to be bigger than she was.

He slipped past her, back into the shadows, and Eve sidled into the outhouse and closed the door behind her. She instantly felt claustrophobic. It was pitch black, as though she'd been swallowed. Lighting her phone torch made her feel slightly better. She surveyed the room. The place smelled of oil and was full of tools: a mower, loppers, shears and spades. Plenty of things to use as improvised weapons, but she wouldn't and couldn't. She was in the wrong. She and Robin could both be arrested if they were discovered.

Eve cast her torch over the floor of the outhouse. It looked like concrete, dusted with dirt from the garden. She moved around a workbench. She could see her footprints in the dirt. *Heck.* She crouched down to smooth over the marks she'd made and tried to tread on tiptoe.

It was at that point that she noticed other marks in the dry earth. They were faint, as though someone had swept the floor to try to disguise them, but by torchlight, they showed up. Lines of dirt and scratches, making it look as though something heavy had been pulled across the floor.

Glancing up, Eve could imagine what had caused them. Just beyond the sketchy marks was a large, heavy-looking storage unit. Eve guessed it had been moved recently. Nothing had marked the swept area of dirt since. Why suddenly move a heavy bit of furniture like that, if not to hide the entrance to the tunnel they were looking for? The position of the unit made no sense otherwise. The contents would be harder to reach in its new position.

Eve's phone lit up with a message. Robin's signal for her to get out. Her breath caught.

She retreated as fast as she could. There was no time to mess up the dirt to cover her tracks.

The house was still in darkness as she slipped outside and back into the shadows.

'Someone's hanging around in the pathway.' Robin's whisper was almost inaudible. 'I'm going to lock the outhouse. Then we need to find out who it is.'

Eve watched the back of the house again. It was quiet. Robin returned quickly and melted into the shadows. A moment later, he'd pressed himself into the conifers and was peering into the passageway.

'They're just up the path from us, tucked into the hedge, like we were. Peering in.' He kept his mouth close to her ear and she turned to do the same.

'Do you think they saw us?'

He shook his head. 'Let's leave while their attention's focused on the house. Then we can find out who they are and what they're up to.'

That sounded daunting. Eve followed Robin through the conifers. They were almost silent.

He pulled off his beanie and shoved it in his pocket and Eve followed suit. Then he took her hand, pulled her close and kissed her passionately, as though they were a normal couple, taking the passageway at the end of a romantic evening.

A moment later, he must have decided he was happy for them to be spotted. He shifted to crack a twig underfoot and there was a gasp from behind them.

Robin grinned at Eve, then pulled away as she looked towards the sound.

It was a woman with shoulder-length hair, dressed in a padded jacket and slacks.

She didn't look like your average burglar any more than Eve did. Her head was turned towards them, but she was still pressed in close to Max Bancroft's hedge. Producing an innocent explanation would be tricky. Thank goodness she hadn't noticed Eve and Robin emerge from the garden. It would have been another matter if they'd had to push through a hedge that rustled.

For a moment, Eve thought the woman might run, but when Robin beckoned, her shoulders went down. She approached, and Robin indicated they should all about turn, back towards the church and the village green.

They'd got a certain way when the woman hesitated at the back of another house on Parson's Walk. Eve could see a gap in the hedge, as though someone had recently pushed their way through.

'Your place?' Eve said quietly.

The woman avoided her eyes but nodded.

Suddenly, Eve thought she knew who this woman was. She dredged her memory for the name of Stevie's playmate's mum. 'Are you Rose?'

She blinked at them in the moonlight. 'How did you know?'

'I'm a friend of Stevie's,' Eve said. 'She mentioned your name recently.' And if Rose was out in the dead of night, looking at the rear of Max Bancroft's house, it meant something. 'Should we talk inside for a moment? If you don't mind?'

Rose's eyes were wary but at last she pushed through the hedge and Eve and Robin followed, stepping into a conservatory that she unlocked.

'Stevie mentioned playing here,' Eve said. 'And that she was a terror for wandering off.' She let the sentence hang. She'd rather not say anything too leading.

Rose sank into a sofa. 'I tried to keep a close eye on all my daughter's friends.'

'It's never easy.'

'I was a childminder. It was supposed to be my specialist subject.'

'All the same.' Eve smiled. 'I've got twins. I know what it's like.' She paused. 'What made you look at Max Bancroft's house tonight?'

Rose was silent for a long time. 'I wondered about the flash-back everyone says Stevie had,' she said at last.

'Did Stevie say anything when she was a child to make you think she'd got inside Max Bancroft's place? Or mention anything she'd seen there?'

Rose shook her head. 'Not at all. I just wondered.'

She seemed on edge, but that wasn't necessarily suspicious. If she'd ever had doubts about Max's character, the flashback was enough to justify her nervousness.

'Stevie's sure it was The Briars she went to.' Eve was determined to reinforce that story for now, to keep her safe. 'And besides, I don't see how she'd have got into Max Bancroft's house.'

But Rose bit her lip. 'He and his wife were having an extension done back then. I remember because I went in for drinks and we talked about how shocked we were at Honor's death. Half the back of the house was remodelled. It was only covered with a tarpaulin.'

16

Eve felt like death warmed up the following morning, she'd had so little sleep. It was Sunday and she could have lain in, but worry drove her out of bed early. She and Robin dosed themselves with black coffee then went to walk Gus along the beach.

'What do you think?' Robin said, taking her hand.

'It's all circumstantial, but the storage unit had clearly been dragged across Max's outhouse floor – and recently. It's too much of a coincidence. I imagine he's hidden the entrance to the tunnel. And now we know Stevie could have accessed his house too. It's closer to Rose's place than The Briars.'

'If Bancroft moved Honor's body, he'd have to have done it quickly, or the pathologist would have picked up on it. But the tunnel would have made that possible. He wouldn't have had to wait for nightfall to avoid being seen. I wonder where the tunnel emerges at The Briars. It must be well hidden, or the police would have found it yesterday.'

It was a good point. 'Either way, if Max has hidden the tunnel entrance since Cleo's death, there surely has to be a link between Honor's fall and Cleo's murder. I still feel it's most likely that the flashback caused someone to challenge Cleo and lose control. It would fit with them attacking her despite the crowds milling around.'

Robin nodded. 'Or Max could have murdered Honor alone, then killed Cleo when she guessed.'

'True. And in that scenario, Perry might also want to silence Cleo. Even if he hates his dad, having him revealed as a murderer could ruin his career. He's got some well-to-do clients.'

'It sounds like a stretch, but not impossible. Greg's going to dig out the information you wanted, by the way. Palmer's driving him nuts. He's not willing to believe the police missed anything relating to Honor's death, though he still fancies Stevie for Cleo's killing, driven by baseless rumours. I'm afraid a witness heard her talking to you and Viv about struggling to forgive Cleo.'

Eve remembered her saying it, after Cleo had insisted she must have Honor's drawing. 'But just after that, she made up her mind to accept a gift from her to move things forward.'

Robin grimaced. 'They didn't hear that bit, I'm afraid.'

This was awful.

His eyes met hers. 'You've been getting to know her. She wouldn't do it, would she?'

Eve shook her head. 'I'm sure not. And even if she was the sort, the idea of her committing murder just before her wedding is ludicrous.'

He held her close. 'I've updated Greg on what we found last night, but I doubt he'll be able to do anything without more evidence.' He gave her the flicker of a smile. 'It would be best if it was legally acquired too.'

After they'd discussed Cleo's death, they talked about the cold cases Robin was reviewing for the police down in London. His old employers had been quick to approach him as a free-lancer, now he was no longer in hiding. Eve loved the fire in his eyes as he spoke, and his drive to come up with answers for the families of the victims. Best of all was the fact that he wanted her opinion and trusted her with the information.

Back at home, Eve spent a while digging for leads. She found Cleo's sister online; she managed a farm shop a few miles away. Eve emailed to express her sympathy and ask to interview her for the obituary. She wasn't sure what to expect, given Cleo had ignored her in her will. After that, she messaged Richie and Max to request interviews. They were a top priority and she was already connected with them, thanks to the open-garden WhatsApp group.

As for Abby and Lara, she could see them more informally at Parker's, perhaps. They and Perry didn't feel as urgent but Eve had time to kill, while she waited for Max and Richie to respond.

She glanced at her watch. She could go to Parker's now. She might catch Abby or Lara if they were working.

'Sorry, buddy.' She looked down at the expectant Gus, who'd sensed an outing was in the offing. 'Parker's isn't the sort of establishment that realises the true value of canines.'

He cheered up when he realised Robin was staying at home. *Talk about fickle...* Eve decided to rise above it.

She fetched her Mini Clubman and drove to Blyworth to reach the venerable department store. It was nearing lunchtime, but hopefully she'd catch Abby or Lara before they took their breaks.

In fact, as Eve left the side street she'd parked in and entered a road lined with half-timbered Elizabethan buildings, she saw Abby. She was striding down an alley that led round the back of Parker's, in pursuit of a man, by the look of it. As Eve's eyes focused, she realised it was Max Bancroft.

Abby looked determined and was gaining speed. An interaction between two suspects was too important to miss, but she couldn't eavesdrop from the passage they'd taken. There was no cover. She pictured the surrounding area instead, dragging out her phone to look at a map.

There was a tree-lined car park to the left of where the pair were about to walk. Eve would need to run to reach it, going the long way round. *Game on.* Passers-by stared as she hared off.

She got herself in position at the far end of the car park. Peering through the trees, she glimpsed Abby and Max and heard the murmur of their voices. She stood very still to listen, trying to slow her breathing.

'No,' Abby was saying, her voice breathless too, 'I just caught sight of you and I wanted to express my condolences. I'd fallen out with Cleo, of course, but I know the two of you were close.'

Max's expression was sceptical. 'Thank you, but it felt as though you were chasing me. And it feels a bit odd for someone who hated Cleo to be offering condolences. I can think of other reasons you might want to talk to me though. Past history, is that it?' He looked at her keenly.

What had gone on between them? Max wasn't talking to her like an ex – he seemed too distant for that.

'I don't know what you're referring to,' Abby said.

That settled it. If they had been lovers, she'd have understood his meaning.

She'd stilled now, as though she was trying to gauge something from Max's expression. 'I didn't start off hating Cleo, you know. She probably told you she took me and Sean for fools.'

What did Abby mean by that?

Max asked the same question, but Abby shook her head, frowning as though making a calculation. 'If Cleo didn't tell you then it doesn't matter. I suppose she blabbed about her reasons for retracting her job offer though.'

Abby's secret.

At last, Max nodded. 'I was shocked, I don't mind admitting.'

She flushed. 'I'd like to explain it to you. Will you come and visit me? It's no use talking here, in a rush.'

Max towered over her. 'All right. But when I come to your cottage, I'll be prepared. For all I know you killed Cleo to keep her quiet.'

Abby blanched. 'I didn't!'

But he'd already turned and was striding away. Abby stared after him, then pivoted towards Parker's rear entrance.

Eve retraced her steps, back to the front of the department store. She felt uneasy. If Max had killed Cleo, it made perfect sense for him to accuse Abby to convince her he was innocent. He'd implied he'd visit Abby's cottage armed. That now he knew her secret, he imagined she might try to silence him. But he could be more dangerous than she was. Eve strongly suspected he'd murdered Honor, with or without help from Cleo.

She needed to get enough evidence to persuade the police to look at Max and it was important to find out what Abby was hiding too. She'd be more likely to get that information from one of Sean's friends, but she'd still try to strike up a conversation now. The more familiar she and Abby got, the more clues Eve might unearth.

She entered Parker's to the smell of clean carpet and wafts of scent from the beauty section. There was something comfortingly traditional about it. She went up the escalator to womenswear and began casually looking through the outfits. She'd have to choose carefully if she wanted something with a bit of flair, but there were plenty of classic suits.

Just ahead of her and to her left, Abby appeared. She looked tense.

Eve caught her eye and got a strained smile in response.

'Sorry,' Eve said as she approached. 'It feels as though normal life should be on hold after yesterday. Coming shopping is weird, but I've got a wedding to attend soon. I'll feel twitchy until I've picked an outfit.'

Abby nodded. 'Of course.'

'I'd like something quite,' Eve sought the right word, 'chic.' That cut out around half the outfits.

A knowing smile flashed across Abby's face. 'I understand.' Of course, she'd been working in a fashion boutique in Paris until she'd decamped to Suffolk – all thanks to Cleo's job offer.

Abby did a good job of picking outfits Eve might consider wearing, though when she tried them on, they weren't quite right. Coming out of the changing room with the rejected dresses and jackets, Eve prepared to tackle the business in hand.

'By the way, *Suffolk Monthly*'s commissioned me to write Cleo's obituary.'

Abby tensed as she took the clothes from Eve and handed her another suit.

'I'm sorry. I realise your life's been turned upside down thanks to her, but bad opinions count as well as good. I'm not trying to muckrake, I just want to write a balanced article.' Eve disappeared into the changing room again with the emerald-green dress and cropped jacket Abby had found. Really quite decent.

Abby was quiet until she reappeared. 'That outfit's good, but maybe try another colour. I'm not sure what to say about Cleo. Getting me over here then dropping me like a stone's unforgiveable.'

'Why do you think she did it?' But there was no way Abby would mention her secret.

She frowned as she turned away. 'She preferred Richie all of a sudden. She was mercurial that way.'

But Cleo had made Richie a beneficiary of her will weeks ago now, according to Robin. She wasn't as unpredictable as she'd seemed. Eve pondered the facts. Sean had told her Abby's secret before he died, prior to Abby moving back to England. Eve could only think that Cleo had decided she could overlook it but then changed her mind. Perhaps Abby had won her over initially with her first-class experience and charm.

'I'm sorry. You must have had big plans.'

Abby nodded. 'I'd persuaded Cleo to let me stock some clothes as well as the jewellery. Or at least, I thought I had.'

Thinking of Cleo's change of heart and Abby's comment to Max – that she'd taken her and Sean for fools – reminded Eve of Sean's letter. What if Abby had brought it up the day before and killed Cleo over it? If only Eve knew what it had said.

'Did you ever talk to Cleo about Sean's letter?'

Abby's cheeks tinged pink. 'No, not in the end. I was emotional when I told you about it. I realised afterwards that it didn't make any odds. He was still unfaithful to me.'

That thought mirrored Eve's, but she was sure he'd said something to alter Abby's view of his affair and that Abby was lying to cover that up. The idea of her and Sean being taken for fools presented them as united again. Cleo's joint victims.

Eve was running out of time. She needed to be at Monty's soon. 'Did you know Honor at all?' They must have been around the same age.

Abby's eyes opened wider. 'I thought you said you weren't muckraking.'

'I'm not, but she feels like part of Cleo's story.'

She frowned. 'She was. More than you'd ever know.'

What did she mean by that? But before Eve could ask, Abby went on. 'We were at school together.'

Eve took the suits Abby was carrying before she dropped the lot. Her mind was clearly no longer on Eve's outfit. There were tears in her eyes.

'It was just so sad,' she said, pulling a tissue from her pocket.

'I'm sorry to bring it back. You were close?'

Abby nodded. 'Good friends for years. It ended so abruptly. To hear that she was gone—' She buried her face in her hands for a moment.

'I presume the rumours about Honor keeping a damaging secret of Cleo's were rubbish.' If Eve pretended to dismiss the gossip, Abby might trust her enough to speak honestly.

But Abby shook her head. 'I don't know.' After a long pause she added, 'If there was any truth in it, Honor didn't confide in me.'

Eve hadn't really expected it to be that easy. She lowered her voice. 'What are your plans now? I'm guessing you might not stay at Parker's long.'

Abby took a deep breath and matched Eve's whisper. 'I put out feelers at the beginning of last week, the moment I knew it was all off with Cleo. I've got offers from two London stores where I'd get plenty of autonomy. I just need to make up my mind which to choose.'

If she was telling the truth, that had probably blunted her anger with Cleo, but she could still have killed to keep her secret.

Eve thanked her for her time, said she'd think about the dresses, then went back to the escalators.

She visited Parker's hair salon next, but there was no sign of Lara Oxley. Eve snapped up the first available appointment with her, though it wasn't as soon as she'd have liked.

She pondered the situation as she descended to the ground floor. She'd wanted the informality of the hair appointment – it might unlock Lara's secrets – but waiting that long wasn't ideal. She'd drop in on her as soon as she could and slip in some early questions.

On her way out, Eve passed a beguiling display of cookware. Barnwell and Greene, apparently. Beautifully designed. She was still making up her mind about a wedding present for her son and his fiancée. She glanced at the prices and winced. She'd consider other options too. As she moved off, she realised Lara was there, chatting to the person running the concession. For a moment, she hovered, but she didn't want to interrupt. She'd stick to her original plan and drop in.

17

Eve drove back to Saxford along country lanes, wild carrot and red clover dancing in the verges, the fields beyond full of pigs. It made her think of the contrast between Suffolk and London, where Eve had lived before. And where Richie was about to go. It was ridiculous, the way she kept feeling anxious for him. Surely he'd feel like a fish out of water, though? She'd done it in reverse: lived in Seattle until she was eighteen, then London after that, until her divorce. She smiled for a moment at the memory of her move to Saxford. She'd had to get used to everyone wanting to know her business and talking about her as though she was common property. It had been a shock to the system, but there'd been warmth too – people noticing if she had problems, wading in if she needed help. And often when she didn't. Doing it the other way round might be worse. There was a special sort of loneliness you only felt in a big city.

Eve was normally early for her shifts at the teashop but she forced herself not to dash in before three. She wanted to talk to Toby first, one of the three co-owners of the Cross Keys pub. She needed to find someone who knew Abby's secret. One of Sean's friends was a possibility. Of all the people in the village, Toby or his brother might know someone who'd known him. Ideally, she wanted a long-standing friend. She had no idea how old the secret was.

She went into the pub and offered to buy Toby a drink. He grinned and asked for a Coke. 'Is it me, or do I detect that this is advance payment for something?'

Eve smiled back. 'I can't believe I'm so transparent. You're right, I'm after information.' She explained what she wanted in a low voice, then added: 'I just need to know if there's any chance Abby would have killed Cleo to keep her secret.'

Toby frowned. 'Leave it with me. I'll try to find someone who fits the bill.'

'Thanks, Toby.' She hesitated. 'If you manage it, could you let me know where they work or which bars they go to? I'll try to bump into them, rather than making it formal. I've got an excuse to quiz people about Cleo, but pumping them for information on Abby's secret might set tongues wagging.'

Toby grinned. 'Not a problem. Glad to be part of the team.'

'Thank you.'

As Eve entered the teashop, Viv fixed her with an assessing glance. 'You look like someone who's paused in the middle of a running relay. Have you had lunch?'

When Eve hesitated, Viv steered her to the kitchen. 'Have a summer fruits tart. Now. But between mouthfuls, tell me everything.'

Eve passed on her news.

'How's Stevie?' she said, after she'd answered all Viv's questions.

Viv's eyes filled with tears. 'She was at the police station the entire morning, poor lamb. They knew all about her mum's breakdown. She says they kept pressing her on how she'd felt when she was so ill and rubbing it in about her parents breaking up on the back of it. She seemed so self-reliant yesterday, but there are chips appearing. I heard her crying in her room before I came over here. I had to stop myself dashing in to comfort her. I'm starting to sense she'd rather I gave her some space.'

Poor Viv. Turning inward in times of trouble was alien to her. Eve gave her a hug.

'Blast Palmer, he really is the pits,' Viv sniffed. 'Stevie looked so joyous when she first arrived. I wish she hadn't come up in advance of the wedding. I know it's terrible about Cleo, but this is ruining everything.'

Eve only hoped it didn't get worse. She gave Viv an extra squeeze. 'The police have nothing on her. I'm sure they're just desperate.'

'I can't bear the damage it's doing.' Viv bit her lip. 'I thought Jonah would come back to be with her but she says she's persuaded him to stay in Paris.'

'She'll have downplayed the whole thing. Jonah would be here like a shot otherwise. But the course is important to his business, isn't it? And it was expensive. Competitive too.'

Viv nodded. 'But I still wish he'd come.'

Eve went to help serve the customers. The place was crowded, just as the pub had been the evening before. It was easy to gauge the reaction of the locals. Stevie's flashback and Cleo's death were popular topics of conversation.

When Eve went to the kitchen for a pot of tea, she mentioned the chatter to Viv, who nodded. 'I need to keep Stevie out of sight. A gaggle of the usual suspects rushed up to her when I brought her back from the police station. Did they honestly think it was okay to hound her with questions? One of them said they didn't blame her for killing Cleo! The poor sweet's brought some work to crack on with while she's here but she can't concentrate, of course.'

Eve knew she designed websites. 'How do you know?'

Viv coloured slightly. 'No typing when I listened at the door.'

A resolution to the murder couldn't come soon enough.

Back in the teashop, Eve found the customers staring at the village green. She looked too, and double-took. Daphne was out there with Max Bancroft. She was shrinking away from him, her footsteps hurried. He was so much taller than her, and the more she drew back, the more he loomed over her.

Viv entered the room at that moment and Eve nodded towards Daphne. 'I think I should go to the rescue.'

'Absolutely.'

Eve pulled the teashop door open and strode towards her neighbour. 'Sorry to interrupt, but did you still want to come in for tea, Daphne? We're holding the table for you.'

Daphne looked at her gratefully. 'Is it that time already? Of course, I'm on my way. Excuse me, Max.'

Eve eyed Max, but he wouldn't know she was the one who'd sent the WhatsApp message requesting an interview. Their paths hadn't crossed, except when she'd visited his garden with a horde of other villagers. She'd chase it up if he hadn't replied by evening. At the moment, he looked devastated: eyes red and shadowed underneath. But that didn't make him innocent. He'd told Cleo he wanted to marry her and she'd rejected him. Add panic after the flashback to that and she could well believe he'd lashed out.

Back inside Monty's, the buzz of chat got louder, then quietened as Daphne sat down at a table. Eve waited until the throng had given up trying to listen in. Viv was by her side, her expression anxious.

'Are you all right?' Eve said at last, as Allie came to take Daphne's order.

Daphne nodded, but she glanced over her shoulder, as though checking she was safe. 'You remember I told you that I'd worked with Max's wife?'

'Yes.'

'He was asking me about her. What she'd said to me back in

the old days, *before* she officially found out about him and Cleo. He wanted to know if I thought she'd had any inkling he was being unfaithful.'

'He must have got the wind up,' Viv said. 'If he killed Honor, maybe he'd had a fling with *her*, and he wants to find out if anyone knew.'

It was risky to ask around. It might just jog memories. But Eve could understand him being rattled. 'How on earth did he bring the topic up?' It was on the sensitive side.

Daphne thanked Allie as she appeared with tea and a fruit tart. 'He said Cleo's death had brought it all back. And how guilty he felt over betraying his wife. He said he was worried she might secretly have known what was going on for longer than she admitted.'

Viv tutted. 'It's a bit late for regrets now. And of course she didn't! She exploded with grief when she finally discovered the truth.'

Daphne nodded. 'That's more or less what I said, but he kept pushing. He seemed scared. But his wife always seemed happy to me, and very much in love with Max. That's what I kept telling him. I wonder what he'd have done if I'd said I knew something about him and Honor.'

Neither Eve nor Viv replied. It wasn't a good thought.

18

As Eve left Monty's, she turned her attention to her interview with Richie. It was possible she could combine it with her plan to drop in on Lara. Eve needed to know why Lara had hated Cleo but kid gloves were required. She'd probably have to extract the information by degrees.

As for Richie, she wanted to know whether his memory of his mother was treasured, despite the influence of the disapproving granny. It was crucial to understand how he'd have reacted if Cleo had admitted to killing Honor. Would he have lashed out? Or gone to the police? It all depended on his feelings and his character.

Eve went to fetch Gus before she made for Meadowsweet Grove. Robin would accompany them too. He'd hide in the lane with an open call to Eve, just in case she ran into trouble. She couldn't see Richie or Lara causing problems unless they revealed they were guilty, but as Robin said, you never knew.

Both human and dog greeted her with fervour, which gave Eve a ridiculously sparky feeling inside, despite the current situation. Gus's enthusiasm increased when she picked up his leash. 'Please don't feel I'm using you,' she said. 'We are going for a walk, but it's a walk with a purpose.' She bent to fuss him. 'Your presence will make my conversations a lot more informal.'

Gus put his head on one side.

'It's just because you're adorable. You should be flattered.'

Eve and Robin cut across the village green and along Parson's Walk to reach Meadowsweet Grove. Eve couldn't help glancing to her right as she passed Max Bancroft's place. It looked shut-up but her skin still crawled. She wondered if he'd noticed any disturbance in his outhouse. He might know someone was on to him; he seemed to be panicking.

The police had left The Briars, but there was still tape across the doorway.

Robin's eyes were on Cleo's place too. 'I'll ask Greg if they've discovered anything extra.' He turned to her. 'Let's get the call live.'

She dialled and he picked up.

'All good. I'll go and lose myself up the lane behind that hawthorn. Any trouble and I'll be with you like a shot.'

She nodded and swallowed. That type of talk was enough to get anyone's adrenaline going.

She glanced at her watch. There was just time to call on Lara first if she was back from work. She lived opposite Richie in the second cottage on the left as you walked up the lane from The Briars. Eve could see an open window in the whitewashed house. That was a good sign.

She nipped up the front path, past fragrant lavender and cistus covered in blooms. She was about to knock on the door when she heard crying. That was awkward. Whatever was going on, Lara wouldn't want to be disturbed. But seeing her was important.

Eve knocked and the sobbing stopped, as though Lara was holding her breath.

Eve waited, feeling rotten, then knocked again. It was another minute before the door opened.

Lara's eyes were dry but noticeably red. She flinched at the sight of Eve.

Eve introduced herself, mentioning her job at Monty's before explaining about the obituary. Living and working in the village tended to help people accept her. 'I'm so sorry to bother you.' She gave a sympathetic smile. 'I'm in the grove to interview Richie, but I'd love to have your thoughts on Cleo too. I've booked a hair appointment with you. Perhaps we can chat then. I know you and Cleo had had a run-in over the necklace she stole yesterday, and maybe you didn't get on, but that makes your opinion even more important. Obituaries are only worthwhile if they're balanced.'

Lara stood back a little, her face swallowed by shadow. 'Seeing the necklace knocked me flat. But what makes you think we didn't get on in general?'

That was easy to answer. 'When you realised Cleo had taken something of yours, you said it fitted and that she was cruel, without a shred of conscience.' A strong hint, on top of the look she'd given Cleo in the Cross Keys.

Lara closed her eyes. 'I'd forgotten I'd said that. It was in the heat of the moment.'

'Could I possibly come in for a minute? I had a couple of quick questions for the obituary now, if you don't mind.'

Lara clearly did mind, but politeness stopped her from saying so. 'All right.'

Eve wanted to know why Lara had been crying. Something in the house might give the truth away. You didn't usually sob over the death of someone you hated. She was curious to see how Cleo might have pinched the necklace too. As Lara guided her and Gus through to her living room they passed a door to the kitchen and some steep stairs coming off the hall. Cleo could have reached them easily enough while Abby was feeding Lara's cat but it still seemed odd.

Lara sank onto a sofa and looked at Eve accusingly. 'So, what do you want?'

Eve's eyes ran over the tiny room. There was nothing to indicate the source of her emotion there, but it wasn't surprising. There'd been a mug on the kitchen table as they'd passed. She'd probably been sitting in there.

'I wondered if you could tell me how long you'd known Cleo for? And what kind of interactions you had? It will help shape our chat when I come in for my hair appointment.'

Lara looked tired, her shoulders sagging and rounded. 'I've known her since she arrived in the village. And she's made her presence felt ever since she bought The Briars and turned this lane into her fiefdom. I'm sorry, but she liked power, and she operated in an underhand way. You can see that from the theft.'

'That seemed odd to me: that she'd take such a risk when she has a successful business.'

Lara opened her mouth and closed it again before replying. 'She was acting oddly towards the end. Look at the way she treated poor Abby, despite her having way more experience than Richie. I think Cleo was cruel to force the job on him, just as she was cruel to take it away from Abby.'

'You and Abby are good friends?'

Lara nodded.

'Though she's only recently come back from Paris, I gather.' Lara seemed very partisan, considering.

'We knew each other a bit before she went.'

'And did you know Honor, by any chance?'

Lara frowned. 'What is all this?'

'She seems like an integral part of Cleo's story.'

'I suppose she was. I knew her. Everyone in the village did. But not well. She didn't clean for us – we couldn't afford it after my father died.'

'I'm so sorry for your loss. What did you think of her? I had the impression Cleo thought she was special, despite all the rumours about their fight.' Eve was thinking of the way Cleo had talked about Honor's drawing. Whatever they'd argued about the day Honor died, they'd clearly had a close connection.

Lara looked irritated. 'I barely knew her.' Her eyes met Eve's and she sighed. 'I can imagine Cleo might have liked her spontaneity. I saw her swimming in the sea once in a summer dress, her hair all straggled and wet. Immediately afterwards, she went to clean for Gwen Harris, dripping everywhere. Opinions were mixed, as you can imagine. Look, I'm sorry, but can we leave the rest until your appointment? I was in the middle of something.'

'Of course.' Eve needed to get to Richie anyway.

She glanced through the kitchen doorway as they crossed the hall again. There was something flat on the table next to the mug, but she couldn't see what.

After she'd thanked Lara and said goodbye, Eve heard the stairs creak from beyond Shell Cottage's closed door. For a moment, she hovered, wondering. But the longer she left it, the riskier it would be.

She caught Gus's eye, put her finger to her lips, then manoeuvred to the still-open kitchen window. She hoped to goodness Richie opposite didn't see her. Very briefly, Eve poked her head inside.

On the kitchen table was a photograph of a young man – in his early twenties perhaps. He had one of the most radiant smiles Eve had ever seen and an eager innocent look. It clashed with the soldier's uniform he wore.

It must be Lara's brother – so alive in the photo, yet now frozen in time after he'd drowned in the river a little way outside Saxford.

19

Eve crossed Meadowsweet Grove, glancing up the lane for any glimpse of Robin. There was none – he was too subtle for that – but she knew he was there. That was enough.

She allowed her thoughts to fasten on to Cleo's death again as she walked towards Richie's cottage. Abby had speculated that Lara's hatred of Cleo dated back to when her brother had died, and now, here was Lara, crying over his photo the day after Cleo's death. If the murder had brought it all back it looked as though Abby might be right. But had her hatred led Lara to kill Cleo? If it had, it would make the timing of Stevie's flashback irrelevant. Eve found that hard to swallow, despite Robin's warning to consider other motives.

The reports on Freddy's death said he'd been alone when he crashed, but Cleo might be implicated in some other way. Perhaps she'd plied him with drink before he took to the road, just as she'd got Honor drunk. She'd ask Greg if any toxicology tests had been done after the crash.

As for Honor, Lara had sounded irritated when Eve mentioned her. It might have been the young woman's behaviour that got her goat, or just Eve's questions. The scene she'd described reinforced the image of a woman just into adult-hood and young for her age. Either way, Lara hadn't rushed to champion Honor. Eve couldn't see her killing Cleo in revenge for involvement in her death, real or imagined.

Eve had arrived at Richie's door. It was time to switch focus. She took a deep breath and knocked. This would be a tough conversation. He'd clearly been fond of Cleo even if he'd ended up killing her.

At last, he opened up. His thick, dark, wavy hair was ruffled and his white shirt was open at the neck. He could have walked straight off a classic Hollywood set.

'Thanks so much for seeing me.'

Richie nodded. 'Of course.' His voice cracked as he stood back and gestured for her to come past.

He directed her to his sitting room – the cottage was similar in layout to Lara's. 'Would you like tea?'

'Just a glass of water would be lovely.'

He disappeared and Eve looked around the room. There on the wall was a photograph of a young woman on a bike, her red hair flying, signalling to turn right onto Church Lane by the village green in Saxford. The photo was taken from behind and had captured the moment she'd looked over her shoulder to check for traffic before crossing to the centre of the road. Eve's heart contracted as she saw the watch on the wrist of her outstretched hand. It had a large face and she could pick out the Mickey Mouse design. The woman must be Honor. She looked desperately young and she was laughing. Carefree. Behind her was a man, also young, also on a bike. Eve had the sense he was battling to keep up with her. He wore jeans and a stripey shirt.

'My parents,' Richie said as he came back into the room. 'In the early days when they were happy.'

Though Richie's father was almost sneering in the photo as he glanced behind him. Eve remembered Viv's words: *He wasn't kind or romantic. Mum said he treated Honor like a brainless skivvy.*

How differently life might have turned out if she'd found someone who valued her. 'What was your father called?'

'Aiden.'

'Did your granny put the photo up?' Eve was curious, given her reported dislike of Honor, who was definitely the star of the photo.

Richie shook his head. 'I found it in a trunk in the attic after she died last year. She wouldn't have pictures of either of them on display. She hated my mother and I think reminders of Dad were just too painful. He never came to see her. I haven't seen him since I was tiny.' His dark eyes were full of emotion. 'I remember Mum telling me Dad would never have chosen to leave me.' He picked up a Mini key fob and toyed with it absently, shaking his head.

'But you're here to talk about Cleo. It was a horrible week, even before she died.' He shook his head and attempted a smile, which crumpled.

'That's rough. What happened?' Eve moved to a squishy chintz-covered sofa at a gesture from him. 'The job offer must have been a shock, I suppose, though good news.'

Richie nodded and perched on an armchair opposite her. 'But horribly awkward too. Abby lives diagonally opposite me. Cleo promised to explain why she'd decided against her, but nothing she said quite squared it. I found myself trying to avoid her, though I bumped into her in the end.'

Tackling it head-on was probably best anyway, but Eve could see it was difficult. Cleo must have decided to keep Abby's secret from Richie, then. Maybe her ruthlessness had had its limits.

'How was Abby when you finally spoke?' Eve sensed Richie wanted to offload. She needed to take advantage of that, however vulnerable he was.

'She seemed angrier with Cleo than with me.' He blinked, his eyes damp. 'Not that I think she'd have got violent over it. She told me yesterday she'd got other offers.'

'That's good news.'

He nodded. 'It was so humiliating, what Cleo did to her.'

'Was it out of character?'

'I think so. She was very tough, but she didn't often change her mind.'

Eve nodded. 'So that awkwardness kicked off a bad week?'

Richie closed his eyes. 'That's right, thanks to the villagers. Or a section of them.'

'Why on earth?'

'Some of them hate me for "stealing" Abby's job. But others loathe me for working with Cleo, given the rumours about her and my mum. Accepting the promotion stirred them up again. Some of them told me what they thought to my face, the rest whispered about it as I passed by.'

It figured, after what the man in the navy T-shirt had said in the Cross Keys. Poor Richie. He'd been through enough, without all this.

'You see, Cleo was always kind to me,' his eyes were pleading, 'and she had an alibi for Mum's death. I asked Lara about that. Even though she disliked Cleo she reassured me it was true. And I think... well, it sounds disloyal, but I think Mum was a difficult person.'

'It was your granny who made you think so?'

Richie nodded. 'But she wasn't just making it up. She had evidence.' He reached for a battered notebook that lay on top of a bookcase and handed it to Eve.

'You're sure it's all right to look?' She desperately wanted to but she felt she had to ask. It was so personal and nothing to do with Cleo's obituary.

'I've been wishing I could show it to the gossips in the village. They might understand then. Mum was complicated; she had faults.'

Just like everyone else, but the spin 'Granny Joyce' had put on them would make a difference. And if she'd noted them in a book, she must have had a purpose. Eve imagined her revelling in them, using them to berate Honor and influence other people's opinions.

Richie held out the volume like a child seeking approval. He seemed young for his age, just like Honor. And now Cleo was gone he was without support. Mother and grandmother dead, father absent.

Eve steeled herself and opened the book. The content was horrific. A very detailed catalogue of every mistake Honor had made, by the look of it, all timed and dated. Appearing in church with her top hanging off one shoulder, seen kissing an old school friend when she was already married to Aiden, forgetting to keep a cleaning appointment. She'd garnered complaints from another client too, and those had been passed on to Joyce, not Honor herself. Joyce had noted it with apparent relish. The pen had flowed and there were lots of exclamation marks. Between times there were entries that mentioned Honor 'sitting around crying'. It made the other behaviour sound like an attempt to escape, though Joyce had painted everything, including the crying, as wicked self-indulgence. Poor Honor. She'd needed a hug, a listening ear and some guidance. But when things had gone awry, she'd had no one.

As Eve turned the pages, she knew she was working towards the dreadful day when Honor had died. It was the last sad entry in the book.

Called out of school by Martha Goodhew who said she thought Honor might have left Richie at home on his own. How right she was. I found him in his playpen. And then came the news that Honor had been found dead after drinking too much and trespassing at The Briars. I shall be looking after little Richie, of course. I've handed in my notice at school. I'll be able to give him a proper upbringing.

Eve looked up to see Richie was leaning forward, his eyes on the words she was reading.

'Dad had already left by then.' His gaze met hers now. 'Granny Joyce said he went because of Mum. Perhaps that's what Mum meant when she said he'd never have chosen to leave me. Maybe she knew she'd driven him away.' His voice cracked. 'Unless she was lying to comfort me.' He put the key fob he'd been tatting with in his trouser pocket, then patted it. 'She gave me his old key ring. I slept with it under my pillow for years.' He blushed.

Eve's chest felt heavy. It was heart wrenching that he'd clung onto it with such fervour when his dad had abandoned him. As for Honor, she'd been neglectful and the consequences could have been terrible, but Viv's parents had called her vulnerable. It looked as though she'd been sad and unable to cope.

'What about your mum?' Eve asked. His strength of feeling towards her was more relevant to his motive.

'I loved her, but I never believed Cleo had killed her, so I had no reason to distance myself.' He got up, his face strained with emotion. 'You have to understand that they were fond of each other. Cleo had lots of Mum's drawings, though she gave me plenty. And Cleo gave Mum presents too.' He opened a box on top of a cupboard, drew out some material and turned to show it to Eve. It was handmade Christmas bunting. 'I found it in the attic amongst Mum's things with a note underneath it.' He passed Eve some paper, fragile where it had been folded.

Don't let anyone tell you it's not worth putting up decorations. If Aiden won't buy you any, here's one from me, with my love.

It made Eve emotional. Cleo had certainly minded about Honor once upon a time. The idea of a rupture between them followed by a conspiracy to murder was achingly sad. Eve wished Cleo had been innocent, but their blazing row, and

Cleo's death so soon after Stevie's flashback, must mean something. And if Cleo had murdered Honor, Richie had every reason to put Eve off the scent. It made him an obvious suspect for her death.

Eve handed the note back to Richie. 'It's good to know your mum had a friend.'

He nodded. 'You can see why I liked Cleo. And of course, Granny Joyce and I lived in one of her houses. She was almost like a second mum to me.' He shivered.

Eve wanted to reassure him. 'I understand.' But had Cleo acted out of kindness or guilt?

His shoulders went down a little. 'Some of the villagers are saying Mum might have died at Max Bancroft's house.'

Eve tried to keep her expression neutral. 'It wasn't unnatural for Stevie to have the flashback in a house that matched the layout of The Briars.'

'I know.' Richie's voice was mechanical now, as though he was blocking off something too painful to consider. She was pretty sure he *had* rethought Cleo's possible involvement.

'Did you have the chance to talk to Cleo about it, before she died?'

Richie's eyes filled with tears. 'There was no time.'

But he wasn't meeting her gaze.

20

Eve used the open call to locate Robin. As she hung up and set off to find him, she got a text. Sylvia.

> *Yoohoo! We can see you! We're up in the hide. We had to share with a couple of birdwatchers earlier, which cramped our style. We're alone now and getting stiff. Nothing to report. Might call it a day soon.*

Eve looked in the direction of the hide and smiled to herself. Her neighbours were pure gold. She texted back, thanking them and promising drinks in the Cross Keys as soon as possible.

Robin reappeared as subtly as he'd melted away. He raised an eyebrow, but they didn't discuss her meetings until they were back at Elizabeth's Cottage.

At that point, they agreed Eve should write up her notes while everything was fresh in her mind, after which they'd reconvene and chew the whole thing over. Robin went to the spare room to look at the cold cases he'd been working on, and Eve sat at the dining room table, her workspace of choice. She liked that they had their own territory.

Eve found that Beth Marbeck, Cleo's sister, had emailed to

say she could see her on Tuesday – it was her afternoon off. She explained she and Cleo had been estranged but Eve figured that just made it more interesting. She replied to confirm, then got everything down from her two meetings.

An hour later, she and Robin met in the kitchen. He poured her a drink while Eve gave Gus his supper, then they aired ideas while cooking pasta with a cream and mushroom sauce.

'Do you think the records would show if Lara Oxley's brother was driving drunk when he was killed?' Eve said, giving the food a stir.

Robin raised his eyebrows. 'I can ask Greg.'

'Thanks. His name was Freddy.'

They were still dissecting Lara and Richie's possible motives when Eve's mobile rang. It was Toby.

'*I've found a friend whose elder sister knew Sean.*' Eve could hear the smile in his voice.

'You're a marvel. Thank you!'

'*You're welcome. She's called Jill and she works at a baker's in Blyworth.*' He gave her the details. '*She'll be there tomorrow if you can catch her then?*'

'Perfect!'

'*Want me to happen to be there when you arrive, to oil the wheels?*'

'Are you sure?'

'*Yep. No problem.*'

They arranged a time, then Eve thanked Toby and hung up.

'Back into town tomorrow morning.' She explained the plan to Robin as they sat down to eat at the kitchen table. 'Sean clearly knew Abby's secret. I'm hoping his friends might have got wind of it too. I still think Cleo's death probably relates to Honor's, but I know we need to be thorough. And if the secret wasn't worth killing for, it'll help rule Abby out.'

'But keep an open mind.' Robin sipped his drink. 'Abby would have been primed to lose it with Cleo after she lost the

London job. Anything that made her angry enough to swing that statue would have been enough.'

It was a chilling thought. One second of lost control, and Saturday had changed from an ordinary day to one of utter horror.

The following day, Toby was in the bakery as planned when Eve arrived. She sized the place up as she entered. It was quiet and with luck it might stay that way on a Monday morning during office hours. There were a couple of tables at the back for anyone who wanted to eat in. That could be handy if Eve could get Toby's friend's sister to sit down for a chat...

Toby acted the whole thing perfectly, turning as Eve entered the shop, then widening his eyes in mock surprise. Eve hoped she could perform her part with equal aplomb, despite her hatred of roleplay.

'Eve! How's it going?' He turned back to the woman behind the counter. 'Jill, this is one of my neighbours, Eve. Her dog Gus is Hetty's best friend.'

Jill smiled. 'You have a schnauzer too?'

Mentioning the dogs was a neat move. So wholesome. Eve smiled back. 'A dachshund. They're rather mismatched, size wise.'

Jill laughed. 'What can I get you?'

'Four almond croissants please.' Her mouth watered. Thank goodness Viv wasn't there to see her looking so covetous of someone else's bakes.

Toby smiled. 'Good choice! I often get some if I pop in. Jill's the elder sister of Spike, one of my school friends. And in fact, Jill was a friend of Sean's. Spike mentioned it only yesterday.' He turned to Jill. 'Eve's interested in Sean, because he knew Cleo and she's writing Cleo's obituary.'

Jill's eyes narrowed slightly as she reached for the pastries and put them into a striped paper bag. 'It's true. We'd kept in touch since school, but to be honest that was down to Abby. She's one of my best friends.'

Toby shot Eve an apologetic look, but she smiled at him. It was true that this might spoil things, but Toby wasn't to know. As a friend of Abby's, Jill wasn't likely to give up her damaging secret, but she knew about Sean. That was something. And more background on Abby could only help.

'I didn't see so much of Sean just before he died,' Jill went on. 'Abby was away in Paris so the pub trips tailed off.'

It was the perfect time for Eve to leap in. 'She mentioned her job out there. She said they had to take their relationship long-distance. It sounded tough.' The more familiar Eve seemed with the pair, the more likely Jill was to talk.

She shook her head. 'That's right. It was a three-year contract but too good an opportunity to miss. She and Sean took it in turns to travel to see each other at weekends.'

'That sounds fun but hard to sustain, I guess. Poor Abby. She told me about Sean taking up with Cleo Marbeck. She was very upfront about it.'

'She always is.' Jill set about tidying the cake displays. 'She and Cleo used to joke about it. I couldn't believe it when she told me about their bust-up over the London job. They seemed like the best of friends before that. That's six pounds please.'

'I can imagine them bonding over Sean's bad behaviour. It sounded as though he was spilling her private business to Cleo too. Pretty unforgiveable.'

Jill met her look head-on, unblinking. 'I didn't hear about that.'

Eve was sure she was lying; her denial was too studied. But there was no point in pursuing it. Eve needed to speak to someone less protective of Abby.

Then Jill sighed. 'I think Abby felt she and Cleo had had the last laugh, initially at least.'

But Sean's letter had changed Abby's mind, Eve was sure.

'I'd better dash.' Toby gave them a wave and they said goodbye.

'Actually, can I get a coffee while I'm here?' Eve leaned on the counter. 'I've got a busy day coming up. I might as well go into it wide awake. Can I get you one?'

'That's kind.' Jill glanced outside. 'I'd love one and we'll probably be quiet for a bit. What would you like?'

Eve asked for a cappuccino. 'I suppose Sean must have found it hard when Abby went to Paris.' She knew Jill was biased now, but she'd still like her take on it.

'He should have understood.' Jill was busy with their drinks. 'He was set on furthering his career too.'

She'd have to be more honest now. 'I never knew him. What was his surname again?'

'Arnold.'

'And what did he do?'

'Designed the most beautiful bags. Very exclusive. He went to great lengths to market them. It was probably that which triggered the affair with Cleo.'

Eve raised a questioning eyebrow.

'She ended up offering to stock his wares in her shops. Quite a coup, because up until then she'd only ever sold vintage jewellery. I imagine seduction was part of his pitch.'

'Ah.'

'Yeah, I know. So yes, he of all people ought to have understood Abby's move to Paris.' She looked cross. If she'd been bottling up her feelings about him, it was good news. With any luck she'd be dying to offload. After a moment, she leaned forward and lowered her voice, though they were alone. 'His sleeping around was nothing new. Abby should have ditched him long ago. She could never pull free, unfortunately. I bet they'd have got back together again if he hadn't died. It was a toxic relationship.'

Jill brought their coffees to a table and perched next to Eve. 'He and Abby first went out at school.'

'Wow. That is a long time to stay together, considering he strayed.'

Jill nodded. 'He was already at it when we were in sixth form.'

Eve would have told him to take a hike. 'And Abby forgave him?'

'It took a while. Not least because it was with her best friend.'

Eve felt the faintest pricking sensation as suspicion swept over her. 'Was that Honor?'

Jill nodded.

Eve thought of Abby's tears in Parker's: *It ended so abruptly. To hear that she was gone*— Maybe they'd never made it up. 'What happened?' she said to Jill.

'They were very close, until that flirt Sean put a spanner in the works.' She puffed out her cheeks. 'That was some row. Sean did all the running, I have to say. I don't think Honor was that keen but Abby caught the pair of them kissing. Honor hated conflict and Abby went berserk, understandably. But ultimately it was the friendship that ended, not the relationship with Sean.' Jill shook her head. 'Honor married someone else of course – that Aiden Hamilton. A slimy, selfish guy with the most impossible mother. Sean punched Aiden when he heard about the engagement.'

What a mess. Sean sounded like a menace. As for Honor, she felt like a victim, not an operator, a pawn being used by other people.

Eve thought of the implications. A bust-up might put Abby in the frame for Honor's murder, but in reality, Eve imagined the heat had gone out of the quarrel. Honor had been twenty-three by the time she'd crashed to the bottom of the stairs. She was married with a child and Abby was back with Sean. And besides, Eve couldn't see Abby working with Max. She'd sounded terrified when she'd discovered Cleo had told him her secret. That would make no sense if Max also knew she was guilty of murder. Nothing could trump that.

Abby's secret was still a motive for killing Cleo though. If she couldn't get it out of Jill, she'd try Sean's family instead. His business connection with Cleo gave her the perfect excuse to talk to them. 'Do you know if Sean's parents are still living?' she said to Jill. 'I'd love to ask them about his bags. Stocking them must have been one of Cleo's last business decisions; it would be great to mention that in her obituary.'

Jill sipped her drink. 'Oh yes, they're still around.' She sounded reluctant. 'They live on the Old Toll Road in Saxford. The blue house, next door but one to the doctors' surgery.' She frowned and got up from her seat as a potential customer glanced through the window.

Eve thanked her and was about to leave, one hand on the door, when Jill spoke again. 'By the way, I wouldn't take too much notice of anything Sean's mum and dad say about Abby. The relationship was tempestuous, as I said, and they always took Sean's side. You know what parents are like.'

Eve did. She was full of anticipation now. The less Mr and Mrs Arnold liked Abby, the more likely they were to give up her secret. She only hoped they knew what it was.

21

Before Eve left Blyworth, she checked her messages. Max Bancroft had replied at last, offering her a slot that afternoon. She responded to confirm, then texted Toby to thank him and report interesting results. After that, she bought some notepaper and envelopes from a stationery store. She was going to write to Sean's parents. She looked up his bags on her phone as she sat in the car and saw what Jill meant. They were exquisite, embroidered with birds and flowers, decorated with tiny sparkling jewels. Eye-wateringly expensive.

Eve put pen to paper and explained about the obituary and her desire to talk about Sean's work. *Suffolk Monthly* wouldn't give her many column inches; she mustn't make false promises when Mr and Mrs Arnold were mourning a son. But the bags were a genuinely fascinating part of Cleo's story; she was sure she could slip in a line or two. Sean could have changed Marbeck's entire direction.

She sealed her letter in one of the envelopes and dropped it at the blue house near the doctors' on her way back into Saxford. She hoped the Arnolds would call her soon.

She was back at home, communing with Gus, when her mobile rang. Sylvia's name flashed on the screen.

'Sylvia. How are things?'

She laughed croakily. *'We're up in the bird hide again.'*

'Heck, this is good of you.'

'We haven't had so much fun in years. I've been photographing the wildlife.' Photography was her profession. *'But Daphne's been keeping watch over the village.'* It would be less easy to make ceramics up there.

'You've seen something?'

'We have indeed. Abby Porter and Perry Bancroft, Max's son. The pair of them were having a ding-dong. Well, that's what it looked like. Daphne saw Perry grab Abby's arm and Abby jerked away and threw him off.'

'Are they down in the grove?'

'No. They were walking along the river. They've just disappeared beyond St Peter's.'

Eve visualised their position.

'We thought you might like to know in case you want to intercept them and listen in.'

In the background, Eve could hear Daphne questioning the wisdom of Sylvia's idea, and asking if Robin was around, as backup, which he wasn't.

'Thanks. I might just do that.'

Eve texted Viv at Monty's. Calling would involve explanations which would take too long.

Please look out of the back window and text when you see Perry Bancroft and Abby Porter go past. Will explain later.

A text came back immediately.

You'd better.

Eve was dashing down Haunted Lane towards the estuary, Gus by her side, his ears inside out, when Viv's next text arrived.

They're passing now.

By Eve's reckoning they'd cross the path that led from Haunted Lane to the estuary in three or four minutes. Eve wanted to get beyond them and into the reeds that bordered the Sax. She could listen from there, then follow them. With Gus in tow, Eve would have the perfect excuse for being there if they spotted her.

Gus seemed thoroughly overexcited by her unusual turn of speed and bounced this way and that, so that she had to change course to avoid tripping over him.

At the end of the path, she stopped and listened hard over the top of her own breathing and the rustling reeds. She could just hear voices and they were coming from her left. She'd beaten them to the path.

She dashed on and found a bit of firm ground between the reeds which would hide them from view, then turned to Gus and put her finger to her lips. He gave her a resigned look.

The voices were getting nearer now.

'Stop walking away from me, Abby! You never minded talking to me before.'

'That's because you weren't like this!' Abby sounded breathless. 'I don't know what's got into you.'

'I told you. I want to know why you let my dad into your house. When I took you into my confidence, I didn't think you'd be fraternising with him!'

Of course, Abby had begged Max to visit her. She'd wanted to put her side of the story when he admitted he knew her secret.

'You're making a mountain out of a molehill!' Abby said.

'He's a neighbour. Neighbours sometimes have coffee. I'm sorry he wasn't a good father to you but it's not my battle!'

'Coffee? Pull the other one. What are you playing at? I wish I'd never told you how I felt about him and Cleo. Did you discuss it?'

It made sense for Perry and Abby to bond in this way – they'd both suffered because of Cleo. But now, Perry sounded panicked. Perhaps he was worried they thought he was guilty.

'Don't be ridiculous!' Abby shouted.

'Cleo was the most selfish, heartless monster and Dad is too. You need to stay away from him for your own sake.'

'Ow!' That was Abby again.

Eve risked peering through the reeds. Perry was trying to grab her arm. Eve would have to move if she wanted to carry on listening.

She signalled to Gus. They left the marshes and followed, Eve tiptoeing quietly, still holding her finger to her lips to keep Gus subdued.

They were getting near the sea now. They passed Ella Tyndall's new boat, moored at the end of Ferry Lane. The estuary mouth was in sight.

The breeze in the reeds made it hard to hear what Abby and Perry said. Eve thought of what she'd already heard instead. Abby clearly thought there were two sides to the story of her guilty secret, but had she convinced Max? It was interesting that he'd agreed to hear her out. Maybe he had his own agenda. He could have decided to blackmail her.

She continued to follow Abby and Perry. For a while, all she could hear were murmurs, but when they reached the woods that bordered the estuary path, they paused. That was good, but Eve would have to creep through the trees to reach them and the ground was dry. The crack of a twig snapping could give her away. At least the wind in the branches would help cover any noise she made.

She signalled to Gus to stay, then slipped from tree to tree, grateful for the shadows.

'This is getting us nowhere!' Abby's raised voice made her easier to hear. She was facing Perry, her eyes blazing.

'Why were you so pally towards him? I need to understand!'

'It's none of your business!'

'All right then! Go ahead and be his friend! But you're a monumental fool after that Stevie woman had the freak-out in his house.'

'She still thinks Honor died at The Briars! And in any case, she was four years old. Besides, why would your dad kill Honor?'

'Maybe she made herself inconvenient! I expect she fell in love with him. Everyone else seemed to! And she babysat me, don't forget. She had time to fall under his spell. You don't know what it was like! He'd be out with my poor mum, keeping up their sham marriage, dressed up in his best. And I'd know he and Cleo were sneaking off every five seconds to be together. I didn't trust any woman who went anywhere near him. Would it surprise you if Honor and my dad had had a fling?'

Abby folded her arms. 'Not if Max did the running. We all know what Honor was like.'

'A complication too far, I'll bet that's what she was. If she threatened to upset Dad's phoney life, you're probably befriending a killer!'

22

Eve didn't move until Perry and Abby reached the beach. They were still arguing. Abby kept flinging her arms out and rounding on Perry, who was hurling stones into the sea. The stones spun off into the distance. He was strong.

Eve had no hope of more eavesdropping, so she messaged the WhatsApp group to thank Viv, Sylvia and Daphne and suggest a catch-up over lunch at the Cross Keys. Robin had a gap between clients then, and Monty's schedule was fixed to give Viv an hour's break.

Viv responded immediately, the rest in dribs and drabs as she walked home. Gus trotted ahead of her along the rutted estuary path.

Half an hour later, she and the gang were at the pub, shaded under a white parasol in the far reaches of the garden, away from prying villagers. Gus and Hetty were amusing themselves, not far away.

Eve swigged her Coke; she needed to cool down and stay sharp. There were too many facts flying around her head.

'So where are we?' Viv said. 'What was all that about Perry and Abby?'

Eve explained.

'Blimey. I wonder if Perry's right about his dad and Honor.'

Sylvia frowned and sipped her lime and tonic as a waiter arrived with the first dishes of food. 'I need everything summing up.'

'Agreed.' Robin thanked a woman who'd put a fish pie in front of him. 'As soon as we're sorted.'

He meant as soon as they were alone.

Once they all had plates in front of them, Eve took a forkful of goat's cheese tartlet and ordered her thoughts.

'First things first, I still strongly suspect that Cleo's murder relates to Honor's death and the flashback. I think Honor died in Max Bancroft's house and that he killed her, then used the tunnel Ella told me about to move her body. Someone's moved furniture in his outhouse, probably since Saturday. I assume it was Max, covering the tunnel entrance.' She turned to Stevie. 'It would have been easy for you to sneak into his house when the back was covered with tarpaulin. And Perry was impressing it on Abby that Max could have killed Honor. I'm not sure I buy his idea of a relationship between them though. Cleo didn't like sharing Max with his wife. I can't imagine her putting up with a three-way split, and I bet she'd have found out. She and Honor saw a lot of each other, and Cleo was sharp.'

Eve ran her eyes over her notes. 'If we take it that Max killed Honor, Cleo could have orchestrated things. She got Honor drunk. Perhaps she planted the idea of visiting Max too. In that case, it would be natural for Max to talk to her after the flashback. Like I said before, he could have killed Cleo if they fought over what to do next.'

Once again, she imagined Max saying they should silence Stevie, and Cleo saying it was too risky.

'The other possibility is that he murdered Honor without Cleo knowing and the flashback led her to put two and two together, so he killed her to keep her quiet.'

'He still seems like a strong possibility to me,' Robin said.

'He definitely looked nervous when we spoke.' Daphne twisted her hands. 'And it wasn't idle chat. He was checking what I remembered from the old days.'

'He really wanted to marry Cleo, just before she died.' Eve remembered the crash and the broken decanter. 'She was cruel when she rejected him. That could have exacerbated things. He's agreed to talk to me this afternoon, so that's something.'

Robin sat up straighter at the news. 'I don't think you should see him alone.'

'We could station ourselves outside his house,' Viv put in, glancing around the group.

Eve imagined Viv, peering from behind a bush, her green hair gleaming in the sun.

'Don't worry,' Robin said. 'I've got a gap after lunch. I can keep watch.' It was as though he'd read her mind.

'You can probably come with me openly.' She met his eye. 'Maybe you could ask to wait in the garden with Gus while we talk inside. I doubt he'd do me in then.'

'Very reassuring.' Sylvia laughed and sipped her drink.

Eve smiled. 'Right. So, sticking with Honor-related suspects for Cleo's murder, the second candidate is poor Richie.' She told them about her interview with him. 'His view of his mum up until now must have been influenced by his granny, who drummed it into him that Honor was no good. But he's put a photo of her and his dad on the wall since the granny died. He's emotional about Honor, despite his nuanced feelings.

'His turmoil's probably been compounded by some villagers who attacked him for accepting a promotion from Cleo; they didn't think he should be working with her in the first place. I'm sure he never suspected her of conspiring to kill his mum as he grew up, but he might have reconsidered after Stevie's flashback. Cleo's longstanding affair with Max is common knowledge now.'

'I can imagine him wanting to talk to Cleo in those circumstances,' Daphne said quietly.

'I'm afraid I can too.' Eve glanced at Stevie. It was horrible to be pondering her cousin's possible guilt like this.

'Poor Richie,' Stevie said, but she didn't argue.

'If he did attack Cleo, he was probably overtaken in the moment.' Robin leaned forward. 'He's had an awful lot to cope with. He might have knocked her out then got scared and thrust her head underwater. A court would take all the background into account. But of course, it might not be him.'

'Absolutely.' Max looked just as likely to Eve. Where was she? 'We're on to suspects who could have killed Cleo for reasons that have nothing to do with Honor's death.' She checked her records again. 'Abby has a secret she wants to keep, on top of being furious with Cleo for withdrawing her job offer. That must have stung like heck, especially given she left Paris to take it up.

'And she found a letter from Sean that made her feel differently towards Cleo too. Before that, she hadn't blamed her for the two-timing; afterwards, I sense her feelings changed. I think that letter is key, along with Abby's secret, if Cleo was set to reveal it.'

'More important than Abby's anger and humiliation after being passed over for the London role?' Simon said.

'I think so. Abby got two job offers within a couple of days of being dropped, if she's to be believed. Either way, I can't see her killing Cleo over it several days later. But with any of her motives, it's like I said before, why kill in the middle of a village event?'

'Cleo could have goaded her,' Viv said.

'It's possible – but to the degree that Abby lost all control?'

Sylvia shook her head. 'It doesn't seem likely to me.'

'And killing over the letter contents would involve a delayed reaction, just like the job.' Robin swigged his beer. 'She found it last Thursday.'

Eve nodded. 'You're right. I can only see Abby killing Cleo if she'd threatened to reveal her secret in the middle of the open-gardens event.'

Robin raised an eyebrow. 'Not impossible, but not likely?'

Eve nodded. 'There's one other development of interest. Abby and Honor were friends in school, but then Sean made a pass at Honor and they fell out. It was at least five years before Honor died, but it's worth bearing in mind.

'Then we're on to Perry. He agreed to work for Cleo, despite the trouble she caused his mum. There has to be a reason for that. But he's here for several months, so if he's guilty, why choose to kill in such a risky way?'

'Cleo could have taunted him, just like she could have goaded Abby,' Viv said. 'But why would she? She ought to have felt guilty if anything.'

Eve nodded. 'Guilt would explain her offering Perry the job. It would be interesting to know what she's paying him. If it's over the odds that would reinforce the idea.'

'So Perry doesn't seem super likely, despite his hatred of Cleo,' Stevie said.

'I agree.' Simon speared a chip.

'Me too.' Eve looked at her notes. 'But I won't feel happy until I understand why he agreed to work for her.'

'Who does that leave?' Daphne asked.

'Lara Oxley. Another one who puzzles me. Abby thinks her hatred of Cleo dates back to when her brother Freddy died. He was driving alone and skidded on ice not far from here. He bumped his head, landed in the Sax and drowned. I wondered if there was any way Cleo could have been involved, but I don't see how, unless she got him drunk before he set off. And I've no reason to think they even knew each other.'

'I've got news on that.' Robin leaned forward. 'Greg says they did a blood test at the time and there was no alcohol in Freddy Oxley's system. And nothing suspicious about the car or the road.'

Eve sighed. 'Back to square one. But when I called on Lara yesterday, she'd been crying over a photo of Freddy. Why would she do that in the immediate aftermath of Cleo's death if there's no connection? Then again, all this happened twenty-five years ago. Even if there's a link, why take revenge now, and in the middle of a crowded event?'

Robin nodded. 'So we're left with Richie and Max as the top suspects, one acting out of revenge and the other out of fear.'

Eve sipped her drink. 'Yes. But we don't know it all yet.' Her thoughts were interrupted by a text coming in for Stevie.

'Oh no!'

'What?'

Her eyes were still on her screen. 'The firm who're doing the menu cards and orders of service have pulled out!'

Viv sat bolt upright and reached for Stevie's phone, scanning the message. 'Talk about last minute.'

Eve happened to know they'd only been booked a week ago, when Stevie had finally (sensibly) seized control of that bit of admin. 'How come?'

Viv was still reading. 'Something about a fire, followed by a flood. Honestly!'

'Well, quite. Desperately selfish of them.'

Viv looked at her askance. 'I didn't mean it like that. But this is an emergency.'

Stevie put a hand on Viv's arm. 'I'll sort it. Don't worry.'

At that moment, Stevie's mobile rang, making Viv jump. She handed it back.

Eve saw Stevie blanch as she looked at the screen and Viv flushed.

'Hello?' Stevie blinked several times. 'I see. No. No, I can come in this afternoon.' As she hung up, she hugged Viv before Viv got the chance to hug her. 'It's all right. Truly. All this will be sorted before you know it. But the police say they have fresh evidence. They want to interview me again.'

23

Viv's hand shook slightly as she put it on Eve's arm as they left the Cross Keys. 'What can the police want Stevie for? They've already questioned the poor lamb until they're blue in the face.' She glanced over her shoulder to where Stevie was walking next to Simon. 'Why hasn't Greg told us anything?'

Robin was on Viv's other side. 'I'm afraid he can only update me after the event with something like this. I'm sure he's certain Stevie's innocent, but it would be too unprofessional to inform a suspect and her friends of questions in advance.'

Viv opened her mouth to protest, then closed it again.

'I'm truly sorry,' Robin said. 'As soon as we know more we can work out how to help.'

Viv turned to Eve. 'I think I should call Jonah. Tell him to come back. He wouldn't want to be on this wretched patisserie course if he understood what things are like here.' Then she sighed. 'You're giving me that look.'

'Excuse me?'

'Like you've swallowed a bee and you're finding it hard to digest.'

Okay.

'You don't think I should call him?'

'Maybe not without talking to Stevie first. After all, they're going to be married soon. They'll have their own ways of working things out.'

Viv gave a quick sigh. 'I'd hoped he'd come to the rescue whatever she said to him.'

Eve thought of the hug Stevie had given Viv. 'You and Stevie seem different together somehow.'

Viv blushed. 'I was so worried last night that I got a bit tearful after I went to bed. I was thinking of Oliver again. We used to share everything. I just wished I could talk to him about what's going on. Stevie must have heard me. She knocked on my door and we had a good chat. I felt awful afterwards. I should be comforting her, not the other way round.'

Eve suspected Stevie preferred mothering to being mothered. 'I'm sure she was glad to have a focus.' She must have had to grow up fast, after what happened to her aunt and its effect on her mum.

Viv dropped back to join Stevie, putting an arm through hers. 'I'll run you into Blyworth. You don't want to be taking the bus at a time like this.'

For just a second, it looked as though she might protest, but then she drew Viv in close. 'Thank you.'

Eve was glad she was down to interview Max Bancroft that afternoon. She'd never stop thinking about Stevie's summons otherwise. Her stomach skipped uneasily. Poor Viv.

When the time came for the appointment, she and Robin crossed the village green with Gus to reach Parson's Walk and Max's cottage.

Max looked disconcerted to see two humans and a dog, rather than just Eve.

Eve introduced Robin and Gus. 'I hope you don't mind. We have to get to Watcher's Wood afterwards and you're on our way.'

Robin smiled. 'Perhaps the pooch and I could wait in your garden?'

A frown twitched Max's face. He probably suspected Eve didn't trust him but it couldn't be helped. She wondered if he knew about Robin and his police background.

After a moment, Max shook himself and offered them all drinks, then let Robin and Gus into the garden through the French windows. He closed the door on them and motioned Eve to a seat at the table.

'So, you want my memories of Cleo?' He sank into a chair opposite her, his hands clasped in front of him.

Eve nodded. 'Yes please. I understand you were pivotal in the launch of Marbeck's. You helped with her first premises and invested money too?'

Max unclasped his hands and adjusted his shirt cuffs, one by one. 'That's right. The start of a long journey.' His voice cracked and he cleared his throat hastily, taking a sip of water.

Eve wondered if he regretted the past now. He'd made Cleo hang around for him all those years, then lost her in the end. And now that loss was permanent. Whether he'd killed her or not, his emotion made sense.

'What was it like to be involved back then?'

He sighed. 'I was excited. Cleo had flair. I knew she'd do well. She was a go-getter with vision.'

Eve thought of the rumours about her. 'When you say a go-getter, do you think she could be ruthless?' She saw him flinch.

'You have to be, to a degree, to get on in business.'

Of course, Max had got on in business too.

'I wouldn't call it ruthlessness though,' he went on. 'She was efficient, resourceful and single-minded.'

'Were you very hands on?' Heck, she could have phrased that better, given his affair with Cleo.

Max glanced down. His eyes were damp when they met hers again. 'With the premises I was. I showed Cleo the best options, advised on décor, layout and signage, that kind of thing.'

'You must have spent a lot of time together, planning.' Eve's eyes met his.

He put a hand to his forehead. 'You've heard about our affair, of course. Most people know now but I'd rather you didn't highlight it in the obituary.'

Because he was guilty of murder, and didn't want people dwelling on their connection?

'It's my son, you see,' Max went on. 'He was never reconciled to our relationship, even after my wife left. I... well, I didn't handle it well.'

You can say that again. He'd refused to come clean and get a divorce, forcing Perry to keep the secret to protect his mum. Max looked regretful now, but it was way too late. Eve needed to keep him onside, though. 'I understand. I won't mention it.'

Max put his head in his hands. 'I fell for Cleo, hook, line and sinker.'

The old tale. He just couldn't help himself and neither could she. 'You didn't consider coming clean and marrying her?' Eve couldn't resist asking. Surely it would have been better than years of subterfuge.

'I didn't want to hurt my wife.'

Oh, the irony. Eve took a deep breath and attempted to unclench her teeth.

'What about after you'd separated?'

'Too hard on Perry.'

Eve decided to push. 'Even after all these years?'

'He might be here in Saxford, but we're still estranged.' He'd put his right hand to his heart and it looked subconscious. As though he really was still hurting, both for his lost relationship with his son and the missed opportunity with Cleo.

If he minded that much, and Cleo had rejected him, he could have killed her for that. The motive didn't *have* to relate to

Stevie's flashback and Honor's death. But there must have been a trigger so strong that he'd lost control, despite the risks.

'You must have been a great support to Cleo behind the scenes.'

'I hope so.' Max was tatting with his cuffs again. He was definitely anxious.

Eve glanced up at Robin. He was still pottering round the garden. She took a deep breath. 'How did she cope when the rumours about Honor Hamilton went round?'

Max's gaze didn't drop from hers but everything tightened, from his jaw to his shoulders. 'It was a terrible time. The coroner ruled the death was an accident and her alibi was rock solid of course, but that didn't make any difference. Once a rumour takes hold it can be ruinous.'

Eve agreed. 'I'm sorry to ask, but people were still talking about it just before she died. The news reports on Honor's death mention Cleo plied her with alcohol. She was drunk when she fell downstairs.'

Max shook his head. 'Cleo gave Honor a drink to cheer her up. They'd had that row over the way Honor was treating Richie. Cleo said afterwards that she felt guilty, giving the poor kid a hard time. She could drink anyone under the table, whereas Honor had no head for alcohol.'

How would he know that about Honor? Was there any chance it was from personal experience and Perry had been right about a relationship after all? Or maybe Cleo had told him. Either way, it was information they could have used. It would fit with Cleo planning to get her drunk. Whatever the truth, Eve was convinced Max would lie for Cleo, especially if there was an element of self-preservation involved. But he could still have killed her in the end.

Eve glanced up to the window again, safe in the knowledge of Robin's presence.

'What did you think of Honor? Only she was clearly a key connection of Cleo's.'

'Me?' Max's eyes fluttered. It was that same look of fear she'd seen after Stevie's flashback. 'Why would I think anything of her?'

'I understood she was your cleaner, and babysitter too.'

Max blinked. 'My wife saw to all of that.'

Of course she did. They talked a little more, then Eve wrapped up the interview. It was frustrating. She had more hints, but nothing concrete. She knocked on the window and Robin and Gus came back in, after which she thanked Max for his time and turned towards the door. It was only then that she saw something that made goosebumps rise on her arms.

A pretty notebook, decorated with bluebirds and honeysuckle. It was only visible spine-on, amongst a pile of other books, but Eve recognised it. It was an exact match of the one she'd seen Cleo use. Eve glanced swiftly around the room, but Max wasn't one for decorative belongings. His décor was a mix of taupe and slate grey, and minimalist. Eve was all but certain the notebook was Cleo's. And she'd last seen her use it shortly before she died.

After Eve, Robin and Gus had left, they walked in self-conscious silence as though they might be en route to Watcher's Wood as she'd claimed. Eve was itching to share her knowledge but she wanted a safe distance between them and Max first.

When they'd left the vicinity, Robin leaned in close. 'Anything soul-shaking?'

'Some interesting insights into Max's personality. And I'm pretty sure he has Cleo's notebook.' She explained about it. 'Given the row we heard them have on Wednesday night, I doubt she gave it to him. My bet is he pinched it. It makes me wonder if she had something on him. And if he might have killed her and stolen it for damage limitation. Do you think the police will take any notice?'

'Unlikely. We can't prove it was the same notebook. But it'd be good to let Greg know your thoughts. He'll have it in the back of his mind.'

Eve took out her phone to text him, wondering how Stevie was getting on at the station. For just a moment, Robin's query echoed in the back of her mind. *She wouldn't do it, would she?* Eve took a deep breath. There were umpteen reasons to believe in her innocence, from her upcoming wedding to her sense of right and wrong. She dismissed the thought from her mind.

24

Back at Elizabeth's Cottage, Eve put the kettle on. 'What might Cleo have had on Max? If she'd worked out he was guilty of murder, I'd have thought she'd tell the police if she wasn't involved herself. She was pretty disenchanted with him by the end and it would finally put paid to the gossip about her and Honor.'

Robin nodded. 'I know. It's a puzzle. And if she *was* involved, it would be weirdly unguarded to refer to it in her notebook.'

'Either way, I wish the police would put pressure on Max rather than Stevie. And investigate the tunnel too.'

'Greg's frustrated that he can't, but Palmer won't budge. The keys to The Briars have already been handed over to Cleo's executors and he's adamant that Honor's death was properly investigated.'

'That's such a pain.'

'It would be different if Stevie remembered anything concrete that indicated Honor's body was at Max's place. Of course, Max Bancroft is a rich landlord with friends in high places. Palmer won't want to offend him without good reason.'

'Why am I not surprised? I wish we knew what was happening with Stevie.' Eve glanced at her watch.

'Viv will call, won't she, once they're back?'

Eve nodded. She was halfway down her tea when her mobile went, making her tense. But it was Simon, not Viv.

'Hello. All well?'

'Yes, fine, but I saw Max Bancroft go past a short while ago. He wasn't brandishing a blunt instrument or anything, but he was striding very purposefully and looking at his watch. I wondered if he was meeting someone. It's probably nothing but he was heading out of town. It must be a private rendezvous.'

Eve considered. 'I saw him this afternoon. It would be interesting if something I said triggered him into action. It's a long shot, but I might come over and spy out the land.'

'Good stuff. Will Robin be with you? Or I can join, if you'd like company?'

'He's got a job on in twenty minutes. Safety in numbers sounds good. Thank you.'

Five minutes later, Eve met Simon at the stables as planned. She'd broken her habit and taken her car for speed. There wouldn't be much point otherwise. Gus had been tired so she'd left him at home.

They strode towards the lane.

'It's probably a wild goose chase,' Simon said. 'I feel a bit silly for ringing now, but I wanted to do something. It's horrible, being so helpless when Stevie's under suspicion.'

Eve knew exactly what he meant. 'It's got to be worth a peek. The more we see of our suspects, the better we can judge them. The question is, did he head towards the river, or along Blind Eye Lane towards the main road?'

As they walked a little further, Eve heard movement to their right towards the Sax. It sounded as though someone was moving at speed. She doubted it was Max though; he'd had too much of a head start.

Simon raised an eyebrow. He must have heard the noise too.

They reached the place where the paths diverged and looked in both directions. There was no one in sight on the rough track to the river, but there were trees to either side. Someone could have hidden themselves there, and that was where the noise had come from.

Close to the riverbank, they could see a lone house. It was rather grand and had been let out, Eve remembered. She didn't know who lived there now. Through a downstairs window, she could just make out movement.

Simon slapped his forehead. 'Eve, I'm an idiot.'

'What? Why?'

He grimaced. 'I completely forgot. Max Bancroft owns that place these days. It's one of his holiday lets. He's probably gone there to show someone round or sort out a maintenance issue.' Simon was blushing.

'Maybe.' Eve lowered her voice. 'But someone was here, weren't they? I had the impression they ran for cover when they heard us coming. Perhaps the holiday cottage is empty and Max *is* meeting someone.'

Simon nodded and whispered back: 'Think it's worth lying low in case there's anything to see?'

Eve turned to retreat. 'No harm,' she murmured.

They tucked themselves behind some vegetation, back on the lane on the far side of the track to the river.

Fifteen minutes later there was no sign of movement.

'If they worked their way to the river through the trees, they could have hidden themselves beyond the cottage's garage and gone in the back way.'

Simon unbent and flexed his shoulder muscles. 'True. Perhaps we've missed them.'

Eve was staring at the grass to one side of the track, before the trees began. 'Wait a moment, what's that?'

She went to look, Simon hard on her heels.

It was a battered old Mini key fob. Richie's. She remembered it from when she'd visited him because she had a Mini too.

She picked it up and pocketed it. 'I know who owns this.' She stared into the trees, willing Richie to come out if he was there. The desire to talk to Max alone could have been triggered by Stevie's flashback. He'd want to understand how his mother had died. But the mission could be dangerous.

'Richie!' She couldn't bring herself to leave without calling out.

But there was no reply.

On impulse, Eve turned to Simon. 'I don't like it. I feel like we should go and knock on the door. It's a lovely house. I can say I'd like to hire it for some of my wedding guests.'

Simon nodded. 'Okay. Let's do it.'

Eve hadn't seen anyone leave the house but when she knocked, there was no reply.

If only she was wrong about Richie going to meet Max…

After she'd left Simon and the stables, she went to Richie's cottage on Meadowsweet Grove and knocked on his door. There was no reply. Perhaps she should have left the fob where it was. He might have gone back to look for it. *Too late now*. She posted it through his letter box.

Half an hour after she got back, Robin reappeared and she updated him. She was halfway through when Viv called.

'*We've only just got back. Stevie told me all about it in the car on the way home. Apparently she wrote some angst-filled letters to Cleo as a teenager and the police have found them.*'

That sounded like bad news. Whatever she'd written didn't prove anything but Palmer would make a big deal out of it. 'What kind of thing?'

'*Blaming Cleo for her mother's breakdown. Asking why she'd let Honor get drunk when she was supposed to be looking after a child. Letting rip, basically. Stevie said she'd got past that stage. She never imagined Cleo would have kept them.*'

It was interesting that she had. They must have hit home. 'Did Stevie keep Cleo's replies?'

Viv groaned. '*The police asked the same question. Stevie had to admit she'd burned them. But this was when she was sixteen, Eve. Years ago. You know what it's like when you're that age. Jonah texted to ask if we were okay just after we got back. Stevie saw it before I could reply and insisted that I should say it's all fine. She keeps telling me it will be but I know she's protecting me.*'

'Hang in there. I'm sure she's right.' There wasn't much point saying anything else. 'Look, is there anything practical I can do to help? What about wedding stuff? Did you get the printing crisis sorted?' It was the kind of thing that might get overlooked when everything was so stressful. Or even when it wasn't, if Viv was in charge.

'*Stevie called "Brown's of London".*' She said it in a snooty voice. '*Moira recommended them, as though any lesser firm would be unacceptable, but they seem quite reasonable, honestly. Isn't Stevie a marvel to organise it when everything's so difficult?*' But then her voice cracked. '*I hope to goodness they can get married. What if it's all still hanging over them and everyone's talking about it at the wedding?*'

Eve wished it wasn't quite so soon. 'We'll crack it, Viv. Something will come clear.' They just needed to make sure it was sooner rather than later.

After Eve had rung off, she wondered if she'd been right to encourage Viv not to interfere between Stevie and Jonah. Things really were rough.

Eve and Robin had just finished supper when there was a knock at the door of Elizabeth's Cottage.

Eve stepped over a bouncing Gus and opened up to find Sylvia and Daphne.

'Have you heard the news?' Sylvia looked at her keenly.

Eve blinked. 'What? I don't know. I don't think so.'

'Max Bancroft's in hospital. Someone pushed him down the stairs of one of his holiday cottages!'

25

Within ten minutes, Eve, Robin, Sylvia, Daphne, Viv and Stevie were sitting around the dining table at Elizabeth's Cottage, each with a coffee in front of them. Eve had tried Simon but there was no reply.

'We don't know much,' Sylvia said. 'Daphne and I were out for an evening stroll and we bumped into Moira who'd heard it from someone up that end of the village. The word is, Max is seriously injured but he managed to call for help himself. I'm surprised Simon hasn't been in touch. The place where he was pushed is near the stables.'

Eve explained they'd been there earlier. 'Do you know when it happened?'

'Not precisely,' Daphne said.

'If only it was while we were at the police station.' Viv put her head in her hands. 'It would put Stevie in the clear.'

Stevie patted her shoulder and Viv clutched her hand.

'What did you and Simon see while you were watching Bancroft's holiday let?' Viv asked.

Eve explained.

'Blimey. Do you think Richie could have killed Cleo then tried to take Max out as well, all in revenge for his mum?'

Eve shivered. 'It seems quite likely, if everything was triggered by the flashback. Unless someone's trying to frame him.' She thought through possibilities. 'Abby might feel vengeful over the London job, but we've already agreed she doesn't seem likely as Cleo's killer.'

'Whereas Richie has a believable motive for Cleo and Max.' Robin sighed. 'I'm sorry to say it. There are reasons he might act on the spur of the moment, too, unlike Perry for instance, who also had cause to hate both victims.' He sipped his coffee.

'I can't bear the thought of it being Richie after all he's been through.' Stevie clutched at her curly hair.

'What other possibilities are there?' Viv asked as she pulled her tattered notepad from her bag. Several of its pages were almost dislodged.

Eve resisted the urge to push them back into place. 'Whoever pushed Max might not be the same person who killed Cleo.' She breathed in the steam from her drink. 'If you look at him in isolation, Abby could have tried to kill him if he was blackmailing her, or Perry might have done it in revenge for the pain he caused his mum. I can't think of any motive for Lara though, unless she'd killed Cleo and he knew it.' Eve thought it through. 'For Perry, my question would still be why act now, if it's unrelated to Cleo's death? He could have sneaked back to Suffolk at any time.'

Viv chewed her pencil. 'That's a point. So Richie seems most likely, because he only realised on Saturday that Cleo and Max could have collaborated to kill his mum.'

Eve nodded. 'That's the way I see it.'

'But the timing would make sense for Abby too,' Sylvia put in, 'if Max had just started blackmailing her.'

It was possible. 'Of course, Max might have seen his attacker for all we know.'

At that moment, Eve's mobile rang. Simon.

'*Have you heard?*' His voice sounded tense and weary.

Eve explained the extent of their knowledge. 'The whole gang's here and we're all ears. I'll put you on speaker.'

'*I wanted to call you first, Eve. The police have just been. I expect DI Palmer will get to you soon. We were seen watching Bancroft's holiday house, right around the time he was pushed. Palmer didn't give much away, but Bancroft can't have seen who attacked him.*'

Simon didn't have much more to add. After they'd said goodbye and ended the call, Eve turned to Stevie. 'The thing to hold on to is that you might have an alibi this time.' She could have done without being a replacement suspect though.

DI Palmer called on Eve first thing on Tuesday morning. Eve had spent all night worrying about Richie's key fob.

Robin had taken her in his arms after she'd turned over for the umpteenth time. She must be driving him up the wall.

'It's not your fault, but you'll have to tell them.'

'I wish I hadn't seen it. Or that I hadn't known it was his.' At least she hadn't seen Richie himself. That was something. She hated having to point the finger. Whoever had pushed Max had done something terrible, but if Richie was convinced he'd killed his mother, the situation seemed tragic as much as anything.

DI Palmer sat opposite Eve on one of her couches. His judgemental gaze met hers.

Gus sat at Eve's feet, staring back at Palmer as though poised to attack. His loyalty was bolstering but was probably making the situation more tense.

'So, Ms Mallow,' Palmer leaned forward, 'perhaps you'd like to begin by explaining your visit to Mr Bancroft yesterday afternoon.'

'I was interviewing him for Cleo Marbeck's obituary. He was

a close friend of hers and instrumental in establishing her business.' *Put that in your pipe and smoke it.*

'I'd also be *very* interested to know why you told Mr Bancroft you were on your way to Watcher's Wood with your partner and dog.' Palmer peered at Gus accusingly. 'We're reliably informed you did no such thing.'

This wasn't good. 'I was wary of Mr Bancroft. I wanted someone at his house to keep me company but without causing offence. I made up the story to explain my partner's presence.'

'And where *is* your partner?' Palmer looked around as though Robin might spring out from behind a bookcase.

'He's at work.'

'Gardening, or playing detective?'

Eve counted to ten. 'He doesn't "play detective". The London police employ him as a freelancer. Today he's gardening.' Keeping her temper was the best way to annoy Palmer but oh boy, was it challenging.

'Now, Ms Mallow,' Palmer leaned forward further, looming towards her, 'perhaps you'd like to continue in this creative vein and tell me why on earth,' he slapped her coffee table, 'you then followed Mr Bancroft to his holiday cottage where he was pushed downstairs? You and Mr Maxwell were seen. There's no point denying it.'

'I wasn't going to.' What did he take her for? 'We were all wary of Max Bancroft, as I said, after Stevie Witham's flashback.' She matched his posture, leaning in. He needn't think he could intimidate her. 'Honor Hamilton could have died in his house, not The Briars. There's a tunnel linking the two.' She might as well present it as fact. 'Simon – Mr Maxwell – thought Bancroft was acting oddly and we went to look. In fairness, if someone pushed him downstairs, then Simon was right. There *was* something odd going on.'

She'd swear she could hear Palmer's teeth grind.

'You have no business to be following anyone anywhere!

There's not one jot of evidence that Honor Hamilton died anywhere but The Briars. Stevie Witham has been interviewed. None of what she remembers even hints that Ms Hamilton's body was moved. The death was expertly investigated and ruled accidental.'

'And the tunnel between the two houses?'

'An irrelevant, unsubstantiated rumour!' Palmer slapped the table again and Gus barked.

Eve stroked her dog, her eyes on the detective. She didn't bother mentioning Cleo's notebook. She knew he'd dismiss it out of hand.

'What did you see while you were spying on an innocent pillar of the community?'

Eve's heart was thudding hard, part adrenaline, part worry over Richie. 'We thought there was someone hiding in the trees. We waited a while but they didn't appear. Then we went to knock on the door of the house but there was no reply.'

'What time was this?'

'About a quarter to five. Max Bancroft must have decided not to answer or he was already injured.' She hoped he'd reveal the time of the attack in response, but he didn't.

'Could the person you heard in the trees have got into the house?'

'Only if they'd managed to reach the river path unseen and entered by the back door.'

'But they could have done that?'

Eve nodded at last. 'It's possible.'

'I understand you found a key ring close to the house.'

The time had come. Eve nodded. 'I recognised it. I picked it up and dropped it back to Richie Hamilton on Meadowsweet Grove.'

'He was in?'

This was the worst. 'No. He was out.'

Palmer grunted. 'Richie Hamilton's mum's death was an accident, but that's irrelevant. It's entirely possible he fell for this ridiculous village rumour and lashed out in what he thinks is an act of revenge. This looks very bad for him indeed. Perhaps he and his cousin worked together.'

And there she was, thinking Stevie might be off the hook.

26

Once Palmer had left, Eve had the urge to talk to Richie. She wanted to explain that it was she who'd returned his fob and to warn him that the police would be on their way. She snatched up Gus's leash and dashed across the village green towards Meadowsweet Grove, but it was no good. By the time she got there she could see Palmer's lumbering form through Richie's window. And perhaps Richie really was guilty. On paper, he seemed most likely.

She decided to walk the rest of the way along the grove then cut through to Parson's Walk to give Gus a proper airing. What if Richie was arrested? If years of lies had fallen away when Stevie had her flashback, the hurt would have hit him at his core. Lashing out at Cleo then finishing the job in desperation fitted. Just as pushing Max down the stairs did. Both attacks were full of emotion. That or desperation. And the key fob placed him close to the latest crime scene. If she and Simon had caused Richie to run, that could be when he'd dropped it.

But in the back of her mind, Perry's conversation with Abby played too. He was full of hatred for his father. He could have shoved him after years of hurt. He'd come home and accepted a commission from an arch enemy for a reason. But why strike now?

On impulse, she doubled back and knocked on Perry's door. She hadn't talked to him for the obituary yet. It would be natural to express her sympathy over his father too.

He opened up. His eyes were puffy, as though he hadn't slept well.

Eve held out a hand. 'Eve Mallow. I'm so sorry to bother you. I interviewed your dad yesterday for Cleo Marbeck's obituary. I heard what happened afterwards and I wanted to say how sorry I am.'

Perry grunted.

'Do you know how he is yet?'

'Out of danger. In fact, I'm not sure he was ever in it.' He sounded scathing.

'It's terrible timing, but I wondered if I could talk to you for Cleo's obituary.'

'Me?'

Eve nodded. 'You were working for her when she died. You must have got to know her quite well as you researched your book. On top of your previous contact.' She needed to get him to open up. She wanted to know if he'd hated his dad enough to kill him, and why he'd agreed to write about Marbeck's when he'd loathed Cleo.

Perry's eyes narrowed. It might be guilt or simply suspicion.

'I'm happy to provide examples of my work.' She handed him a business card. 'I promise I don't do gutter journalism. I just want to get the obituary right. It shouldn't be a puff piece, but it will be if people are too polite to speak out.' She hoped it would tempt him to air his grievances. In her experience, most people wanted to set the record straight.

At last, he took out his phone. 'All right then.' They agreed a time on Thursday.

'Why did you agree to work for Cleo? Your dad said you weren't reconciled to his relationship with her.'

Perry's eyes met hers steadily. 'She made me an offer that was too good to refuse. It was business, pure and simple. What happened with my mum was a long time ago.'

But there was a tic going in his cheek. She bet it felt like yesterday. Eve wouldn't have accepted the work in his place. It wasn't as though he was short of commissions. The excellent package Cleo had offered would fit with her feeling guilty, but Perry accepting it was suspicious.

Then beyond him, in the depths of the shadows of his cottage, she caught movement. Someone was there. Someone who wanted to know who was calling but was anxious not to be seen.

As they said goodbye, and Perry closed the door, she wondered. She'd like to get inside. Find out who had been eaves-dropping. She kept thinking of defenceless Richie, stuck with Palmer. Whatever he'd done or not done, she was certain there was more going on than the police knew.

She grimaced, walked into the passageway to Parson's Walk and glanced over her shoulder. She was alone. She knew what she needed to do, but it was hard. A moment later, she was drag-ging her hand along the pavement, pressing her palm against the flagstones. *Ouch.*

Gus looked at her and whined.

'It's all right,' she said, under her breath. 'All in a good cause.' She'd drawn blood. She pressed a couple of bits of grit into her palm and smeared grass along her wrist so it was stained.

A moment later, after squeezing her graze to redden it and draw a few extra droplets of blood, she was knocking at Perry's door again. There was no one out in the grove. Whoever was skulking at his place must still be there.

'So sorry.' She showed Perry her palm when he answered and pulled a rueful face. 'I tripped over Gus's leash and grazed myself. Would you mind if I came in for a moment and gave it a quick wash? I don't like to leave it until I get home.'

Eve was banking on him being too polite to say no.

Sure enough, he stood back in the doorway, but she sensed his stiffness. She stared into the shadows. She couldn't see anyone but there was a creak on the stairs. What the heck was she doing, coming in without backup? She'd acted on instinct, and it was too late now.

'Here. There's a downstairs cloakroom.'

Upstairs might have revealed more. 'Thanks so much. You don't have any cotton wool and disinfectant, do you?'

If he walked through the house to fetch it, he might interact with his visitor. She could listen from the door. At last, he went.

She turned the tap on full blast, then abandoned it and crept after Perry, pulling the cloakroom door to, to drown out the sound of running water.

She could hear his footsteps overhead. She stood at the bottom of the stairs, straining to catch any conversation.

'Thank you.' That was Perry's hushed voice. 'I know it goes both ways but I mean it.'

'... going to go.' A woman. Abby?

'Why don't you stay? She'll be gone in a minute.' Perry sounded exasperated. 'We need to make sure—' She couldn't catch the rest.

'No! I was never intending to stay. I'm going right now.' It *was* Abby, Eve was sure of it.

She heard her stumble at the top of the stairs and visualised her falling. She didn't, but she was bolting down as Eve dashed back inside the cloakroom and got to work on her grazed hand.

Abby had sounded frightened.

27

Back at Elizabeth's Cottage, Eve found an envelope on the table and a note from Robin. Greg had come through with the information on Honor's death. He'd risked everything to take copies of the reports for Eve to see. Robin was still out, but he'd texted to say he ought to have updates on the attack on Max later that day too.

Eve glanced at her watch. She just had time to look at Greg's information before she went to Monty's. She sat at the dining table with Gus at her feet and the envelope in front of her, surprised to see her hand shake as she opened it.

It was hard to read the description of Honor's death. She'd been so young. Eve kept thinking of her unhappiness and her search for support and love. It was tragic that she'd never found it.

The notes said she was found lying on her left-hand side, left arm underneath her, the right arm flung out. The report mentioned the Mickey Mouse watch, cracked beneath her. It put the time of death at 3.35 p.m., which tied in with the pathologist's estimate of between three and four. The window was relatively precise, because her body had been discovered quite soon after she'd died.

Livor mortis – the pooling of blood in her body after death – was consistent with where she was found. But it was as Robin had said: if Max had moved her quickly then he'd have avoided gravity doing its work in her original position.

The police had interviewed Cleo at the time, of course, on the back of her row with Honor, as well as everyone on Meadowsweet Grove and Parson's Walk. No one had seen Honor enter The Briars. That would fit if she'd been carried there through the tunnel. The familiar names on the list of interviewees were Rose Hobson, the mum of Stevie's friend, Max Bancroft, and Lara Oxley and her mum.

As Eve knew, it had been Lara who'd provided Cleo with her alibi. The pair of them had bumped into each other up the river just after 3.30 p.m. Cleo said she'd been walking off her upset after quarrelling with Honor and Lara's reasons for being there were also emotional: grief over Freddy had left her constantly restless. They'd been well beyond the mill at the time, a good forty-minute walk away. Neither of them could have been at The Briars or Max's place during the time-of-death window if they'd told the truth, and as Eve had thought before, it was unlikely that Lara would have lied for someone she hated.

Max said he hadn't seen anything. He claimed he'd been out visiting one of the properties he owned when Honor had fallen. There was a witness to back him up. But if Max had killed Honor and moved her body, he could also have altered the time on her watch before smashing it, to give himself an alibi. He'd been much closer at hand.

As Eve knew, it had been the estate agent and Cleo who'd found the body. The viewing had been at half-past five. The estate agent had had to unlock the front door as expected to enter the property, and the back had been secured too. There were no open windows.

The notes said that in the recent past, some local schoolkids had been found monkeying around inside The Briars. They'd cracked open a window and climbed in, but as they couldn't have re-latched it on their way out, the police decided they hadn't been inside the day Honor died. One of the kids involved caught Eve's eye: eleven-year-old Perry Bancroft, interviewed in the presence of his father, Max.

Honor had had a gap in her schedule that afternoon. She was meant to be at home, looking after her son, but her mother-in-law had stepped into the breach. Eve remembered reading about that in Joyce Hamilton's record book. She'd been summoned by a neighbour who'd realised Richie was alone.

Honor's set of keys for cleaning had been on her, including one for The Briars, so everyone assumed she'd let herself in. The only other people with keys to the house were the vendors, who'd already moved out, and the estate agent. But of course, if Max had taken Honor's body there, he could have used the tunnel or Honor's keys to get inside. Either way, it seemed nigh-on impossible that Stevie would have blundered in there.

But Eve needed proof. She explained it all to Gus. 'That fathead Palmer won't budge until we can show Max moved Honor.' Of course, Stevie might remember more in time. The thought made Eve's mouth go dry. Max must be watching her like a hawk.

Eve hid the case notes and turned to Gus. 'All we can do is keep pulling at all the different mysteries we've identified until something comes loose. We need Greg's update on Max Bancroft too.' Waiting was tense. It was just as well she'd got a shift at Monty's and the meeting with Cleo's sister Beth to keep her occupied that afternoon.

She wondered how Richie was getting on. For all she knew he'd been arrested. Perhaps he'd confessed to pushing Max and killing Cleo. Even if he was guilty, Palmer would go on believing the conspiracy against Honor was a figment of Richie's imagination unless she proved him wrong. Richie's future and the leniency Robin had talked about might depend on that.

During her shift, Eve filled Viv in and invited her over to Elizabeth's Cottage later for Robin's debrief on Max's attack. She messaged the rest of the gang too.

'Even if Richie was hanging around Max's holiday cottage it doesn't prove he's guilty,' she said to Viv. 'Max was one of our top two suspects for Cleo's murder. I wonder if there's any chance he could have faked the fall completely. Deliberately flung himself off the fifth step or something.' Just as she'd grazed her own hand.

'You really think he could have?'

She could tell Viv thought it was a long shot. She agreed, in truth. 'It would be hard to do, psychologically. I found faking the graze tricky enough. And even then he'd have to get the right sort of injuries. Bad enough to be believable but nothing life-threatening. I'm afraid Richie is more likely. Either way, it's not a reliable way to kill someone, as the outcome shows. It feels like an attack made in anger or panic.'

'I texted Jonah, by the way.' Viv frowned. 'You'll be proud of me. I just said everything was getting ironed out. I'm seriously hoping Stevie will be ruled out as a suspect after the attack on Max.'

'I'm keeping everything crossed. And I'm glad you've been in touch.'

'Yes, but Eve, do you know what he replied? Something about wedding plans and then he waxed lyrical over a new method for baking mille-feuille. I mean, I'm glad he's not overly worried, obviously, but I'd quite like it if he was a little less practical.' She sighed. 'Oliver was the same, but I'd always thought Jonah was more like me.'

.   .   .

Gus was especially balletic as Eve re-entered the house after her stint at Monty's. She'd left bang on time to make sure she could walk him before meeting Cleo's sister in St Mary-by-Sax. As she and Gus went round the village green, she thought ahead to her interview. She was twitching at being away from Saxford when there'd been such a major development, but she needed to understand everything about Cleo. Talking to her sibling would be invaluable. She wanted to know what had caused their estrangement and why Cleo had ignored immediate family in her will.

St Mary-by-Sax was little more than a hamlet, set in farmland. All the same, Beth's place seemed impossible to find. Eve called to say she was stranded and after more instructions, she found a footpath to the tiniest house she'd ever seen. A one-up one-down, with a lean-to bathroom at the back.

'Thanks for inviting me in,' Eve said. 'You have beautiful views.'

Beth shook hands, her expression rather stiff. 'Cold as the grave in winter but the rent's cheap. It's part of the package for my work at the local farm. Coffee?'

'Thanks.'

'So, you want to know about Cleo.' She put her hands on her hips. 'How long have you got?'

It wasn't unusual for relatives to want to offload. Eve tried not to look greedy. 'I'm not pushed for time. Getting a true picture of Cleo is important. Do you mind telling me why you were estranged?'

Beth's mouth formed a firm line. 'The relationship started to break down long ago. It all began with my dad. She was always his favourite. She can't have been more than eight when he first took her out on business. He bought and sold, just like she did. It was farm equipment first, then second-hand furniture. She soaked up his approach like a sponge. By the time he died, she had more money than the rest of us put together.'

'So his method worked?'

Beth grimaced. 'Yes, and all the better when Cleo employed it. She was good-looking and a risk-taker. Just like our dad, she bent the rules almost to breaking point.'

Almost. That was the crucial word. The theft of the necklace didn't fit.

Beth set their coffees down on a solid pine table and motioned Eve to a seat. 'My other sister and I worked just as hard. I got made redundant twice, and Lynda took time off work sick and got the sack, whereas Cleo came up smiling, time and again. And our dad thought we got what we deserved. Lynda and I were weak and stupid. Not determined enough. He believed you made your own luck. It was all about survival of the fittest. When he died, he left Cleo all his money.'

Eve had come across plenty of divisive bequests in her time. 'Nothing at all for you and Lynda?'

'Nope. He left a letter saying Cleo would make the money count.'

'Did she offer to help you at all?'

Beth huffed. 'Not through handouts. That would have gone against everything she and Dad believed in. She offered work though – for her, playing by her rules. I was stupid enough to accept. I was with Marbeck's for a short time.'

'It didn't go well?'

She shook her head. 'She set me up to fail. Wanted me working all hours. She said I needed to do as she did and live the job. I was sufficiently stubborn to do it for a while. I didn't want to fail the test, but after I'd worked myself into the ground she called me in and told me it wasn't working.'

'Without any warning?'

Beth nodded. 'I don't believe it was anything to do with my work, though.'

Eve waited for her to go on.

'I overheard Cleo lose her temper.' She took out her phone,

googled, and found the article Eve had already read about Honor's death. 'She quarrelled with this woman. The one who fell downstairs.'

'You heard the argument just before Honor died?'

Beth shook her head. 'This one was a short while earlier. It wasn't an argument exactly. The girl was upset. Cleo burst out of the room where they'd been closeted together, gave me the sharpest look and asked me what I'd heard. I said nothing, but the next morning she said she'd decided to let me go.' She leaned forward. 'There was something odd about it and I'll tell you why: Cleo paid me off. A good amount too. If I'd really failed she'd have sent me away without anything. I was still on probation. I guess she coughed up to ensure I left without a murmur.'

Eve closed her notebook – it would look less pressuring. 'It does sound odd. Did you really not hear anything of her conversation with Honor?'

Beth sighed. 'Nothing I could make sense of. All I know is that Honor had fallen in love with someone and the upset was something to do with that. It sounded as though Cleo wanted her to betray him.'

28

That evening, Eve, Robin and the gang sat around the dining
table at Elizabeth's Cottage eating salmon risotto.

Eve passed round a bottle of Viognier as Robin looked at the
notes he'd made when talking to Greg.

'Max Bancroft broke an arm and hit his head when he fell.
According to him, he'd gone upstairs to check on the bedrooms
prior to a new guest arriving. The cleaner had been in but he
likes to make sure they've done a good job. The attack came
from behind. He'd no idea he'd got company and didn't see who
pushed him. The upside is, it was definitely while you were at
the police station, Stevie. Palmer can't pin it on you.'

'Except Richie says Palmer's got it into his head that the pair
of us worked together.' Eve could see the strain behind her
ironic smile.

Robin put his drink down. 'It'll take more than his fairy
stories to make an arrest.'

Eve turned to him. 'How did his attacker escape without him
seeing?'

'He thinks he lost consciousness for a short time. It's possible
it was a standard break-in, and the thief took fright, but a

connection feels likely. Palmer thinks so too, especially on the back of the key ring you found, Eve.'

Her heart still sank at the thought of it.

Daphne patted her arm. 'It's terribly sad, but if Richie pushed Max then it has to come out.'

She was right, of course. 'So long as the truth about Max and Honor does too. I still don't have proof that she died in his house. Palmer thinks Richie's fallen for local gossip. Has he been arrested?'

'Not yet.' Robin sipped his wine. 'He admits he followed Bancroft and that he hid in the trees when he heard you and Simon approach.'

Simon swallowed his mouthful. 'Which doesn't sound great. How did he explain himself?'

Robin sighed. 'He says it was his afternoon off and he wanted to talk to Bancroft about his mum. When he saw him crossing the village, he followed. He admits he felt guilty after the villagers had a go at him for accepting Cleo's promotion. And that Stevie's flashback increased his uncertainty. He wondered if he'd wronged Honor by ignoring the rumours.'

'Oh dear,' Sylvia said. 'He couldn't have done better if he was applying for the role of prime suspect.'

Eve's sinking feeling intensified as Sylvia passed her the wine back. 'Did he tell the police why he hid from us?'

'He said he was embarrassed about what he was up to. And he insists he never went inside the house at all. He spent a while watching and worrying over what he'd say and what Bancroft's reaction might be, after which he bottled it and went home.'

'Did he see anyone else at the house?' Eve pushed the risotto towards Viv, whose plate was almost empty.

Robin shook his head. 'But they could have come and gone the back way, via the river path. The police haven't found any useful witnesses. It was a woman who lives on Blind Eye Lane who saw you and Simon. Simon's a near neighbour, so she recognised him.'

'Just our luck,' Simon said.

'Palmer's trying to place Richie inside the house now,' Robin went on. 'The scientific support team are combing the place, checking for his prints, which he's given voluntarily. Maybe he wore gloves. Or maybe he's telling the truth.'

Eve realised his potential motive was strong, but she still had questions. 'I assume Bancroft was inside the house when we arrived, whereas Richie was skulking in the trees, if it's him we heard. Surely it's more likely that whoever pushed Bancroft got in ahead of him? We knocked on the door and there was no reply. I guess that means he was unconscious or injured by then.'

Robin nodded. 'Probably.'

'The police have spoken to me again too.' Stevie sounded tired. 'They know I've visited Richie more than once since I arrived.'

'Which would make sense,' Viv said hotly, 'as he's your cousin and you didn't have much contact growing up.'

'Inspector Palmer thinks we had a shared interest in getting our revenge, all driven by what he calls "baseless rumours".'

'Ignore Inspector Fathead.'

Eve watched Stevie, mechanically chewing her food. 'We'll sort this. We have to. Then the pressure will be off and you can enjoy your wedding.' But what if they failed? She took a deep breath. 'How would anyone know Bancroft would be at his cottage?'

Robin gave her a wry smile. 'He went to the village shop first thing yesterday and Moira asked him about his plans. He wasn't specific about the timing, but he said he'd visit the cottage in the afternoon. Someone could have lain in wait inside, or out in the woods like Richie did.'

Eve thought of Bancroft looking at his watch as he'd dashed

to his property. But maybe he'd just been running late with his to-do list. She could relate to that.

'If the police are convinced Richie's lying, how do they think he got in?' Stevie asked.

'Bancroft used his own keys, but there's a key safe with another set by the cottage gate. He hasn't changed the combination since he bought the place, so anyone might know it via previous owners or tenants. It was set to 1066, so it was easily memorable.'

Everyone groaned.

'On top of that, a sociable artist stayed there for six months a year or so back. Lots of the villagers went in and out for drinks. She was perpetually forgetting her keys, apparently; she used the safe as backup all the time. Richie attended one of her parties but he claims he never knew the combination.'

'Before we leave Honor-related suspects behind, you ought to tell everyone about your visit to Beth Marbeck,' Robin said.

Eve nodded. 'There was certainly no love lost there.' She explained the background. 'The crucial point is that Cleo paid Beth off after Beth overheard her arguing with Honor a few days before Honor died. She must have worried that Beth had heard too much. I'm still puzzling over it. Beth said Honor had fallen for someone and Cleo wanted her to betray them. I wonder if Cleo was losing patience because Max wouldn't leave his wife. Maybe she sent Honor to his place to stir up trouble.'

'So you think Honor loved Max?' Daphne frowned.

Gus pottered in and Eve bent to give him a pat. 'I don't believe they had an affair. I can't see him stringing her and Cleo along at the same time. Cleo would never have worn it and I'm sure she'd have found out. But it's possible Honor had a crush on Max. She might have felt it was love. And if she went to his house to make mischief, it could have angered him enough to kill her.'

Sylvia glanced at her. 'How will you find out more?'

Eve had been thinking about that. 'I need people with long memories. Would you put the word out to the villagers that I'll be in the Cross Keys tomorrow evening from eight, collecting stories for Cleo's obituary?' She needed to go wide. Someone, somewhere might have a hint as to the task Cleo had given Honor. 'I'll put a message on the open-gardens WhatsApp group too.'

'And I'll let Moira know.' Viv gave a wry smile. 'That ought to bring in the hordes.'

Eve smiled back. 'Good thought. Right, time to get back to the attack on Max Bancroft.'

Robin nodded. 'We need to consider the suspects with motives that don't relate to Honor.'

'Do any of them have alibis?' Eve reached round the table to top up wines here and there.

Robin's eyes met hers as she refilled his glass. 'Abby and Perry vouch for each other.'

'What? Really?' Eve put the bottle down with a thump. She hadn't had the chance to tell him what she'd heard at Perry's house yet.

Robin nodded. 'You've got news?'

Eve explained how she'd inveigled herself into Perry's cottage. Robin put a hand to his forehead and looked horrified.

'I still can't believe you did that,' said Viv, who'd heard the tale at Monty's.

Daphne was peering anxiously at Eve's hand.

'It was largely cosmetic,' Eve said. 'I was too much of a wimp to do a proper job.' She explained what she'd heard. The thought made her shiver. 'Now I know they're vouching for each other, Perry thanking Abby seems significant. That and the way she acted with him. He was trying to get her to stay but she couldn't leave fast enough. I'd say she was scared. What if he persuaded her to alibi him?' She remembered his words as Abby had cut him off. *We need to make sure—* Sure that they got their stories straight, perhaps? 'He hates his dad, and Max knows Abby's secret. They have a shared interest in getting rid of him.

'Maybe they did a deal. I can imagine Abby feeling anxious about it. I still suspect Perry accepted the contract with Cleo with a plan in mind. And it brought him back into his dad's orbit too. But if he's guilty it doesn't explain why he'd kill Cleo in a frantic hurry.

'I should find out more about the pair of them tomorrow. Abby's ex's parents, the Arnolds, have agreed to see me in the afternoon, followed by Cleo's second-in-command at Marbeck's. I hope I might discover Abby's secret and find out how Perry's approaching Cleo's commission.'

Each of them was harbouring strong feelings: fear, anger, hatred and vengefulness. For Perry, Eve's question was still why act now? But Abby was another matter.

29

The following morning, Eve was thinking ahead to her planned trawl for information in the Cross Keys. She was confident lots of villagers would turn up; everyone had had plenty to say about Cleo when she was alive. They'd want to add their two cents' worth to the obituary. She could get them on to Honor easily enough from there. Maybe, just maybe, someone would know more about the secrets the pair had kept. In the meantime, it would be useful to home in on anyone who'd known the key players well back then.

As she walked Gus on the beach before breakfast, the sun sparkling on the waves, she ran into Toby, airing Hetty, and asked him for ideas.

'Ella Tyndall might be your woman,' he said, as they watched the waves break on the shore. 'Richie's granny, Joyce, was a colleague of hers. She stopped work when Honor died, but I believe they overlapped and Ella taught Richie. She might remember something useful.' He shook his head. 'I shouldn't speak ill of the dead, but Joyce Hamilton was a poisonous woman.'

Eve went straight to Ella's house on her way back from the

beach, and managed to catch her as she left for work.

She looked anxious when she saw Eve. 'I heard about Max Bancroft. I gather Richie's in the police's sights.' She shook her head. 'He was always a gentle boy, Eve.'

'He doesn't strike me as the type either, but he's been pushed far further than most people.' Eve walked alongside her as she made for the Old Toll Road and asked if she'd be willing to talk. They arranged to grab a word during her lunch break.

After that, she'd got her meeting with Sean Arnold's parents, which might uncover Abby's secret, then a chat with Jason Dempsey, the deputy executive director at Marbeck's. She'd had to push for that one. Even his PA sounded snooty. *Suffolk Monthly* didn't cut ice in the way *Icon* would have.

Gus had had a decent walk now, but Eve had one more errand before they went home. Richie weighed on her mind. She made for Meadowsweet Grove.

He looked ashen when he opened his door, and bewildered to see Eve.

'I'm glad I caught you before work. I wanted to apologise. I think you've been wondering about Max Bancroft, just like I have. I wish I hadn't found your key fob on the track near his holiday rental. I wanted to explain before the police came to interview you, but I was too late.'

Richie winced. 'It's not your fault. I shouldn't have dropped it.' He shook his head. 'I never would have normally. It shows how rattled I was. The police think I pushed him. But you didn't see me go in, did you? Do you want to come in?'

Eve was about to agree when the faintest alarm sounded in the back of her mind. Yes, he'd had rotten luck and he was Stevie's cousin, but right now he looked desperate and desperate people did desperate things.

'I'd better not. I'm due to work a shift at Monty's and I haven't had breakfast yet. Thanks anyway.' He was too close in age to her own son. She couldn't look at Richie without thinking of Nick. It made her unreliable.

She needed to get back to thinking clinically if she didn't want to land herself in trouble.

She just had time to check her email before she was due at Monty's. She was surprised to see one from Grace Witham, Stevie's mum and Honor's sister. Eve double clicked to open it.

Dear Eve,

I wanted to thank you for the efforts you're making to find out who killed Cleo Marbeck. I can't bear it that Stevie is under suspicion and I'm not with her. I asked for emergency leave but the hospital can't spare me.

I feel so guilty for everything that's happened. If I hadn't stopped talking to Cleo, the rumours about her and Honor might have died down. And Stevie might not have grown up thinking of her as our enemy. Truth to tell, I've always blamed myself in part for what happened. I wasn't around to look after Honor when she was vulnerable. If I'd been in the village, she might not have turned to Cleo for support and ended up drinking that day.

I went where my career took me, to look after people I didn't know, when my own sister needed care. She was a very special person, Eve. She might not have been mature and logical, but she was full of love. I remember her sitting with me for a whole week once when I had flu. She made me warm drinks, which were disgusting, and read to me when I longed for silence. All she wanted was to help; she just couldn't work out the right way. I wish I'd taken her with me when I left Saxford. I could see she wasn't happy with Aiden.

Thank you again. I hope to meet you at the wedding,

Grace

Poor woman. Uprooting Honor would have been a big decision and she might not have agreed, anyway. Besides, Grace could never have imagined her sister would meet such a tragic end. Eve did her best to come up with a suitable reply and sent it off.

Eve was subdued when she reached Monty's. The shift was a weird mix of baking apple cakes, talking about the case and telling Viv off for drawing wedding-cake designs on a linen napkin. (Viv had protested that it was an emergency and there was nothing else to hand.)

Eve couldn't bring herself to be too strict. Viv desperately needed some light relief between bouts of worrying about Stevie. And if she didn't finalise the design soon, it would be too late. Assuming everything went ahead as planned. Eve tried to moderate her nerves.

A high point was the arrival of the menu cards and orders of service for the wedding. The menus were beautifully decorated with a green and white botanical design. Moira had been right; the firm was good.

Viv's eyes were glistening. 'If only the occasion is as beautiful and trouble-free as Stevie and Jonah have a right to expect.'

'Moira did well, putting Stevie on to the supplier.'

Viv smiled. 'She heard about them through Lara, it turns out. Her cousin runs the place. Just like Moira to take the credit.'

They were distracted by a neighbour who came to tell them Max Bancroft was out of hospital. 'His arm's in a sling, head all bandaged up,' the woman said. 'He looked shifty when I asked how he was. Scuttled off inside his house. Some people are saying he killed Cleo then threw himself downstairs to fool the police.'

Emily, one of their new waitresses, was drinking it all in, and not focusing again. She swiped a half-eaten chocolate heart cake from under a customer's nose. Eve heard the woman cry out in what Viv later called 'understandable alarm' and apologised, ushering Emily back to the table. She always cleared too quickly. Tilly, the other new recruit, was her polar opposite. She tended to forget to do anything but chat. Eve had been sure they'd settle down in time. Hope was now waning.

Eve told Viv about her planned interviews after her shift.

'Update me the moment you're back. We desperately need a breakthrough.'

'You can come and see me in the pub with the other villagers. Though you mustn't make it obvious if you listen in. They'll clam up.'

Viv looked scandalised. 'As if I would. I've been telling everyone you'll buy them drinks, by the way. They seem very keen.'

At lunchtime, Eve fetched Gus, then walked up the Old Toll Road to Saxford's primary school. It was a classic red-brick Victorian building with a pantiled roof and an arched doorway. Ella came to meet her and they sat at a picnic table with their sandwiches.

'Don't worry,' Ella said, as three small boys hurtled past and threw themselves onto a heap of tyres, 'I'm not on playground duty. If anything drastic kicks off I'll muck in. Other than that, I'm all yours.'

Gus was watching the boys. Shifting excitedly this way and that. Waiting to see if there was a chance to join in. Eve had a feeling it would be against some kind of rule.

'What can I tell you?' Ella asked.

'I'm trying to find out what secret Honor and Cleo might have been keeping.' Honor could have been killed because of it, so it was crucial. 'I know you teach primary, but I thought you might have got gossip about Honor when she was older, via Joyce.'

Ella nodded. 'We overlapped for a bit. We were never exactly friends, but she enjoyed sounding off. I might be able to help.'

'She sounds like a forceful woman.'

'And then some.'

'Did she kick up a fuss when her son and Honor decided to marry?'

'It was before I knew her, but she often referred to it.' Ella unscrewed the lid of her thermos flask as two girls hurled mini bean bags at each other, narrowly missing their table. 'She talked as though Honor had cast a spell over Aiden. She was a monumental snob about Honor's work as a cleaner. They went off and married in secret after a whirlwind romance. I suppose Aiden must have seemed dashing and he had a steady job in sales.'

'What did you think of Honor?'

'She was sweet in many ways but not a bit worldly. She spent her whole time looking for love, and never in the most sensible places.'

Eve thought of Max Bancroft and wondered again if she had had a crush on him. Poor Honor. It sounded as though she'd been rootless and ill-equipped for the situation she'd found herself in. 'How long did it take for Honor and Aiden's marriage to come unstuck?'

Ella sighed. 'It was three and a half years before he left, but I think they realised their mistake much sooner than that. I imagine the day-in, day-out grind of living together, with Joyce breathing down their necks, was a world away from their courtship. And of course, they had Richie to look after before long.'

'Richie said he wondered if Honor drove Aiden away.'

'That's sad.' Ella chewed her lip. 'I suspect Aiden made his own decision. He wasn't the sort to pick up the reins if Honor wasn't coping, especially not with a baby.'

'Ah.' Not something she could comfort Richie with. 'Richie remembers Honor telling him Aiden would never have chosen to leave him.'

Ella grimaced. 'Poor thing. I suspect that was Honor protecting his feelings.' She glanced over her shoulder, then turned back to Eve. 'I remember the woman who taught Aiden gossiping about him when Joyce's back was turned. She said he was a selfish obnoxious boy even then. Joyce wouldn't admit it, but you could see how hurt she was when he left. *She* blamed Honor, of course, but he never came back, even once she was dead. He might have wanted to escape the marriage, but I imagine leaving Joyce was a bonus.'

'What about Honor and Cleo? I know Honor cleaned for her, but did Joyce ever say anything else about their connection?'

'She didn't approve. She said they spent too much time together and that Honor was getting stars in her eyes.'

What had she meant by that? Cleaning was a worthwhile job, but not glamorous and without a career path, Eve guessed, if you were freelance like Honor. There'd been talk of Cleo offering Honor extra work, but only running errands.

'I remember Joyce shaking her head,' Ella went on, 'and saying no good would come of it. Of course, she made a massive thing of Honor leaving Richie home alone when she had a drink with Cleo, that last day. But I heard Honor had asked a friend of hers to drop in and watch him. The friend never made it, clearly. Honor was careless and impractical. She should have waited to make sure Richie had a minder, but I don't think she meant to leave him unattended. She loved him like anything, Eve. I can still see her hugging him tight.'

The thought was agonising. All these years, Richie had had the book of Honor's sins by his side, telling him she'd abandoned him that day without a second thought. 'Have you ever told Richie that?'

Ella frowned. 'No. Should I have?'

Eve explained about the record book Joyce had kept.

'Good grief. She was an awful woman.' She sat up straighter. 'I'll tell him the moment I leave today.'

Eve thanked her and got up from the table. She was glad Richie would hear Ella's story, but everything else left her feeling dismal. Joyce Hamilton wouldn't have regretted Honor's death and there was no sign that her son had ever thought of her or Richie again. Honor had minded about Richie's feelings, though, telling him his father wouldn't have left by choice. He'd lived off that crumb of comfort. Then all too soon, she was gone too and all he had left was a memento of his dad, and Joyce's catalogue of Honor's failings.

Eve felt for the children Joyce had taught. As for the extra work, she wondered if Cleo had started to use Honor as a sort of personal assistant. It might fit with the task Beth Marbeck had heard Cleo set her. An underhand mission. It could have helped Cleo make it sound exciting and prestigious. Eve still wondered if it related to Max Bancroft.

30

It was time for Eve to drop Gus at home and go and find Mr and Mrs Arnold to ask about Sean and his bags. She hoped they might shed light on Abby Porter's secret too. Abby's friend Jill from the bakery was clearly worried they'd say something which showed her in a bad light.

Eve was about to set off when she got a call from Sylvia.

'Hide team, reporting for duty.'

'You and Daphne are stoics. What news?'

'We've just seen the strangest thing. Max Bancroft approaching Abby Porter's house looking remarkably shifty. We lost sight of him briefly, because of our viewing angle, but he reappeared as he climbed over her back gate.'

'Really? That is odd.' He had a hold over her. If he wanted to get into her house again, he could just ask. What was he up to?

'That's not all.' There was a note of relish in Sylvia's voice. *'Once he was in her back garden, he crept into her house. He managed to get a side window open.'*

Perhaps he'd planned ahead – tampered with the window when he visited Abby. Eve had always wondered why he'd agreed to see her. Blackmail was one possible reason. Wanting access to her house could be another. But why would he need time alone there?

'*He had a carrier bag when he went in,*' Sylvia went on. '*He must have let himself out the front way, because the next time we saw him he was back on the path to Parson's Walk.* Without *the bag.*'

Had he planted something in the house? 'I don't like the sound of that. I'm on my way out of Saxford for an appointment but I'll call Abby at Parker's.'

'*Good idea.*' Sylvia's tone had turned sober. '*We thought she should be warned.*'

Eve thanked her, then rang off and tried to reach Abby. The operator said she was with a customer, doing a 'personal styling' session. She was in all afternoon, though. Eve left a message, asking Abby to call her urgently.

She was preoccupied as she drove to see the Arnolds at the plant nursery they ran. Perhaps Max had planted something to incriminate Abby. Or maybe Abby suspected him. He still seemed like a strong candidate for Cleo's killer. If so, and Abby had become a threat, the package might contain something harmful. It didn't bear thinking about.

Eve found the Arnolds hard at work in their herb section, surrounded by fragrant rosemary, buzzing bees and creeping thyme. They must be past retirement age, Eve guessed, but it looked as though they lived their work. They introduced themselves as Janet and Pete.

Janet pulled off some gloves to shake Eve's hand, then cupped her eyes to shade them from the sun. 'We've a café for visitors. Why don't we have a cup of tea while we chat?'

As they sat down and a waitress took their order, Janet leaned forward and took Eve's hand for a moment, squeezing it. 'I'm glad you want to mention Sean in Cleo Marbeck's obituary. We're still aching for the loss of him.'

Their pain would be unimaginable. Eve felt a stab of guilt, but she'd have included his work even if she weren't digging for dirt on Abby Porter.

'I'm so sorry for your loss. I've seen pictures of Sean's bags. They're beautiful.'

His dad nodded. 'When the kids were little, we hoped they'd take over the business here, but Sean's creativity took a different form. His brother's waiting in the wings to make the most of this place.' He sighed. 'He doesn't have Sean's vision, but we'll make an entrepreneur of him yet.'

Janet was frowning. 'Shhh.' She turned to Eve. 'He's doing fine. We just can't bring ourselves to retire yet.'

Eve looked out over the plants, the smell of lavender wafting on the breeze. 'It's a special place. I can see that.'

Pete smiled. 'So, how can we help?'

Eve asked if they knew how Cleo had discovered Sean's talent.

'It was tremendous good luck,' Janet said. 'Sean was so gifted but his bags weren't well known. He had a website, but you had to go looking. Cleo found him through that. She told him she wanted to support someone from Suffolk.'

Eve made a note. 'They got to know each other well, I imagine. I gather he moved into one of Cleo's cottages.'

Janet and Pete exchanged a glance and Eve wondered if they knew about their affair.

'They certainly seemed to hit it off,' Janet said at last. 'Cleo was older than Sean but not by so much. It makes less difference at that age, doesn't it?'

This might be the opening Eve needed. 'You think they were romantically involved? Only I thought Sean was Abby Porter's partner.' She pulled an apologetic face. 'It's just what I heard. I live in the same village.'

They exchanged another glance, then Janet looked at her lap.

Pete took his wife's hand and clutched it. 'We weren't so fond of Abby, to be honest, though she was Sean's long-term girlfriend.'

Eve sensed she'd have to sympathise if she wanted more. 'Ah, I see. Look, I'm sorry to ask, but what made you hesitant about her? I'm having to spend some time with her at the moment, and I suppose forewarned is forearmed. I sensed...' She hesitated deliberately. 'I sensed she was holding something back. That she might have a secret in her past.'

If the Arnolds were already lukewarm about her then at least she wouldn't be influencing their opinion.

Janet seemed eager. 'It's very interesting that you should say that, isn't it, Pete?'

He nodded.

'Our worries about her went way back, if I'm honest, and we haven't any proof.' She looked at her husband.

He leaned forward. 'You'll laugh, it's so long ago, but back when Sean and Abby were at school together, they had a massive row over another girl. It almost split them up.' He sighed. 'We used to wish it had.'

Janet bit her lip. 'Sean didn't tell us about the blow-up between them; we heard it on the grapevine. The event was so acrimonious it caused a lot of gossip. And then, a day later, Sean went off to see this other girl again. But we heard he'd bumped into Abby on the way. Or she'd followed him. That was our impression.'

Pete pushed his hand through his thinning hair. 'And the next time we saw him he'd been injured.'

They thought Abby was responsible? 'That sounds bad. What happened?'

'There was a massive gash on his cheek. He'd had stitches.' Janet's jaw was tense, her eyes haunted. 'We asked him about it of course. He said he'd fallen but that wasn't believable. We were sure he'd been in a fight.'

'What made you think Abby was to blame?'

Pete shook his head. 'We pieced it together. Someone saw them disappear into a pub garden in Blyworth. Then someone else saw them reappear separately, Sean's face dripping with blood. Sean swore it wasn't Abby who'd hurt him, but he would, wouldn't he? He wouldn't want to lose face. We were pretty certain. It was a cold night. Everyone else was indoors in the bar. We guess Abby had been drinking. The people we spoke to said she and Sean were both carrying bottles of beer.'

Janet looked into Eve's eyes. 'How could she do it? I'll never know why he went back to her. The scar lasted, of course. It was a constant reminder, as if we needed one.'

That could definitely be the secret Cleo had referred to when she'd rejected Abby for the London job. Perhaps she'd thought she could overlook it but when push came to shove, she realised Abby was too much of a risk.

Eve sat back in her chair. If Cleo had threatened to tell, it could have been enough to kill over. Would Abby still have her new job offers if her prospective employers knew she'd assaulted her ex? The attacks on Cleo and Max made perfect sense if Abby wanted to kill the story. They were sure of their ground, whereas Janet and Pete only suspected. Cleo *could* have threatened to tell in the middle of the open gardens if Abby had brought the topic up. And Abby would still have been angry with Cleo after she'd dragged her to the UK.

Eve moved on to talk about Sean's creative process, how he'd got started and what the Marbeck contract would have meant to him. As they chatted, she was aware of a man of around forty-five, hovering nearby, doing something to some roses. Eve wondered if he was the other son; he looked very like Pete.

When the time came to say goodbye, Eve promised to send Janet and Pete a copy of her article and made her way towards the main entrance.

The hand on her elbow made her jump. It was the man who'd been tending the roses.

'You're the obituary writer?' His angry eyes met hers.

'That's right. Eve Mallow. How can I help?'

He drew her to one side. 'It might be that Abby lashed out at Sean one day, but he wasn't perfect, you know. She went too far, but I dare say he deserved it.'

'Because of the fight over the girl? I can imagine Abby hated him for flirting, but they were young. It happens. She shouldn't have attacked him. If she did.'

'Yes, but Sean used to pester women. He didn't take it too kindly if they rejected his advances. I hear he went after that girl from his school again. He wouldn't leave her alone, even after she was married. That's all I'm saying. Abby and Sean only got back on an even keel when she was dead.'

His words made Eve shiver.

31

Eve drove back to Blyworth. Abby hadn't called her back, but she just had time to dash into Parker's before she was due at Marbeck's. Her mind was full of what Sean's brother had said, but that would have to wait. Warning Abby was most pressing.

She breathed a sigh of relief when she saw her, standing in the womenswear section. She looked up as Eve approached.

'This is going to sound a bit odd, but one of my friends saw Max Bancroft climb into your back garden.'

Eve watched Abby's eyes. Shock, confusion and anxiety. Eve doubted she had any more idea than Eve did what Max had been up to. At least she was warned now.

'The weird thing is, he was carrying a bag, but when he reappeared, he didn't have it any more. They wondered if he might have broken into your house and left something there.' It was best to make the information a little sketchy; she didn't want to reveal her neighbours' habit of watching from the hide.

It looked like Abby was still processing the information as Eve said goodbye.

Eve dashed round the corner to Marbeck's.

The firm's offices were above their main outlet in the town.

Eve entered through a royal-blue door adorned with a brass name plaque and was greeted by an impossibly svelte receptionist in vertiginously high heels. She was wearing some of the firm's wares by the look of it and screamed wealthy elegance.

'Jason Dempsey is ready for you. I'll show you in. Coffee?'

Eve accepted and the receptionist knocked on an office door. The building was as immaculately presented as she was. Posh modern interiors in a charmingly olde worlde shell. The office Eve was invited to enter smelled of polish and Jason Dempsey's cologne. He must bathe in the stuff.

He leaned forward to shake her hand, his rings flashing in the light from his desk lamp. He looked as though he'd spent many years living well. His receding grey hair was neatly swept back and his bronzed skin spoke of foreign holidays. Eve guessed his watch had cost a small fortune.

'Afternoon.' He motioned her to a leather chair on the other side of his huge table. 'Please, make yourself comfortable. Now, what can I do for you?'

Eve explained her mission and began with questions about Cleo. (What was she like in business? *One hundred per cent driven, determined to win.* How closely had they worked together? *Very* – with an unpleasantly suggestive smirk. What was her management style? *Up front, exacting, and non-hierarchical.*)

After that, and the delivery of coffee, Eve moved onto Cleo's decision to hire Perry to write about Marbeck's.

Jason leaned back in his oversized chair, swinging this way and that. 'It's interesting you should ask about that. Cleo said the book would boost our reputation and she wanted Perry because he was classy. He's done some of the minor royals. So I said, yeah, sure babe, if that's what you want. But I have to tell you, he's a piece of work. His questions are a lot more intrusive than yours and with less bedside manner.' (With a leer at the word 'bedside'. This was a man who'd never grown up, clearly.) 'Now poor old Cleo's a goner I've written to her heir to query Perry Bancroft's appointment.'

That was interesting. 'Does he get access to your confidential files?'

'Not if I can help it. But he asks for them, and I saw him once, in one of the archive rooms. God knows how he got in. They're kept locked. I bawled the staff out over it. One of them must have let him in as they went out.'

That figured. Perhaps Perry had been looking for dirt on the firm by way of revenge. It might explain the why now question. That opportunity had come up when Cleo hired him, presumably out of guilt. And then, if he'd scented the chance to get even but been disappointed, he could have lost patience and got violent. But it was as she'd thought before – doing it during an open-gardens event made no sense.

'What about Richie? What did you think of Cleo's decision to offer him the London job? Did she discuss it with you in advance?'

Jason let out a shout of laughter. 'No, she did not! But it was her show. Abby Porter had way more experience but there was some deal-breaker there. She never did tell me what it was. Fact is, I'm concerned about Richie doing it. He hasn't got that cut-throat instinct you need in business. But Cleo was making every effort to mould him. She wanted him hungry and ruthless. You can break most people in in time.'

He made Richie sound like an animal. She felt he'd been buffeted by other people's desires, just like his mum.

'Of course,' Dempsey went on, 'I could see how he'd appeal to the customers. They'll probably visit the new store just to gawp at him.'

This was getting worse. How could Richie be happy in his work with people like Dempsey in charge? It didn't say much for Marbeck's opinion of their patrons either. She took a deep breath. 'One more thing. I wanted to include something about Cleo's planned new line: Sean Arnold's bags.'

Jason nodded, his gold rings flashing again. 'Now, there I did approve. A sound business decision. And it seemed to be going swimmingly. Cleo must have been keen. She was putting Arnold up for next to nothing in one of her cottages and they seemed close, if you know what I mean.' He gave Eve a significant look followed by a wink. Talk about overdoing it. 'But then suddenly it was all off. I can only assume it was a lovers' tiff, though Cleo was adept at avoiding them normally.'

'What happened?'

Jason raised an eyebrow and folded his arms.

'I don't have to put it in the obituary if you'd rather I didn't.'

At last, he nodded. 'All right then.' He leaned forward. A lover of a good gossip, clearly. 'One day, I came in here and all hell had let loose. Cleo's PA had found the entire range of Arnold's sample bags in shreds. Slashed up in tiny pieces on the floor. She thought we'd had vandals in, and that Arnold and Cleo would be livid. But in fact, when I looked at the security footage, I saw Arnold had come in overnight and done it himself. Cleo refused to give me the background, and he dropped dead of a heart attack soon after, so that was that.'

As Eve drove home, her mind played over what she'd learned from Jason Dempsey. So the plans to stock Sean's bags hadn't died with him, but before that, due to some kind of argument. It could have been a straightforward lovers' tiff, but Eve wondered. The letter Abby had found from Sean appeared to have upended her thoughts on his affair with Cleo. And it was clearly Cleo who'd upset *him*, if his destruction of his own bags was anything to go by. What had she done to make him so angry? And why had his letter made Abby feel the same way? She and her ex had both been meant to work with Cleo, but it had come to nothing. Was there a connection?

Cleo had known Abby's secret before she left Paris, thanks to Sean. Surely, she'd already have had doubts about her at that stage? Richie said she seldom changed her mind.

The thoughts continued to mingle as she parked her Mini Clubman by the village green.

By the time Eve walked up Haunted Lane, new patterns were forming in her head. She glanced at her watch. Well past school pick-up time.

Inside Elizabeth's Cottage, she bent to fuss Gus, then called Ella Tyndall.

'Ella, it's Eve. Sorry to bother you again. Can you remember what Perry Bancroft was like by the time he left primary school?' He'd been eleven years old when Honor died. 'I mean physically, though character could be relevant too?'

Ella's answer fitted with her theory. The question was, how had Cleo been so sure of the basic facts? She stood there in the quiet of the cottage, replaying everything Cleo had said and what Eve had found out since.

As she removed her watch to do some washing up, the answer came to her.

32

That evening, Eve sat in the Cross Keys' garden with the gang. She was going inside shortly to meet villagers with memories of Cleo. She only hoped it would pay dividends. She was desperate to discover Honor and Cleo's secret, but all information was useful. In the meantime, she wanted to share the thoughts she'd had earlier. She'd already told Robin of course, and he'd passed them on to Greg.

'Tell me you've got news,' Viv said, leaning forward.

'I've got thoughts. Several came at once, and I wonder now if my perspective's been all wrong. It's like one of those visual games. At first you see two faces, then suddenly you notice there's a wine glass between them.'

'What on earth are you talking about?' Viv looked put out.

'I was considering the people Cleo let her cottages to: Joyce Hamilton with little Richie, possibly from guilt, if Cleo had a hand in Honor's death; Abby, prior to launching the London store; Sean before her, because Cleo was interested in stocking his bags; and Perry, because she picked him to write about Marbeck's, offering an excellent package – again, possibly from guilt.'

'So she was governed by her conscience and her plans for Marbeck's?' Simon said.

'Apparently.' But not in reality. Eve had been through the facts repeatedly; she was sure of her ground now. 'I kept thinking about Cleo knowing Abby's secret before she hired her. There were a number of reasons she might not care about her assault on Sean, but I missed the obvious one.'

A look of realisation came into Stevie's eyes. 'The offer was fake? She never meant for Abby to launch the London store?'

Eve nodded. 'I believe so. I started off thinking we were looking at two groups of suspects, one lot whose motives related to Honor's death, and another who had separate grievances. But now I realise there's a crucial element that links them all.'

Viv frowned.

'Cleo lured them all to Meadowsweet Grove. And it started years ago, before the current suspects moved in. From her oldest tenant, Joyce Hamilton, to her latest, Perry Bancroft, she offered very low rent, according to gossip. That was enough to convince Joyce to take a cottage. For Sean, Abby and Perry, she also dangled the promise of lucrative business deals. I think she was investigating Honor's death herself. They were her suspects.'

Everyone spoke at once.

'But it's years since Honor's death. Why now?'

'Perry? Surely not, he was just a boy when Honor died!'

'Did they really all have motives?'

'If she didn't conspire to kill her, how did she know Honor was murdered?'

Words tumbled over each other until they all stopped.

Eve looked at the notes she'd written. She'd wanted to make sure her theory held water. 'The why now question is answered by Joyce Hamilton's death, shortly before Cleo lured her next suspect to the grove. Everyone says Cleo spent a lot of time with Joyce when she was on her deathbed. The conspiracy theorists decided it was because Cleo was confessing to Honor's murder but that made no sense. Why confess to Joyce, who hated Honor anyway? I think it's more likely that Cleo was convinced Joyce had killed her. She had every reason to want to solve the mystery. She was genuinely fond of Honor and if she got proof, she could finally silence the gossips. As for Joyce, she was a prime suspect. She loathed Honor. I understand that on the day she died, she was called out of school because Richie was home alone. From what I've heard, I could definitely see Joyce chasing after Honor in a rage, finding her drunk, arguing with her, then pushing her down the stairs. I imagine Cleo pictured that happening at The Briars, where she thought Honor had died. She might have offered Joyce the cottage anyway, out of kindness to Richie and sorrow at Honor's death, but I think she also hoped she'd get the truth one day. Those deathbed visits were Cleo's last chance, but I assume Joyce never confessed.'

Daphne smoothed some hair out of her eyes. 'So Cleo decided she'd been wrong all these years?'

'Again, it's guesswork, but it would fit.' Eve glanced at her notes once more. 'At that point, I'd hazard she turned her thoughts to others who might be guilty. Tongues were wagging again after Joyce died but Cleo was tough. I think she wanted justice for Honor as much as for herself.'

'Why Sean?' Simon said.

Eve explained the background. 'His brother said he pestered women and couldn't handle rejection. He was after Honor for years, by the sound of it.'

Sylvia's eyes were sharp. 'So, Cleo traced him, found he had a nice line in bags and used a possible business deal to lure him to the grove. You've got to admire her tenacity.'

Eve agreed. 'It sounds as though Sean was struggling before Cleo's approach. It's no wonder he was susceptible.' She wasn't surprised he'd flown off the handle when he'd found out the truth. She told the others about the slashed bags. 'After that, I assume he wrote that letter to Abby, explaining how he'd been set up. He must have died before he posted it, but when Abby found it, she realised she was in the same boat.'

'Of course,' Simon said. 'Because she'd fought with Honor over Sean. If Sean was showing a fresh interest in Honor, Abby could have seen red.'

Eve nodded. 'I could see how affected Abby was by Sean's letter.'

'But Perry?' Daphne's look was anguished. 'He was only a child when Honor died.'

'A strapping eleven-year-old, according to Ella Tyndall, but troubled by problems at home. She didn't know why I was asking. I suppose we have to remember that Honor was very drunk, standing at the top of the stairs. And all this time, Cleo thought the death took place at The Briars, where Perry and his friends hung out. But if it was really at the Bancroft family home, Perry looks even more likely. I heard him speculate about Honor loving his dad. If Cleo thought he imagined they were involved, I can see why she added him to her list. He was already devastated by Max's affair with Cleo. If he'd come home and found Honor hanging around, hoping to catch Max, I could see him shoving her. And his father could have moved the body to protect him.'

Everyone fell silent.

'So what convinced Cleo that Honor's death was murder?' Viv asked at last.

'The killer must have removed Honor's watch – presumably to change the time and smash it. They put it back on the wrong wrist. I realised as I took mine off this afternoon to wash up. If Honor hadn't been a fair-skinned redhead, someone might have spotted a tell-tale tan line, but as it was, I guess she didn't have one.'

'Wait a moment,' Simon said, 'how did you know which wrist was the correct one?'

'And how do you know Cleo knew?' Viv put in.

Eve might have clicked sooner. 'I had the information I needed as soon as I read the police details of how Honor was found, but I didn't put two and two together. The reports say she was lying on her left-hand side, with the smashed watch on her left wrist, under her body. But in Richie's living room, there's a photo of Honor on a bike, signalling right. The Mickey Mouse watch is on her outstretched wrist.

'I think Cleo must have realised the same thing. She was with the estate agent when Honor's body was found. If she noticed her watch was missing from her right wrist, she had half the puzzle. And she knew Honor; she'd know where she wore her watch. I doubt she clicked immediately. I think she'd have told the police if she had. She must have been in shock, but as details of the case came out, I imagine the facts settled and a lightbulb came on.'

'She could still have told the police,' Simon said.

'True, but I guess by that stage she'd lost faith in them. They'd been suspicious of her involvement to start with, just like the villagers, then written the whole thing off as an accident. Cleo was a feisty character and the police had been wrong on two counts. I think she must have decided she was better placed to solve the crime.'

'Huh, understandable,' Viv said. 'So she began a crusade to prove who'd killed Honor?'

Eve nodded. 'I always knew she cared about her, but I'd set that to one side, because of that final row. Now, everything looks different. I should have given the friendship more weight. They gave each other presents and they were personal. Thoughtful.' She told them about the Christmas bunting Cleo had made for Honor, then turned to Stevie. 'Cleo was fighting tears when I commented on the picture she wanted to give you, too. I suspect she was devastated that their last meeting ended in a row. And it must have been horrific to discover Honor's body at The Briars, just hours later.'

Stevie's breath was unsteady. 'It's not much, but I'm glad we were starting to build bridges before she died.'

Cleo's words about Honor's drawing made sense now. *I never imagined how significant it would prove. Funny how small, chance happenings can alter the course of one's life.* Watching her draw had probably fixed where Honor wore her watch in Cleo's mind. It would have revealed a terrible truth and set Cleo on a mission.

'So Perry or Abby could have killed Cleo if something about my flashback made it more likely she'd guess it was them?' Stevie said. 'It would explain the urgency.'

Eve nodded. 'And Max could have been on her suspect list too. Cleo might have wondered if Honor had found out about their affair. If so, Max might have seen her as a threat. She must have known the alibi he gave could be false, thanks to the killer tampering with Honor's watch. I guess it didn't worry her at the time; I think she was convinced that Joyce was guilty. But it might explain their relationship cooling after she'd decided she was wrong. If she was suspicious, I imagine she kept seeing Max because it was easier to dig for information that way, but she clearly wasn't in love with him any more.

'So, almost all of our suspects have potential motives relating to Honor after all. And Perry, Abby and Max have personal grievances against Cleo on top of that.'

'Almost all?' Simon said.

'Lara is different.' Eve had thought it through. 'She and Cleo alibied each other and the timing still holds. They were too far up the river to have been at Max's place any time between three and four p.m., when the pathologist says Honor died. And if I'm right, and Cleo was innocent, she wouldn't need Lara to lie for her. Equally, it would make no sense for her to lie for Lara. If Cleo had known Lara was guilty, she wouldn't have needed to search for Honor's killer.

'But Lara's not off the list for Cleo's killing. She has a separate grievance as we know. She hated Cleo and there's still this hint that it was something to do with her brother's death. If the theft of her mother's necklace reignited that original resentment, she could have lashed out.'

'But only if she and Cleo had had a massive row in the middle of the event, I'd guess,' Robin said. 'Still, it's possible. On the upside, your theory makes Richie less likely.'

Eve nodded. 'I couldn't see him attacking Cleo without proof that she'd killed his mum. My theory rested on him challenging her and her confessing. But in this scenario, she'd probably have told him she was investigating, if he'd put her on the spot.'

'It would be nice if Palmer had a rethink on the back of all this,' Robin said, 'but there's no hard evidence, unless Greg persuades Abby to hand over Sean's letter.'

Eve sighed. 'And that seems unlikely, given it probably shows Cleo thought she might be a killer. But if Richie's innocent they won't find forensic evidence to put him at the scene of either crime. We have to hold on to that.'

'So what's the end result?' Viv asked. 'Perry and Abby rise up the list of suspects?'

Eve nodded. 'I think so. Perry's top for me. I guess Max would have moved Honor's body like a shot to protect him. On top of all that, I strongly suspect Perry and Abby are lying about being together when Max was attacked.'

33

Half an hour later, Eve had a queue of people waiting to talk to her about Cleo Marbeck. She'd chosen a small table, a little apart from the hubbub. Overhearing what one person said could influence the next, so it was best avoided.

Her first interviewee was Gwen Harris. Not Eve's favourite villager. She'd once told the police that Eve had been having an affair with a murder victim. It had been a figment of her imagination. Eve would treat her 'memories' with caution.

'So anyway,' Gwen was saying, 'we all know Cleo's reputation in the village was tarnished. All that scandal over Honor Hamilton. There's no smoke without fire, Eve. That's what I always say. And the number of lovers Cleo had! I mean, a woman like that, what can you expect?'

Gwen and Moira were good friends. There was a lot of overlap in their prehistoric views.

'And then, just the week before she died, I was convinced we could add theft to Cleo's charges, well before Lara Oxley's necklace was found at The Briars.'

'Excuse me?'

Gwen nodded. 'Soon after she visited about the open-gardens event, I was convinced she'd stolen the topaz pendant my aunt left me.'

This was one of Gwen's non-stories. 'But she hadn't?'

She looked disappointed. 'Well, no, not in the end. It took me days to find it though. I never normally leave it on top of the tallboy and it was half-hidden behind a bottle of scent. But the very fact that Cleo sprang to mind—'

'Yes, thanks, Gwen, but I need to base my obituary on facts. Saying, "Gwen Harris didn't like Cleo Marbeck because Cleo stole her pendant" would be fine. Saying you didn't like her based on village gossip is less so.'

Eve didn't want to cause a row, but there were limits.

It was water off a duck's back. Gwen just looked puzzled. 'I didn't say I didn't like her, Eve.'

It might be a long evening.

Eve asked several villagers about Cleo's friendship with Honor and they were very willing to talk. But no one knew the secret they'd shared. Of course, Eve was now sure Cleo hadn't helped kill Honor to keep it, but she still wanted to know. Max could have killed over it. Any secret of Cleo's might have affected him – whether it related to their affair or his investment in Marbeck's.

As the evening progressed, Eve learned how close to the wind Cleo had sailed. One of the older villagers had had a visit from her soon after Marbeck's was launched.

'She came to ask if I had any vintage jewellery to sell.' The woman laughed and shook her head. 'I had odds and bits, but nothing of any value, or so I thought. There was one particular necklace my niece bought me for twenty pence at a jumble sale. Sweet of her of course, but I never wore it. It struck me as unfashionable. So I told Cleo I had nothing, but when she described the sort of items she wanted, what she said reminded me of that necklace. I went upstairs to fetch it and her eyes lit up. She asked how much I wanted for it.' She put a hand to her face, as though the memory still embarrassed her. 'I had no idea what to say, of course. Eventually I admitted my niece had paid twenty pence for it and Cleo said, "Oh, I think we can do better than that. What about ten pounds?" I was so pleased.'

'Do you know how much the necklace sold for?' Eve had to ask.

The woman's smile faded. 'A friend of mine saw it priced for a lot more.'

Eve wondered how much, but she didn't want to rub salt in the wound. It made sense. Cleo had been a hard-nosed businesswoman, brought up on her dad's principles. She'd have blamed the seller if they weren't savvy enough to know an item's true value.

'But of course,' the woman went on, 'the firm was just getting established. Cleo needed her mark-up. And it was ten pounds I wouldn't have had otherwise.'

It was lucky for Cleo that people didn't like to admit they'd been conned. Because that was what it was, effectively. Of course, she'd needed her margins – that was fair enough – but if they were vast, then the practice became murky in Eve's eyes.

Eve heard several similar stories during the evening. People who'd assumed they had nothing suitable, then produced something on the back of the examples Cleo described. She'd kept pushing. Most of them claimed they were delighted with the payment offered. Only one said they felt as though they'd been robbed. They'd gone to a lawyer about it, but been told Cleo was doing nothing illegal. It would have been different if she'd claimed the price she'd offered had been the true value. She'd been too clever to make that mistake.

There was one other interesting bit of information which came to light. Someone claimed Joyce hadn't gone straight home after she was called out of school to rescue Richie, the day Honor died. The news sat there like a rock in Eve's chest. If it was true, Eve could only think of one reason for it: that Joyce had gone looking for Honor in a fury, to tell her what she thought of her for leaving her grandson alone. To do that in preference to rushing back to Richie fitted exactly with everything Eve had heard about her. And if Cleo had found out, no wonder she'd thought Joyce had pushed Honor down the stairs. Perhaps she would have, if she'd been able to find her.

At a quarter to ten, the queue was almost exhausted. Eve still had no idea what Honor and Cleo's secret had been.

The last interviewee was less anti-Cleo than many of the others. She told Eve some colourful tales of her house parties. Cleo had been generous, vivacious and charismatic, as well as coldly ruthless.

'I felt I knew what to expect with her,' the woman said. 'I'd never have sold her anything without getting it valued independently. She was out to make money. What do you expect? Though I suppose the gossip got to me in the end. It's amazing how it has an effect, even when one thinks one's immune.'

'How do you mean?'

'Cleo visited me in the run-up to the open-gardens event and shortly afterwards I half convinced myself she'd stolen a bracelet of mine. I'd worn it to a party the night before and left it on my dressing table. When I noticed it had gone, it seemed like the sort of thing to catch Cleo's eye. I searched high and low.'

It was almost an exact repeat of Gwen Harris's story. And from a seemingly level-headed villager. 'You found it in the end?'

The woman nodded, shamefaced. 'It had slipped off the dressing table and got kicked underneath. I'm not sure how, but perhaps after a few wines... It was all my own fault, obviously.'

But Eve wondered.

34

Overnight, ideas circled in Eve's head. The revelations from Sean's parents and the villagers indicated another talk with Abby Porter. It was a delicate situation, and her probable violence towards Sean, and possible involvement in the attacks on Max and Cleo, made Eve cautious.

She called and asked if Abby had time for a quick walk along the beach before she headed into work. They wouldn't be alone there. Abby was in the process of fobbing Eve off when Eve cut across her and said she'd spoken to Sean's parents for the obituary.

It did the trick. She'd guessed Abby would want to know what they'd said. She rejected Eve's suggestion of the beach but agreed to coffee and croissants in Parker's café.

Eve bumped into Richie by the village green. He was getting into his car as she climbed into hers. Eve was back to being at ease with him now he seemed less likely as the killer. She hoped her ideas would alter the police's thinking too. Those and the discrepancy with the watch, which pointed to Honor's death being murder. But of course, there was no proof that Max had moved her body. Eve needed more evidence to convince the police to look at him.

She arrived five minutes early at Parker's and was finalising her strategy when Abby appeared. Eve leaped up to buy her coffee and pastries before motioning her to the table she'd bagged.

'Did you ever work out what Max Bancroft left at your house?' she said as they sat down.

Abby looked into her drink. 'No. I didn't find anything out of place.'

It made no sense. Eve would have to think about it later. 'It's my meeting with Sean's parents that I really wanted to discuss.'

'You're going into a lot of depth for this obituary.' Abby's tone was bitter. She didn't meet Eve's eyes. 'Did they talk about me?'

'Yes.' She waited. It was mean, but the more uncertain Abby felt, the more likely she was to slip up.

'What did they tell you?'

Eve sipped her Americano. 'Probably the same thing Sean told Cleo. I'm sorry, but I overheard you talk to her about it, the Saturday before she died.'

Abby paled. 'It was one isolated incident. I'd been drinking and I lost control.'

'You must have been scared when you discovered Cleo knew.'

She shook her head quickly. 'I suppose she asked Sean about his scar.' There was a long pause. 'I was a goth back then, wearing a snake ring. Sharp. I'd never have done so much damage otherwise. We made it up.' Her voice was quiet, with a tremor to it. 'I couldn't believe what I'd done.'

A snake ring? Eve didn't buy it. Sean's mum said he'd had several stitches. And that he and Abby had gone into a deserted pub garden carrying bottles of beer... Maybe she'd smashed hers and glassed him with it. A line she could never un-cross. 'I think I know why Cleo got you here. And Sean too.'

Abby shrank back like a cornered animal. 'Why?' She mouthed the word.

'The same reason Sean gave in the letter he wrote. She suspected one of you might have murdered Honor.'

Suddenly her head was in her hands. 'You're right, but I didn't. I can see why she wondered. But what happened with Sean was a one-off. I haven't touched alcohol since. I wouldn't risk it.' Then her eyes went fiery. 'Why the heck couldn't Cleo have challenged me over it in Paris?'

She was still angry, as well as scared and sad. 'Abby, I know what you'll say, but the police need to see Sean's letter. It will help convince them that Honor was killed, and that Cleo knew it.'

Abby took a deep breath. 'They might agree with Cleo, and treat me as a suspect. But anyway, I can't show them. I burned it.'

Eve's heart sank. 'You could tell them about its contents though. Please. Give it some thought.' But she could totally see why Abby wouldn't. 'Did Sean guess Cleo was investigating him? Or did she confess?'

Abby took a deep breath. 'She confessed. Whereas I'd never have known if I hadn't found his letter.'

'Did you ever wonder if Sean might be guilty? I hear he was obsessed with Honor in the run-up to her death.'

Abby paused a second too long for Eve to believe her. 'No. Never. We all thought Honor died by accident.'

Cleo must have decided Sean was innocent though. She wouldn't have admitted why she'd lured him to Saxford otherwise. It was different with Abby. The news that Cleo had ditched her for the London job had come out before she'd planned. Abby could still have been under investigation.

'I have one other question. The necklace Cleo apparently stole from Lara's house while you were feeding her cat.'

Abby frowned. 'What about it?'

'I wondered if you'd removed it yourself and planted it at Cleo's place. You were upset with her. It would be a good way to get your revenge. Perhaps you saw Cleo sneak in behind you, and realised how bad it would look.'

But Abby looked nonplussed. 'I had no idea Cleo had followed me in. If she did, then it's natural to assume she stole the necklace.'

Eve had almost begun to accept that, but her interviews with the villagers had changed her mind.

'What makes you think the necklace was planted?' Abby's angry eyes were tinged with curiosity now.

'Two locals I spoke to yesterday told me they'd been convinced Cleo had stolen from them in the week leading up to her murder. But a few days later, they'd each found their jewellery in places that didn't quite make sense.' The second villager could have knocked her bracelet off her dressing table, but surely she'd have noticed? And then to kick it underneath, also without realising? It was hard to believe. And Gwen Harris, unreliable though she was, had no reason to lie about her own habits. If she never normally left her jewellery on her tallboy, it was odd that she'd found her missing pendant there.

'I'm starting to think that someone really did steal their things,' Eve said, 'but replaced them later. If someone wanted to destroy Cleo's reputation, they could have planned to plant the items in her house, just like Lara's necklace. My theory is that that person put them back when they realised they could use an item from Lara's house instead. Cleo did sneak in after you – I saw her – and in a lane like Meadowsweet Grove there was a good chance others did too. It would look damning.'

Abby pushed herself out of her chair. 'I don't know anything about it, but Cleo played dirty. She upended my life without a second thought. I can see why someone would want to hurt her.'

She was walking away, but Eve followed her. 'Abby, I understand you're upset, but you can't blame me for trying to work out what's going on. I'm sure you would in my place. Listen, I saw you with Perry recently.' Eve wouldn't admit she'd spied on them. 'You seemed scared of him. I know you're his alibi for the attack on his dad, but if you don't really know he's innocent...'

But Abby shook her head. 'You don't understand!'

35

Eve was making some apricot and white chocolate blondies in Monty's kitchen.

'So, what have you concluded about Abby?' Viv asked.

'I think she was telling the truth about Lara's mum's necklace.' Eve had explained what Gwen Harris and the other villager said about their missing jewellery, and the conclusions she'd drawn. 'As for the rest, I'm not sure. I'd say she's haunted by her attack on Sean. She claims it was down to drink and that she hasn't touched a drop since, but it shows what her temper was like back then. I could see her following Honor into Max's house and pushing her downstairs. It doesn't mean she intended to kill her. One shove and it would have been too late. What I don't get is why Max would help her cover it up, unless she threatened to say he was involved.' She tried to remember the pair's conversation outside Parker's. 'Max guessed Abby might have approached him just after Cleo died because of "past history". I still don't know what he was referring to. They didn't act like ex-lovers, and Abby didn't understand his reference, which she would have if they'd been involved. Without that sort of relationship, it's hard to imagine them collaborating.

'Besides, if Max knew Abby had killed Honor, why would Abby panic afresh when she realised he also knew about her attack on Sean? It sounds serious, but it hardly trumps murder. Abby's least likely to know the combination of the key safe at Max's holiday let too, after being away in Paris.'

Viv shook flour over her worktop, distributing a liberal dose on the floor. 'Nothing quite seems to fit.'

It was true. Eve sighed and tried not to take it out on the blondie mix. 'One way or another, Perry comes into it. I'm sure the pair of them lied about being together when Max was attacked. Abby looked scared when I asked about it. I don't see why she'd lie for him unless he's discovered her secret too, and he's blackmailing her. He might lie for her though, just because he hates his dad.'

'What about Stevie's flashback?'

Eve still felt it was crucial. 'Knowing Honor might have been killed at Max's place could have given Cleo the hint she needed to identify the killer, for some reason we're not aware of.'

'Were there any other useful leads last night?' Viv weighed out the ingredients for some scone dough.

Eve told her how Cleo had called door-to-door to source jewellery at knockdown prices. 'Did she ever ask your parents if they had anything to sell?' They'd lived in Eve's cottage, once upon a time.

Viv frowned. 'I don't know. I hope they were wise enough to tell her where to get off if she did. Let's ask Simon.' She went to message but her hands were doughy.

'I'll do it.' Eve pinged off the query.

Simon rang back a minute later. '*I remember Mum joked about being affronted that Cleo* hadn't *approached her.*' He laughed. '*She said she felt judged. She and Dad probably looked down-at-heel. I have a nasty feeling they spent everything on our school fees.*'

Viv shuddered when Eve relayed what he'd said. 'And I hated that school. Except for the cooking. What a waste of cash.'

· · ·

After her shift at Monty's, Eve nipped to the village store. It was always useful to check for gossip with Moira.

'Ah, Eve dear!' Moira looked up eagerly as she walked in, the shop bell jangling. 'What news?'

Anything she said would be broadcast round the village by teatime. Eve picked out a block of cheese from the chiller cabinet. 'No breakthrough I'm afraid. But what have you heard?'

Moira enjoyed dispensing information almost as much as receiving it, luckily. 'Well, let me see, there's been lots about your session with the villagers last night. People have been telling me what they told you. I'm quite shocked at the scandalous way Cleo took advantage when it came to buying stock.'

'Did she ever approach you?'

'Oh no!' Moira frowned. 'Of course, I'd never have sold her anything anyway. Even if she'd offered me a great deal of money. Sentimental value, you see. But it's funny she never asked. You'd have thought she'd have looked at what I wore and considered dropping in…'

Eve steered her onto actual news. 'What about things I won't have heard about yet?'

'Oh, well, yes! There was a bit of a to-do this morning, in fact. I've heard on the grapevine that Cleo's heir in Canada received an anonymous email telling her that Cleo made a mistake, offering the London job to Richie rather than Abby. Of course, Abby does have a lot more experience, but she's clearly a sore loser. I think we must assume she sent the email.'

Eve never assumed anything.

Moira let out a sigh. 'Fancy sending it anonymously when it's so obvious who it's from. Really quite embarrassing. I gather from Gwen Harris's niece, who's a sales assistant at Marbeck's, that it included some information about poor Richie's past failures in business.' She leaned forward and looked horribly eager.

'Apparently the Canadian heir is taking the matter seriously. She's doing some background research and has asked Abby and Richie to attend interviews with her on Zoom this afternoon! So that's set the cat amongst the pigeons.'

After Eve had paid for her cheese, she thanked Moira and turned to leave. She was almost at the door when the storekeeper gave a small cough, causing Eve to look over her shoulder.

'Sorry, Eve dear.' Moira's cheeks were slightly pink. 'Only I just wondered, what with you living with Robin, whether you'd heard any discussions following the open-gardens competition. I mean, obviously, I *completely* understand why they had to cancel the event, but it was such a shame. I imagine the judging was almost finished and I did get quite a reaction from everyone who saw my design. I suppose Robin knows who would have won...'

Seriously? Eve thought of Moira's ornamental elephant and stifled a snort. 'He'd never tell me, Moira – not when it won't be announced publicly. It wouldn't be ethical.' She tried to look as prim as possible.

'Ah, well, no. Of course not. Dear Robin.' Moira looked deeply disappointed.

After Eve had said goodbye, she bumped into Richie. She was interested to see he was carrying paperwork decorated with the Marbeck's logo. He nodded at Eve and she thought there was a new determination in his eye. When Cleo had offered him the London role, he'd looked scared. Now, she thought he might fight for it. And so might Abby if she'd sent Cleo's heir the information on Richie's past failures. In truth, it seemed quite likely. Unless Lara had. She and Abby were good friends.

That afternoon it was Eve's appointment with Perry Bancroft. She looked at him differently now. She imagined a surge of fury as he pushed Honor, his shock and perhaps relief when she didn't get up. If he'd thought she was after his dad, she could see it.

Perry had suggested meeting at his cottage, which had worried her, but she'd discovered he had a secretary working there all day. It would be all right.

She wanted to know if he realised Cleo had suspected him of Honor's murder, and to watch his reaction if it came as news. Of course, Eve couldn't prove Cleo had been sleuthing, but it fitted. And if Perry *had* known, or was guilty and knew he'd been found out, then he could have killed her for it.

They sat in the room he'd adopted as his study.

'It's a beautiful desk.' It struck Eve immediately. It was inlaid with leather, classic in style and made from mahogany.

'Cleo bought me some additional furniture when I accepted her job offer.'

'Very generous.' Eve's eyes met his. 'Was that typical of her?'

Perry nodded, but his whole body was stiff. She sensed he hated paying Cleo a compliment.

'She treated everyone the same?'

Now he blinked. 'It was in her nature. She had good points and bad. But she was exceptionally generous when she offered me my role.'

'I can see why you accepted.' Eve kept her voice warm. Non-accusatory. But if Perry had felt conflicted about coming it would hit him where it hurt. Sure enough, he winced.

'I didn't come for the money.'

Eve allowed herself a gentle frown. 'Why, then? I mean, Marbeck's is an interesting firm, but it's not as prestigious as some of your clients.'

'I thought it might be good to be near my dad for a bit. We're still estranged and he's not getting any younger.'

'You wanted a reconciliation?'

He nodded. He was a good liar. Eve wasn't sure she'd have

seen the truth if she hadn't heard his conversation with Abby. As it was, she was quite clear on how much he hated Max.

'Did you ever wonder why Cleo was so generous?'

He frowned. 'No.'

She was sure he was lying again. 'It seems a little unusual to me. Understanding it might help me get to the bottom of her character.'

At last, he sighed. 'All right. I thought she was acting out of guilt. You already know she had a long-term affair with my dad. I don't care if you mention it. She was right to feel guilty. They should have been ashamed of themselves. But I didn't kill Cleo because of it or shove my dad down some stairs, if that's what you're thinking. I've heard about you. How you've worked with the police.'

Eve took a deep breath. 'That always gets exaggerated. The local DI hates me getting involved and ignores what I say. I'm sorry about your mum and dad, though. It must have hurt. I wondered if there was another reason Cleo might have angered you.'

His frown deepened. 'I expect there were any number. But what are you driving at?'

Very carefully, Eve talked through Cleo's tenants with him, from Joyce Hamilton and Sean Arnold, to him and Abby Porter. 'Do you see how she tempted everyone in? And what you all have in common?'

When he shook his head, she listed the reasons each of them had had to hate Honor, ending with him.

Shock. He hadn't guessed what Cleo was after, she was sure of it. He opened his mouth then shut it again.

'You never sensed she was investigating you?'

Perry was still coming out of his apparent disbelief. 'No. Though now you mention it, she did try to talk to me about the old days. Good grief. She asked me if I'd thought Dad had other women in his life, back when I was a kid.' He closed his eyes for a moment. 'I shut her down. I guessed she was implying it wasn't just her, in the hope that it would dilute her guilt. But she *was* his only lover as far as I knew. I suspected Honor was keen on Dad. Everyone always was. But I never imagined it was an actual affair.'

'I suppose the question is, did you give Cleo the impression you hated Honor back then?'

He put his hands over his face. 'Once, when I saw Cleo in the village, I tried to make out she wasn't Dad's only lover. I exaggerated the way Honor behaved towards Dad to make her jealous. Then I told her I hated all the women who were running after him.' His eyes met hers for a moment. 'But I was just lashing out. I never saw Dad and Honor together. And I would never, I'd never...'

He seemed lost for words, but Eve had already decided he was a good liar. He could have killed Honor and Cleo, and attacked his dad. And if he'd killed someone when he was eleven, he'd had a long time to create an alternative history. He'd want to block out the truth.

At that moment, there was a knock on the door. A woman Eve recognised as a local appeared. 'I'm so sorry, Perry, I was on the phone. Now, can I get either of you a tea or coffee?'

But Eve wasn't thinking about refreshments. The sight of Perry's secretary had stirred a memory. She was trying to identify it.

She was gathering up her notebook when the answer came to her.

Perry's secretary was the woman who'd knocked Cleo's box off her table, the day of the open-gardens event, revealing the supposedly stolen necklace.

Perry employed her and he had every reason to get back at Cleo; he might have paid her to send the box flying. And he could have sneaked into The Briars to plant the necklace. He might know about the tunnel. She imagined him spying on his dad as he disappeared down it to see Cleo.

'Was it you who pinched Lara's mother's necklace and planted it at Cleo's house?' She met his gaze head-on. 'Because it was your secretary who revealed the theft, seemingly by accident.'

Was there a faint flicker of reaction? Eve wasn't certain. If she was right, he must have been prepared for someone to ask that question.

'Of course not! What do you mean, planted it? I'm sure Cleo stole it. She was unprincipled. And I don't know how you imagine I'd have taken it from Lara's house.'

Eve had to give it up. She thought it through as she walked home. Perry's cottage was diagonally opposite Lara's. He could have spotted Cleo sneaking in, just as Eve had, but it was true, pinching the necklace would have been a challenge. The fact that his PA had stumbled into Cleo's box could be coincidence.

36

Eve and Robin both made it home for lunch. They tucked into crusty white bread supplied to the village store by Toby at the Cross Keys. There was no purer pleasure than eating it with butter, hunks of cheese and flavoursome plum tomatoes. Eve had hers with coffee and felt restored as she updated Robin on that morning's events. But good food and drink didn't alter the facts. They were stuck in a holding pattern with no proof that Max had moved Honor's body to The Briars. And even if they had it, it wouldn't prove he'd killed her.

'Any ideas on how to break the impasse?' Robin asked as he topped up her coffee.

'Nothing firm.' She'd been wondering whether to try and tease out Stevie's memories, but it felt risky. What she'd seen back then was traumatic. She needed to think further on it. 'Later this afternoon, I want to find out how Abby and Richie's interviews with the Canadian heir have gone.' Eve checked her notes. 'Norah Campbell, that's her name. If it really was Abby who sent the anonymous message then it proves she's more bothered about the job than she's made out. It would increase her motive to kill Cleo.'

Her first task after lunch, though, was dog-related. Gus needed a walk before Eve's shift at Monty's.

They'd been down to the beach and back and had just paused for Gus to sniff a lamp-post when Eve heard a shout from the doorway of the Cross Keys.

It was Jo, and she was waving. 'Got time for a quick word? I've got news for you.'

That triggered a faint spark of hope. Unlike Moira, Jo was well aware when something was important.

Gus needed no encouragement. The promise of Hetty was enough. He and the schnauzer normally modified their boisterous behaviour when Jo was on the scene. She had no time for shenanigans, dog- or human-related. But today, her eyes were on Eve. As they entered the pub, Eve glimpsed Gus hesitate, then bound towards the schnauzer with a tap-tapping of paws.

'Bit of information from Gwen Harris, only she clearly didn't realise the significance.' Jo raised her eyes to heaven. 'You know what she's like. Head so full of other people's business that it's too crowded to make the connections.'

Eve failed to suppress a smile.

Having finished insulting a customer, Jo lowered her voice. 'So, this news is a few days old, but she heard Max Bancroft talking to Lara Oxley about the alibi she gave Cleo for Honor's death.'

'That's interesting.'

Jo nodded. 'The way Gwen tells it, Max was pestering Lara, asking her if she was *sure* Cleo was up the river when Honor fell. Lara ended up getting quite irate with him apparently. She said she'd never liked Cleo and if she was the least bit uncertain she'd have said so at the time.' She shook her head. 'I was just about to call you when I saw you through the window.'

'Thanks, Jo. This makes all the difference.'

Jo nodded. 'Thought it might. Glad to do my bit. We need this village back to normal, ready to celebrate a marriage.'

Eve popped home to Elizabeth's Cottage to drop Gus off, then dashed over to Monty's to start work.

The teashop was busy, and it was a while before Eve managed to grab Viv for long enough to impart her news. Her reaction was worth waiting for.

'I can't believe it. Tell me it all again.' Viv plonked a packet of icing sugar on the worktop, a plume of white puffing from its unsealed top.

'Unless I'm much mistaken, Max is another one trying to work out who killed Honor. From the way he spoke to Lara, he still wonders if it could have been Cleo.'

'So he doesn't know who did it?'

'That's what it looks like. I assume he came home and found Honor dead, then moved her to avoid suspicion.'

'So she could have fallen by accident?'

Eve had already dismissed that idea. 'I don't think so. If Max is investigating, I'd guess he knows she was killed. Maybe something about the scene he came home to gave it away. Now I think about it, it fits with other events too. The way he was questioning Daphne about the past, for instance. Perhaps he wondered if his wife had killed Honor. She could have assumed they were having an affair if she came home and found her there. It might even explain him breaking into Abby's place. I assumed he was planting something there, but maybe she's on his list of suspects, just as she was on Cleo's. It would fit with what he said to her outside Parker's. He sounded as though he was testing the water when he asked if she'd sought him out because of "past history". I think he was wondering if she'd pushed Honor and was looking for a reaction. Then when he visited her, perhaps he pinched something – a diary, say – then sneaked in to return it after he'd checked it for clues. I'll bet he stole Cleo's notebook too – to find out who she suspected. Only I doubt it helped him. She was too clever to leave anything sensitive lying around.'

Viv started to beat her icing, her eyes still on Eve. Eve watched whipped butter and powdery sugar work their way up the bowl and tried not to twitch.

'Why investigate now?'

'I imagine because of Stevie's flashback. He's probably scared she'll remember more. He might be worried for himself – because people will imagine he's guilty – or for Perry, if Max is scared that he did the pushing. He'll want to find out who knows what. And I suspect he's hoping he'll find proof that someone else was responsible. After all, he was badgering Lara for information on Cleo, as though he still wondered if she could have done it.' Either way, he was only digging for information now. It implied he hadn't been bothered until he or his son might become suspects. What an appalling man.

Viv was getting her icing back under control. *Good.* 'So Max is innocent of the first murder?'

'It looks like it. He could still have killed Cleo, either from passion or more likely to protect Perry if he was one of Cleo's suspects.' He was still a strong possibility in Eve's mind.

'So what now?'

'I've texted the police to tell them what Gwen Harris told Jo, but I doubt it'll make a difference. We need proof that the body was moved, so they'll interview Max. But even that won't lead us directly to Honor's killer, much less to Cleo's.'

'Thanks for filling me in. Who else have you told about this?' Viv had adopted a casual tone. 'I suppose Robin was first to hear?'

'He was out gardening. You're the first to know, hot off the press.'

Viv was smiling as Eve fetched the hand-held vacuum to sort out the stray icing sugar.

'I'll message the WhatsApp group now, so everyone knows.'

With that done, Eve asked Viv what she thought about teasing out Stevie's memories. 'I've got some thoughts on how to do it, but it might not work of course, and there's the risk of bringing back something even more horrific.'

Viv frowned as she spoke. 'She's putting on a brave face, but she's under a lot of strain. I'm not sure anything could be worse. How would you go about it?'

Eve began to beat some butter and flour as she explained.

After her shift, with everyone updated, Eve got in touch with Rose Hobson, Max's neighbour on Parson's Walk. She needed more information if she was going to try to jog Stevie's memory. Rose remembered Max having building work done at the time of Honor's death, and she'd mentioned visiting the Bancrofts back then. Eve didn't want to ask Stevie leading questions, but painting a picture of the scene might trigger her memories. It would be risky to tell Rose what she was up to though. She'd need a cover story.

In the end, Eve managed to bump into her then worked her questions into conversation, pretending she was planning building work on Elizabeth's Cottage. Rose was even more helpful than Eve had hoped. She and Max's wife had been friends.

After hearing her memories, Eve prepared to ring Jason Dempsey at Marbeck's. She wanted to ask about Abby and Richie's interviews with Norah Campbell. With any luck he'd have news by now.

'*Eve, good to talk to you again.*' She pictured him lounging in his oversized chair, the tan, the slicked-back hair and open-necked white shirt. '*What can I do for you?*'

Eve explained her query then added: 'It'll affect what I write in Cleo's obituary if Abby gets the London job after all.'

'*Of course, of course.*' Dempsey paused. '*Well, it's not official yet, but it will be by the time your article publishes. Richie keeps the London role, but Abby has been offered the management of the three shops here in Suffolk. And I'll report direct to Norah, so everyone's happy. I think we have a diplomat in charge. Though to be fair, it sounds as though she was thorough. She thought the same as Cleo: that Richie's past problems in business had been down to bad luck. And I suppose whatever Cleo had against Abby died with her.'*

But of course, Eve knew it hadn't. Max knew her secret. And Max had recently been pushed down some stairs.

'You know, Abby swears she didn't send the note about Richie's failures to Norah. She sounded so definite about it that I almost believed her, but who else would bother?'

After Eve had thanked him and rung off, she googled Richie, searching for information on his past ventures. It still seemed odd that Cleo had chosen him, with his flawed track record and lack of experience. She no longer believed Cleo had acted out of guilt, though it could have been from kindness and pity.

Finding details wasn't easy. At last, she dredged up advance publicity about an upmarket kitchenware company he'd hoped to launch somewhere down south. The local paper raved over it and referred to Richie as an 'innovative young entrepreneur'. It certainly looked as though there'd been a market for what he had to offer. In the end, though, another company, Barnwell and Greene, had beaten him to it, opening a similar store and cornering the market. She found a couple of other hints in the business press too. A manager Richie had picked for another venture had got pinched by a rival company, and an upmarket stationery outfit called Brown's had taken a premises he was after in London, just before he'd signed the contract. It really did look like bad luck. It made Eve wonder if Richie was too innocent for the game, though all the nicer for it, she was sure.

It was after Robin had come home, and they'd caught up and had dinner, that Eve's mobile rang.

Sylvia.

'*There's someone in The Briars.*'

'Don't tell me you're at the hide at this hour.'

'*Just as well one of us was.*' Sylvia let out a throaty laugh. '*Want me to call the police?*'

'I'll do it. And I'd like to get over there for a look. Thanks, Sylvia. You're one in a million!'

37

Robin rang Greg as he and Eve dashed up Haunted Lane towards the village green.

They were both in agreement that it made sense to look themselves. By the time the police got there it might be too late. They went round the back of Parson's Walk to access the passageway that ran behind the houses. It cost them time, but they were far less likely to be seen that way.

As they neared their destination, Eve looked up at The Briars. There was a light on upstairs.

'They're not being very subtle about it. Maybe they have permission.'

'I'll text Greg to warn him in case.'

But there was no one visible upstairs, and as they crept nearer, Eve caught movement on the ground floor. The flick of curtains being drawn in the front room.

She and Robin exchanged a glance and approached the window side-on. They mustn't be seen.

Eve was up against the house now, her cheek pressed to the rough brick. At the angle she was at, she could just see through a gap in the curtains.

Torchlight traced a pattern across the room, coming to rest on a large cupboard. The torch holder was in silhouette; she couldn't see who it was. A moment later, they had the door open, revealing a shallow interior. Eve's breath caught as she watched. The back of the cupboard was false. The figure had bent down to move it and now it was open too. Their torch picked out a trapdoor in the secret compartment's base. It had to be the tunnel entrance. Its hiding place, behind the cupboard's rear panel, was a good one, but it looked as though its designer had also included a bit of false flooring to cover the trapdoor. It was sitting propped against the inside wall of the secret compartment. The person carrying the torch hadn't had to move it. Someone had got there first.

Eve watched as the figure picked it up and looked at it. She guessed they were wondering why it wasn't in place. After a pause, they set it aside again and reached for the trapdoor itself. Eve's view was blocked now, but a moment later the figure stood back. There in front of them was the black pit of the tunnel entrance. They were just making towards it when they stopped, stock-still.

From the front of the house, Eve heard a car's engine.

All at once the figure moved at speed, closing the trapdoor, replacing the false floor and panel, then shutting the cupboard doors. They dashed out of the room again.

'Time to make ourselves scarce,' Robin said. 'I think the police have turned up.'

As they crept back along the pathway, Eve was desperate to know the identity of the intruder and if they'd answered the door or run for it. She could see Robin's point though. It would complicate matters if they were seen there – especially if Palmer was on site. Robin texted Greg to let him know what they'd learned.

Back at Elizabeth's Cottage, they made hot chocolates and Eve updated the WhatsApp group.

The evening had cooled, and Eve and Robin lit a fire and talked quietly about the development as Gus snoozed in his bed. They speculated endlessly but without knowing who'd been in The Briars it was hard to draw conclusions. It was half past midnight when there was a soft tapping on the door.

Eve peered through the front window. It was Greg.

A moment later they were sitting on Eve's couches with more chocolate, warming themselves by the fire.

'Thanks for the call-out,' Greg said.

They had Sylvia and Daphne to thank really, but she didn't want to tell Greg. He might not approve of them spying.

'The visitor you spotted was Abby Porter.'

Abby. Abby who'd now got a plum job with Marbeck's despite the secret she was hiding, and who'd had a grudge against Honor Hamilton. What was she doing searching for the tunnel? If she'd killed Honor, she might want to check for anything that could give her away, though if Max had moved the body, it seemed more likely that any remaining evidence would point to him. Perhaps she was innocent after all, and wondering who was guilty.

'She seemed to be there openly,' Eve said. 'But she didn't want anyone seeing her investigating the tunnel.' That could mean guilt, or fear of the killer. 'What did she tell you?'

'That Cleo's solicitors gave her the key to The Briars as instructed by Cleo's heir, Norah Campbell. Apparently, there are lots of papers relating to Marbeck's in the house. Campbell wanted Abby to start swatting up. She's down to start the new job immediately.'

Tonight would be the first chance she'd had to investigate the tunnel then. 'So she went in to burn the midnight oil?'

'So she says. She might be after something else, but her story checks out. We can't make her leave or prove there's anything more to it.'

'What did she say when you asked her about the tunnel?'

'I implied I'd seen her. She said she was curious. Someone mentioned playing in it as a kid, so when she stopped for a break, she went to see if she could find it.'

'Secretly, by torchlight.' Perry might have told her about it, Eve thought.

Greg gave a wry smile. 'She said the bulb had gone. We didn't have just cause to check.'

It was very frustrating.

After Greg left, Eve sent the gang another update. They'd get it in the morning if not before.

She slept badly that night, conflicting ideas about Perry or Abby's possible guilt cramming her thoughts each time she woke. Then, at half past three, she found herself in a cold sweat, with echoes of running feet in her head. Robin stirred as she got up to look out of the window. All was quiet in Haunted Lane, just as she'd known it would be. Eve tried to convince herself she'd conjured the echoes up, but downstairs, she heard Gus whine.

She couldn't sleep after that. In the end, she wandered into the bedroom that looked up the lane, opening the window and peering into the night, as though the answers she needed might be out there.

What the heck?

The sky glowed orange and the smell of smoke filled the air.

Fire. Across the village from where she and Robin were. In the direction of Meadowsweet Grove.

She dialled 999, but the operator said they were already on the scene. The Briars was ablaze.

38

Eve had woken Robin after she'd called the emergency services, her head crowded with panicky thoughts. Was Abby caught in the fire? Had she intended to work through the night? Or had she set the fire to destroy something?

And then, as they'd watched from the window, they'd seen an ambulance rush past the village green. Eve felt sick. Someone had been injured or worse.

The wait for news was horrible. Abby had a troubled past. There was something both vulnerable and desperate about her. Eve could imagine her killing Honor and Cleo and pushing Max, but it looked as though she might be a target now. Perhaps she was innocent and under attack because she'd explored the tunnel. But if she'd looked inside and found something, how would anyone know?

Eve was due to have her hair done by Lara that morning. *Heck.* She'd be devastated if something had happened to her friend. Eve went to the village store where Moira confirmed her worst fears – Abby was dead.

'Yes, Eve dear, that's what I hear. So tragic. She was working at The Briars overnight. Everyone says she was a true professional. Something of a workaholic. And of course, this was the first time she'd been in charge – and of three stores. I doubt anyone knew she'd be there. I suppose the fire was an accident.'

Eve walked home in a daze, thinking of Abby trapped as the fire blazed below her. She imagined her terror and desperate attempts to escape. Windows cracking, curtains going up. The poor, poor woman. Who could have done this? Eve couldn't believe it was accidental. She made a desperate attempt to think analytically, despite the horrific news.

This surely had to be linked to Cleo's murder and the attack on Max, but there *were* oddities. Even if Abby had told a neighbour she planned to pull an all-nighter, setting fire to the house was a chancy way to kill her. If she was awake when the fire started, she could have escaped before she was harmed. Eve wondered about smoke alarms, though it was possible Cleo hadn't had any.

Robin had had to leave for a gardening job, so Eve noted her thoughts to share later.

Perhaps someone had set the fire to destroy evidence which could harm them, not realising the house was occupied. It would mean Abby's death was the most tragic and horrific bad luck. But the aim of destroying something was chancy too; Eve doubted everything at The Briars had burned.

Or maybe someone had slipped Abby something to make her sleep soundly that night. She could have lain down on one of Cleo's beds and drifted off...

But it was all speculation. She'd need to wait until Robin heard more from Greg. In the meantime, she messaged the WhatsApp group to tell them the dreadful news, then called Parker's to see if Lara had gone into work. She had.

Eve made a fuss of Gus, refilled his water, then drove into town.

. . .

Lara Oxley was red-eyed when Eve turned up for her appointment.

'Would you rather leave it for now?' Eve said. 'You must be knocked for six.'

She took a juddery breath. 'I only got to know Abby properly when she came back from Paris, but we hit it off. It's just so unbelievable. When I saw the fire brigade turn up, I had no idea there was anyone inside.' She buried her face in her hands.

'Why did you come in? I'm sure Parker's would have understood.'

'We're short-staffed. Two off sick. I hoped I could blank out the news if I focused on work.'

Eve took Lara by the arm. 'Forget my appointment at least. Let me buy you a coffee. It might set you up for your next client. I'll come back another time.'

'Thank you.' Lara's voice was little more than a whisper.

Eve didn't doubt her sorrow, but there was still a lot she didn't know about Lara, and Abby had speculated about her past. She'd linked Lara's hatred of Cleo to her brother's death. What if she'd gone further and decided Lara had killed Cleo? She might have levelled with her. Sympathised, because of the way she'd been treated. She could have promised not to tell, but would Lara take the risk?

Perhaps Lara had forced a window and set the fire. Or poured accelerant through The Briars' letter box in the dead of night, then ignited it. She'd still be devastated by Abby's death, Eve guessed, warped though that would be.

The objections she had to anyone killing Abby by that method remained. But Eve needed to know why Lara had been crying over her brother's photo in the aftermath of Cleo's death. Was whatever happened enough to kill over?

In the café, Eve bought herself and Lara Americanos and they sat at a corner table. It was early and not yet busy.

'I'm so sorry for what you're going through,' Eve said.

Lara blew her nose. 'Thank you.'

It was cruel, but Abby's death provided the perfect link to the topic she needed to discuss. 'I know you've suffered loss before. I heard about your dad. And then your brother too, at such a young age.'

The tears were spilling now.

'You were very close?'

She nodded. 'After Dad died, we felt it was us against the world, looking after Mum and each other. He was like a light in the darkness. I couldn't believe it when the light went out.'

'The roads around here can be treacherous.' She looked intently at Lara.

'Yes.'

'Forgive me, but I'm still meant to be writing Cleo's obituary, and Abby suggested you disliked her because of something to do with your brother. Was she negligent in some way? They didn't drink together before he went driving?' Eve knew they hadn't, but she needed to probe. 'Only that would add to my picture of Cleo. I need to make my article fair. I don't want to airbrush the truth.'

Eve could see the anger in Lara's eyes.

'Negligent implies not taking enough care. Be in no doubt, Cleo acted very deliberately when it came to her dealings with my family.'

Eve waited, but it was clear she'd need to coax to get more. 'How do you mean? I don't have to quote anything you say if you'd rather I didn't. It will just inform what I write.' Eve was pretty sure Lara was burning to tell her what Cleo had done, yet something was holding her back. Perhaps she was reluctant to reveal her motive for murder.

At last, Lara put her coffee down. Her eyes were still fiery. 'Three days after my brother died, before we'd even held his funeral, Cleo visited my mother. She'd found out about a watch my brother owned, inherited from a great-grandparent. She told my mum she'd come to express her sympathy, but really, she'd come to size it up. She got Mum onto the subject of family finances, what with the recent loss of two incomes, and oh-so-carefully onto the matter of the watch. She presented her offer to buy it as an attempt to help us through a difficult time.

'Mum was torn. It was Freddy's. Something precious. But Cleo offered her seven hundred pounds for it, and things were tight with the cost of the funeral. She wanted to give him a good send-off. And she had other things of Freddy's, she said afterwards.' Lara was sobbing. Across the café someone stared in their direction, but Eve ignored them. 'She said he hardly ever wore the watch – only for best – so it wasn't *such* a wrench. But he'd treasured it. Letting it go felt like a betrayal. I could see her anguish afterwards, when she told me about it.'

'You weren't there when it happened?'

Lara put her head in her hands. 'That's why I wouldn't tell Abby or anyone else about it. I feel so guilty. I should have been there at Mum's side. It was the most horrific ordeal. But instead I'd gone to pieces and gone off on my own. I hid for four days, spending money we couldn't afford renting a room up the coast. I just couldn't take in what had happened. And when I got back, I found Cleo had been busy, taking advantage. One small part of her must have seen a silver lining to Freddy's death. I could never forgive her for that.'

Eve could understand it. She leaned forward and patted Lara's arm. 'I'm so sorry.'

'I heard later that she'd sold the watch for thousands. That hurt, but it was insignificant compared with the thought of her celebrating Freddy's death. She was the most awful woman.'

It was years after the event, but clearly Lara could have killed over it. The apparent theft of her mother's necklace would have brought it all back. But then, suddenly, Eve wondered.

'Lara, Cleo's behaviour back then makes me think of your mum's necklace.' There it was – just the faintest flicker of wariness in Lara's eyes. 'Why do you think Cleo put the necklace in that box in her living room after she'd stolen it? That struck me as odd.'

Lara looked down. 'Who knows why Cleo did anything?'

'Hiding it upstairs would have been more logical. And stealing was an odd thing for her to do. A huge reputational risk, given her profession.'

'And you don't think conning my mum out of Freddy's watch was equivalent to theft?' The words came out quickly and sharply.

'Far from it. I agree it was. But what she did back then wasn't illegal. If she'd started breaking the law, Marbeck's wouldn't have lasted long.'

Lara chewed her lip.

Eve decided to chance her arm. 'It won't make any difference at this stage, I won't tell anyone, but how did you know Cleo had been into your house? You planted the necklace to make her look guilty, didn't you?'

Lara slumped forward, leaning on the table. 'All right. You're close to the truth. A neighbour saw her go in when Abby unlocked my cottage to feed my cat. They told me.'

Eve sipped her drink. 'You said I was close to the truth. I think I know the answer now. You didn't plant it yourself, did you? You gave the necklace to Perry and he did it. He was the person who saw Cleo enter your house.'

Lara heaved a great breath. 'I promised not to tell.'

'I'm sure he'd understand. As I said, it's too late to matter. I'm sorry you've been through so much upset, but why plant the necklace? What Cleo did was terribly callous – I can see that – but it was a long time ago.' But then Eve took a step back. 'Wait. Did Perry suggest it?'

At last, Lara nodded. 'We bumped into each other one night in the Cross Keys and got talking. It soon became clear we had a common hatred of Cleo. I'd heard about her and Max's affair, of course, but we'd never talked about it before. Up until now, Perry's hidden himself away in London, buried himself in his job and blotted out the pain. Then the chance came to work in Saxford, embedded in Cleo's organisation.'

Eve thought of what Jason Dempsey had said. 'I imagine he looked for dirt on Marbeck's while he was trawling through their archives.'

Lara looked down. 'It's true, but he didn't find anything and he was frustrated. He didn't see why Cleo should get away with what she'd done to his mother.'

It didn't seem to occur to her that killing Cleo might have been the answer. Perhaps it was so outside her thinking that she assumed it must have been someone else.

'So he cooked up the idea of faking evidence to get her into trouble?' Eve wracked her brains. 'Of course, you agreed to take Abby's place visiting the open-gardens contestants to categorise their entries. And Cleo was on her way round too, taking photos to drum up publicity. That gave you the chance to steal some jewellery, leaving the villagers to guess Cleo might be responsible.' Eve should have thought of this sooner. The event had been Cleo's baby and Lara had hated her. It made no sense that she'd agree to take on the job. Someone else could have stepped into the breach.

After a pause, Lara nodded. 'It was a crazy idea, but Perry and I talked ourselves into a frenzy. We got to the point where we couldn't let it go. And then Perry saw Cleo sneak into my house. I suppose she wanted to see inside my cottage because she'd been coveting it. Maybe she hoped she'd find something she could use to persuade me to sell. Either way, it was a gift to me and Perry.'

'So you returned the items you'd stolen – dropping in on a pretext, I suppose – and gave Perry your mum's necklace to plant instead?'

She nodded. 'I know it was wrong. But the idea of her being

disgraced so publicly and losing her business was too much to resist. She deserved it, because she *was* a thief. If the law worked better, she would have paid the price. I couldn't wait for the police to arrive. But then events took over. She'll never face justice now.'

39

Eve was distracted as she left Parker's. Lara's hurt had been hard to watch. What Cleo had done had been below the belt. But the upshot was, she didn't think Lara was guilty. She'd had a plan to get even with Cleo but it rested on showing her up in public – bringing down her business and making sure no one trusted her ever again. Eve could see that would fit Lara's emotional needs and it was clear why it had come to a head when it had. She couldn't see Lara flying off the handle if Cleo had taunted her – not when she knew the police would be on their way. She had no obvious connection with Honor either but even if she had, she couldn't have pushed her downstairs. She'd been walking along the river at the time, as witnessed by Cleo, too far away to have made it back within the time-of-death window. And Cleo couldn't have been covering for her, given her investigation into Honor's death. Lara was out of it, but the finding felt like a tiny victory with so many questions still unanswered.

An alert sounded on her phone. Robin on the WhatsApp group, inviting everyone to a catch-up at lunchtime and asking Viv if they could have a garden table at Monty's. He was expecting imminent news from Greg.

Thoughts of Abby filled Eve's head again, making her eyes prick. Once more, she wondered if her death had anything to do with her investigating the tunnel. But who could have known what she was up to? And if she and Max hadn't collaborated then how did she know of its existence and location? She might have heard rumours of course, just like Eve, but her knowledge had been detailed. She'd gone straight to the cupboard after she'd drawn the curtains, and known to remove the back panel. Maybe she'd done some research and set alarm bells ringing.

Perry and his friends had once played in the house, and the tunnel ran to his childhood home. If he had known about it, he and his friends would have kept it secret. They wouldn't have wanted the adults stopping their adventures. It could have been Perry who'd told Abby where to look. But she'd looked scared of him. If she was innocent, and trying to solve Honor's murder having found out that she was one of Cleo's suspects, Eve doubted she'd have risked asking him. But what about the others mentioned in the police report Greg had given her?

She went back to a copy she'd saved on her phone and checked the names. After that she set about trying to trace Perry's former playmates, entering their details into Google, alongside the name of the local school. With any luck she'd get a result on LinkedIn or Facebook.

She came up trumps for two of them, a Bob Finch and a Jeremy Sandhurst, and Finch still lived in the village. If Eve had been in Abby's shoes, she'd have talked to someone out of town. It was less likely to get back to Perry. With that in mind she tried Sandhurst first, telling him she was writing about Saxford's history and trying to trace someone who knew about the tunnel. Sandhurst remembered it all right. He said the boys had gone down there as a dare, but never all the way along. He referred to Honor's death too. They'd stopped playing at The Briars after that. What he didn't mention was anyone asking about the tunnel in the last few days. There was no way he'd have kept quiet if Abby had been in touch. Eve was certain she hadn't got her information from him.

After that, she went back to Bob Finch's LinkedIn profile. He worked at a garage just outside Blyworth. Eve rang and asked to speak to him.

He came on the line sounding curious. Eve gave a false name and fed him the same line she'd used on Sandhurst.

Finch sounded surprised. Someone had asked him about the tunnel and its location just the day before. *Bingo!*

'Oh!' Eve did her best to sound surprised. 'Perhaps it was my assistant, Abby.'

'*Abby, that's right.*' Finch paused. '*She didn't mention a book, though. She said she was researching a lesson plan about local history for a class she teaches.*'

Poor Abby. It was chilling to think she'd been going through such a similar process to Eve. Finch couldn't have seen the news about her death yet.

'We're keeping news of the book under wraps for publicity reasons. Perhaps that's why she made an excuse.' Eve was embarrassed at her flimsy tale, but he didn't question it. 'Speaking of which, did you mention her query to anyone else? I don't want any publicity before the announcement next week.'

'*Ah, sorry. But this Abby woman never said it was secret and I used to play in the tunnel with some mates, I mentioned her call to one of them. Here, there was some bother up at that house last week, wasn't there? Is it really a history book or are you one of those true-crime podcasters? I can do a proper interview if you want? You'd better be quick, though – there's a journo lives locally who's solved a few murders. Eva... Something.*'

In less dire circumstances Eve might have laughed, but the fact Finch had told someone about Abby's call had set alarm bells ringing. 'No, just a history book. Sorry it's nothing more exciting! You said you'd told someone about Abby's enquiry?'

'*Yeah – a friend from back then who's recently come back to*

Suffolk. Thought it would tickle him. The tunnel went all the way to his house, you see.'

Heck. He'd told Perry. 'Not to worry. I don't suppose it'll do any harm.'

But in fact, as she thanked Finch and rang off, she wondered if his little bit of gossip had cost Abby her life. The chain of events seemed utterly tragic. Eve doubted Abby would have found evidence in the tunnel, but going in search of it fitted with her homing in on Perry or his dad. That could have been enough to panic a jittery killer.

When Eve arrived at Monty's, she seated herself at the table Viv had reserved. Tilly and Emily were serving so she and Viv could stand down, in theory. In practice, they kept leaping up to remind Tilly that waitressing involved the delivery of refreshments.

It was Emily who brought them their drinks, along with scones and a tower of mixed cakes. There was slopped tea in Eve's saucer. She turned it so Viv wouldn't see. Her blood pressure must be high enough as it was.

'Just what I need,' said Sylvia, diving in for a berry cupcake. 'Difficult client this morning. Expected me to work miracles but there's only so much I can do. His head will always look like a potato, however I take his picture.'

Sylvia's work was sought-after. She was a past master at conveying a person's character but as Viv had once said, that was of more benefit to some people than to others. She was booked to take the photos at Eve and Robin's wedding and Eve was glad. When she looked back at them she wouldn't just see who was there, but what they were thinking and feeling too. There was no hiding from Sylvia's lens.

With scones or cake in front of them according to preference, they all looked at Robin.

'So?' Eve said.

'The fire investigators will need longer to work out exactly what happened. The intensity of the heat makes it difficult, but they've decided it was definitely arson. It looks as though the perpetrator got inside the house; the investigators believe the fire started under the stairs. And there's no trace of an accelerant so far, just the remains of an exploded aerosol can or two. It looks as though they got the fire going some other way. They might even have set it, then escaped.'

It sounded so weird, though Eve could see that laying the fire under the stairs would make Abby's escape more difficult.

'They think the stairs went up quickly. They were completely destroyed. Most of the landing too.'

Daphne's kind eyes filled with tears. 'Where was Abby? Did she try to escape?'

Robin sighed. 'I'm afraid she didn't get the chance. The tech team say she'd compiled several documents about Marbeck's which were synced to the cloud around two a.m. After that, it looks as though she stopped work. She was found lying on one of Cleo's beds. I guess she decided she might as well sleep there. She died of smoke inhalation.'

'No smoke alarms?' Eve had made a note to ask.

'A couple, but someone had removed the batteries.'

'The killer.'

'Quite possibly. If so, they'd have needed time alone. There's no sign the house was broken into, but the police are investigating the tunnel at last. They'll be looking for signs that someone came in that way. Max Bancroft's being questioned, in any case.'

Eve looked up. 'Thank goodness.' They could ask why he'd moved that storage unit to cover the tunnel entrance in his shed.

Robin nodded. 'Abby's phone's intact, unlockable with a fingerprint so they managed to check her activity.' Stevie winced. 'She called Max Bancroft just after she'd saved her last file.'

'I wonder if he'd asked her to ring.' Eve was musing on the facts she'd unearthed. 'Perhaps he wanted her to do something for him in the house.'

Viv raised an eyebrow. 'What kind of thing?'

'I'm not sure, but he already had Cleo's notebook. Maybe he was worried she thought Perry was the killer and had evidence to back that up.' Eve picked up her tea. 'He had a hold over Abby, he could have asked for her help.'

'If Abby did find evidence,' Sylvia put in, 'Max might have wanted to destroy it and her in one fell swoop. She'd have become a dangerous loose end, poor woman.'

'But relying on the fire still seems risky.' It niggled at Eve. 'Abby went to The Briars to work. She could easily have been awake when it started, and any notes Cleo made could have survived.'

'Maybe Abby told him she'd destroyed the evidence, so it was only her he had to worry about,' Robin said. 'Though your point about her being awake still stands.'

Eve frowned. 'Either way, he's not the only suspect.' She passed on what she knew about Abby researching the tunnel and Perry's old school friend telling him about it. 'He or his dad could have got into the house via the tunnel to set the fire, then escaped again. It looked as though someone came and went that way. The tunnel entrance should have been hidden by some false flooring, but it had already been taken up.' Icy goosebumps crawled up her arms. 'Maybe whoever set the fire was already inside the house. What if Perry and Max worked together, despite Perry's feelings? Max could have tipped Perry off when Abby decided to go to bed. Perhaps he asked if she was planning to sleep there when they spoke on the phone.'

Viv's eyes were wide. 'It sounds possible.'

Eve's thoughts ran on. 'Except I'm sure Abby and Perry were lying to alibi each other for the attack on Max. And I'm certain Perry hates his dad. That makes a father–son collaboration less likely. But if Abby knew Perry pushed Max, he could have decided it was safest to get her out of the way.'

'What about Richie and Lara?' Simon asked.

'I think Lara's out of it.' Eve explained why. 'And I can't see Richie's motive for Cleo any more. I think he'd only have killed her if she'd admitted to murdering his mum.'

Viv nodded. 'Fair enough. I'd love to be a fly on the wall when the police interview Max.' There was hard relish in her tone.

'Me too.' Stevie folded her arms and smiled.

'I want to speak to him and Perry as well, once the police have finished, to see how they explain themselves.' Eve looked at Sylvia. 'I can tell Max I need to talk to him again for the obituary. I'll ask him to meet me in the Cross Keys at eight, assuming he's not under arrest. Do you think you could invent a reason to get Perry there?'

Sylvia let out a quick cackle. 'Maybe I should put myself forward for some kind of collaboration? A book about Suffolk perhaps?'

That would do nicely. 'He'll be off balance in the wake of Abby's death, especially if he killed her, but I think he'll still be interested. He'd be lucky to have you.'

Sylvia nodded. 'He would. You're on.'

'What we still need, though, is proof that Max moved Honor's body. It would strengthen the police's hand.' Eve glanced at Stevie. She looked exhausted but she was a tough nut, and there was some colour in her cheeks now Max was under investigation. Perhaps Eve could try to tease out her memories.

Stevie met her gaze. 'Viv told me the idea you've had. I'm up for it. Nothing can be worse than not remembering everything.'

40

After the gang broke up, Eve took Stevie to the hide, where they could look down on the back of Max Bancroft's house. She'd taken care over their approach, checking repeatedly for anyone who might be watching. She was pretty sure Max had seen her in the hide previously – and known she wasn't spotting birds. She didn't want anyone thinking Stevie was involved in the sleuthing too.

As they peered cautiously out of the hide door, Stevie twisted her fingers. 'The back view's not triggering anything.'

She was primed to panic and that wouldn't help.

'Don't worry. It's not meant to. It looked different back then anyway. But coming up here means we can look down on the path you took from Rose Hobson's house. Wherever you went that day, you started there. Can you remember what it was like? Overgrown or tidy? Could you smell the hedges?'

Stevie closed her eyes. 'Yes, I could. I remember the scent of conifers. And laurel. And earth. Everything was bushy. Very tall compared with me, and a luscious green. It was hot.' Her eyes were open again. 'But I can't remember any more!'

'There's no pressure. You might never recollect that day properly.' Eve hoped she was managing to disguise her tension.

She went on. 'Rose Hobson says when the Bancrofts had their building work done, at least half of the back of the house was covered in tarpaulin. It was pinned down at the corners with tent pegs but it flapped in the summer breeze. She remembers the draught inside.'

Eve had claimed she wanted to know how uncomfortable her own fictitious extension might be. It had worked a treat.

'Inside, beyond the tarpaulin, there was a big back room, which was covered in dust at the time. Lots of tools. It smelled of plaster and sawn wood.' Eve had asked Rose about that. She said she liked the smell.

Stevie had closed her eyes again, but her mouth was moving, as though she was committing the images to memory. Then suddenly she spoke.

'I *can* remember the smell of the tarpaulin – plastic warming in the sun. And the feel of it slithering over me as I crawled underneath.'

Was this real, or was Eve planting memories? And how could she ever know for sure? Palmer would say she'd been leading Stevie, and maybe she was.

Stevie's eyes were wide now. 'I didn't come straight off the footpath into the garden. I went into his next-door neighbour's garden first. It was a dare. She was the one who used to chase us, banging a saucepan. But she didn't come out when I sneaked in, so I pushed my way through to Max's place.'

'And then you crawled under the tarp?'

Stevie nodded, her gaze still far away. 'I could hear voices behind me. I was scurrying suddenly, in case I was spotted.'

Voices? That could be significant. But Eve didn't want to stop Stevie's flow. And of course, neighbours chatting as they walked along the pathway wouldn't be unusual.

Stevie pressed her hands to her eyes and spoke again. 'The

door between that back room and the hall was off its hinges. It was leaning against a wall.'

Eve held her breath. Rose Hobson had described just that. She said Max's wife wished they'd done the work in a different order, so she could shut out the dust.

Eve waited. She needed to let Stevie do it for herself.

'There was plastic across the doorway. To keep the dust out of the rest of the house, I suppose. But it was flapping loose at the bottom. I can remember I didn't like the feel of it. It was heavy on my back as I went underneath.'

Eve could hardly breathe she was so tense. This was different from the flashback. She was reliving the whole experience. How would she feel when she saw her aunt's body again? This might be a terrible mistake.

'There was light coming from the window over the door.' Stevie gasped. 'The body. I stepped over her legs. Her skirt was rucked up. I touched her arm. And then I was scared. I stepped back and stumbled over her.' She put her hand over her mouth. 'And then I looked up at the walls!'

Her eyes were open again now. 'There was red writing on them. I think it was done in lipstick. Yes. Yes. There was one by her hand. I kicked it accidentally and it rolled away.'

She sank onto one of the benches in the hide and took a long, shuddering breath.

41

Stevie couldn't recall anything about the voices she'd heard to the rear of Max Bancroft's house. She hadn't seen people and they hadn't spotted her, thanks to her entering via the neighbour's garden. The sight of the body and the red writing on the wall seemed to have wiped out the earlier memory. But those recollections were enough. Even if Palmer decided Eve had influenced Stevie by mentioning the tarpaulin, Eve could swear that Stevie had remembered other crucial details on her own. The fact that some of them tied in with Rose Hobson's memories should help.

They spent the next part of the afternoon at Blyworth police station. The scientific support team were still busy at The Briars and other officers were dashing in and out of reception, but Eve managed to get the attention of DC Olivia Dawkins.

She instantly appreciated the importance of Stevie's new memories. By the time they left it was on record that Stevie now recalled finding the body in a house matching the description of Max Bancroft's. Eve told Dawkins what Gwen Harris had overheard too. Might as well report it twice and drive the message home.

'It looks as though Bancroft had no idea who'd killed Honor, but equally that he thought her death was murder.'

Dawkins nodded. 'We'll speak to Gwen Harris.'

Gwen would love the spotlight. Moira would be jealous.

'And to Mr Bancroft too of course,' Dawkins added. 'He's already here.'

If he wasn't in custody by that evening, Eve was still determined to get him to the Cross Keys. Sylvia had texted to say Perry had agreed to meet her for a drink at eight. He said he needed something else to think about in the wake of Abby's death.

Even if Max *was* under arrest by then, Eve was sure someone else had killed Honor. She thought of Abby, who'd attacked Sean for flirting with her. How far would she have gone, back then?

But if Abby had killed Honor, and possibly Cleo, then who had killed her, and why? Eve's mind turned to Richie, a hurt young man who'd been made to feel he'd let his mother down. He could have lashed out if he'd discovered Abby had killed her. Maybe they were looking at more than one killer. There was the attack on Max to consider too. Eve was still sure Abby and Perry had lied for each other where he was concerned.

Perry was her top suspect now. He had motives for Honor, Cleo and Max – and potentially for Abby as a weak link, if she'd given him a false alibi. But she kept her thoughts to herself; Stevie had enough to deal with.

There was still a chance that Cleo had played an accidental part in Honor's death. Why had Honor gone to Max's house in the first place? It sounded as though it was she who'd written on the walls, given the lipstick Stevie had seen, close to her hand. Cleo had got her drunk that day, and not long before, according to her sister Beth, Cleo had asked Honor to betray someone she loved. Might that have been Max, if Honor had had a crush on him?

Cleo could have asked Honor to scrawl over Max's walls to get him into trouble with his wife. The pair of them had argued over Cleo's request, according to Beth. And at the end of their second row, they'd agreed Honor should keep something quiet and work for Cleo. She'd already been doing Cleo's cleaning, so this was something else.

Eve had left a message on Max Bancroft's voicemail, asking if he'd be willing to answer a couple of extra questions in the Cross Keys at eight. Even if he was free, it would be the last thing he'd feel like, but she had a hunch he'd come. It was common knowledge that she'd accompanied Stevie to the police station that day. If he was running scared, he'd want to know what she knew.

Eve had almost given up hope when Max texted her at seven forty, agreeing to the meet-up.

It was too early for an update from Greg. She was going in blind without any idea of where Max stood with the police. Just the same, she texted Sylvia to say it was all on and walked around the corner with Gus in tow. She'd be safe in the pub, so Robin was staying at home to avoid cramping her style. She and Sylvia could walk back together.

Sylvia gave Eve a wave as she entered the bar. There was no sign of Perry yet, but Max was already sitting at a table. Eve went to get him a whisky and a white wine spritzer for herself.

As she joined him, her plan was clear in her head. Now the police were on to Max, it wouldn't hurt to show more of her hand. As for Perry, when he turned up, Eve would watch the fall-out. Max was after a reconciliation, but Perry wanted none of it. It was understandable. Eve could barely look at Max without boiling over herself. How could he have moved Honor's body and covered up her murder?

Eve hoped the stress of Max and Perry bumping into each

other might reveal something important. They'd feel trapped, their appointments with Eve and Sylvia keeping them at the pub. Perhaps Max would accuse Perry of pushing him down the staircase. He might not believe his son's alibi any more than Eve did.

She faced Max. 'I realise now that Cleo was trying to work out who killed Honor when she died. She went to vast lengths, so it's relevant to her obituary. And maybe it's why she was killed.'

Max had looked tense to start with. Now his back was a straight as a rod, his hands on the table as though he'd like to push himself up and escape.

'From what I hear, you didn't know Cleo was investigating, but you've been digging into the mystery yourself since. You thought Cleo could have been guilty, despite her alibi. You talked to Lara to see if you could break it.'

Max looked down. 'I loved her, but I had to be certain.'

'So you know *someone* murdered Honor. The death wasn't accidental.'

His eyes flicked away from Eve's. There was a long pause before he said: 'There's always been talk. Then your young friend had her flashback and Cleo died within hours. I assumed there must be a connection.'

Eve was sure he knew more. 'So you can't confirm personally that it was murder?'

He did his best to look shocked. 'Of course not. How could I?'

There was a pause, and Eve was conscious of a shadow across the table in front of her, a microsecond before she heard Perry's voice.

'*How could you?* What kind of a question is that? I've heard what happened at the police station this afternoon... Dad. I hate to even call you that! Honor died in our house. Admit it!'

How had that rumour got out? Someone from the police must have talked. It was frightening.

'Perry.' Max got up, moved around Eve and tried to take his son's arm.

He stepped smartly away from him. 'You're despicable. You cheated on Cleo, as well as on Mum.'

'I swear I didn't!' Max was moving towards him again. 'I fell out of love with your mother and in love with Cleo. I didn't have eyes for anyone else.'

'So what was Honor doing at our house, scrawling graffiti on our walls?' Perry scoffed. 'You rejected her and killed her in a row, I suppose?'

'No! Perry, I— Please, let's sit down and talk.' His eyes flitted around the room.

Jo had appeared from the kitchen and was speaking to Toby. Eve hoped to goodness the Bancrofts didn't get thrown out. She should have primed the Falconers in advance.

'I didn't kill Honor.' Max's voice was still just about level. 'She never made up to me!'

'Let's have no more of this!' Jo's voice carried across the room. 'This pub is a place for people to relax.'

She marched around the front of the bar and made for Perry. Eve couldn't guess what she was saying to him but a moment later, his expression changed. His eyes were still mistrustful but there was a hint of query in them now. Perhaps Jo had told him Gwen Harris had overheard Max investigating Honor's death.

Either way, it looked as though the stand-off had been defused.

Sylvia glanced at Eve, received her nod and stood up to shake Perry's hand. It looked as though he was apologising.

'*You* know I didn't kill Honor.' Max fixed Eve with his gaze and sipped his whisky. 'I wanted to know who took her life.'

'Yes, so you *knew* it was murder, though I don't know how.' It was unforgivable not to call the police.

Max twitched in his seat.

Eve sipped her spritzer and changed tack. 'Perry was very

keen to put the blame on you. I've heard some gossip suggesting it was he who pushed Honor.' She needed to test the water.

'No!' Max's eyes were terrified now. 'You've got it all wrong.'

Eve was convinced Max suspected it was true. She couldn't imagine the agony he'd feel as a father. But he was no angel. Perhaps he had enough conscience to blame himself. He might not have had a fling with Honor, but Perry would have been primed to suspect it, given his affair with Cleo.

'Honor's body was never at our house.' Max's lips were working. 'Your friend was four! Her memories aren't reliable! She could have found her way into our house any time and explored. She must have superimposed those memories on the ones she had of finding the body at The Briars.'

'What about the lipstick on the walls? It wasn't there when Honor's body was discovered.'

'Someone must have cleaned it off.'

'They'd done a thorough job.'

'Well, they would, wouldn't they?'

He'd probably rehearsed his lines. He was certainly protective of Perry. The whole situation made Eve mad. He'd put the kid through hell when he was little, forcing Perry to watch his mum disintegrate when she found out about his affair. Now, he finally wanted to make up for lost time. Why couldn't he have tried to protect Perry back then?

As thoughts of his actions swirled in Eve's head, realisation hit her.

'Oh my goodness. You think Perry tried to kill you, don't you? Just as you're worried he killed Honor. I can see why. You gave him every reason. I think I understand about his alibi now.'

Max went absolutely still.

'You had a hold over Abby Porter, so you asked her to alibi Perry. If she refused, you'd give away her secret: that she'd attacked her partner Sean long ago. I'm guessing she used a weapon and that's why she was so scared the truth would get out. It would make her future employers think twice.'

Max said nothing.

'Do you *know* Perry pushed you?' This was crucial. Eve stared into his eyes, wondering if she could possibly divine the truth.

When the words came, they were in a whisper. 'No. No, I don't.'

'So the alibi was an insurance policy. You wanted to protect Perry. But in fact, it could have been Abby who attacked you. Or anyone.'

But Max shook his head. 'You're putting words into my mouth. I'm not saying anything more.'

42

Max Bancroft left the Cross Keys but Eve stayed on, chatting to Toby behind the bar. When Perry's meeting with Sylvia broke up, she nipped over to intercept Bancroft junior.

'I can guess what you're going to say.' Perry declined the offer of a drink but perched on the edge of the seat his dad had occupied, opposite Eve. 'Lara told me you'd spoken.'

Eve nodded. 'I know you worked together to frame Cleo for theft.'

He shrugged. 'There's not much point in denying it now Lara's told you.'

Eve thought of the tunnel entrance at The Briars, with the false floor which had been removed before Abby discovered it. 'Did you use the tunnel to sneak in and plant the necklace?'

He gave a small shudder. 'No. I haven't been back to Dad's since I left home. I wouldn't use the tunnel now. I visited Cleo to ask something about my writing project and slipped the necklace into the box then. She richly deserved it, and worse. I'm not sorry someone killed her.'

She understood his anger, but his brutal comment was unnerving. 'What about your dad? You seem to hate him just as much. Do you really think he killed Honor?' She watched his eyes. Saw the shiftiness there. 'Only I hear he was trying to find Honor's killer, just like Cleo was.'

Perry leaned forward. 'He's a mean man, but he's not stupid. If he wanted to give the impression he was innocent then what better way?'

'I think he's scared you might be guilty. Not that he said so, but I could see his fear.'

Perry's eyes were still on hers. 'I'd never have killed Honor, Cleo, him or Abby. The fake theft was my plan to pay her back.'

But Eve wasn't sure he'd have felt it was enough. 'You must have wanted to get even with your dad while you were here too. I know Abby gave you a false alibi for the afternoon he was pushed. And that it was your dad's idea.'

The anger blazed in his eyes. 'She admitted that in the end.'

He'd have hated it: the thought of her working with his dad to shield him, treating him like a little boy. If he also feared Abby might change her mind and give him away, she could imagine him killing over it.

Perry leaned forward. 'Whatever the case, I didn't push my dad. Getting my revenge on Cleo would have covered him too. He still had money in Marbeck's. If the firm went under, he'd have lost the lot. As for the alibi, when Abby came to talk to me about it, I was grateful. I knew I'd be a suspect and it would save me trouble. But I thought it was she who needed protecting. That she'd done the pushing. She admitted my dad had something on her. I was happy to help; Dad deserved it.'

And all the while, Eve was sure Abby had been scared of Perry – convinced *he* was guilty. And he still might be, if he was lying.

Sylvia leaped to her feet as soon as Perry left.

'Sorry to be so long,' Eve said.

She smiled. 'I was looking on. I had plenty of distraction while I waited.'

They walked home, talking in whispers about the evening's events. Daphne waved to Eve from the door of Hope Cottage as Sylvia retreated inside, a friendly glow of light shining around her.

Half a minute later, Robin welcomed Eve in. 'Nightcap?'

Eve yawned. 'I feel like putting one on rather than drinking one, but yes please.'

He poured her a small brandy and they sat by the fire. Gus had taken himself to bed. He was there in the corner, making funny little scampering movements with his legs. Dreaming of rabbits, perhaps.

They discussed what had happened in the pub.

'I must let Greg know the upshot.' Eve closed her eyes for a moment. 'Not that there's any proof Abby lied for Perry.'

Robin nodded. 'Go for it.' When she'd finished texting, he leaned forward. 'Ella Tyndall dropped round.'

'Oh yes? What did she have to say?'

'She's been in touch with a friend who used to live here. A history enthusiast like her, but a keen photographer too. Ella remembered that she used to record day-to-day life in the village and asked if she had anything from around the time Honor died, just in case it's useful. She says she knows it's a long shot, but the photos capture a lot. She gave me copies.'

He handed them to Eve and she peered at them. The pictures were fascinating in their own right, giving her a glimpse of Saxford twenty-five years earlier. The buildings looked the same but the cars parked outside were different, the fashions dated and the sign over the village store less classy. Monty's frontage had been updated since too. Viv and her late husband would only have recently taken it over. One of their children wouldn't have been born yet, another had been a babe in arms.

Jonah would have been around five years old. It must have been
hard work.

And then, suddenly, Eve sat up straight. There was a photograph of the marsh meadow round the back of Parson's Walk.
The bird hide hadn't been there back then, but otherwise it
looked the same. And there, in the corner of the meadow, near
to The Briars, was a face she recognised.

Honor's husband. Aiden Hamilton.

Eve pointed him out to Robin. 'Aiden was meant to have left
the village before this. He was gone well before Honor died.'

She checked the date Ella's friend had written on the back of
the photo. One week before she was killed. What the heck had
Aiden been doing there, and who knew he'd been around?

Eve thought of the key ring Richie's mum had given him,
belonging to his dad. The assurance that Aiden would never
have chosen to leave. Perhaps he hadn't left. Or not when
everyone thought he had.

Could he have killed Honor? Eve wondered if he'd been on
Cleo's suspect list.

How would Richie have felt if Cleo decided Aiden was guilty
and shared her theory with him? Could he have killed her to
protect his dad? According to Ella, Honor must have bigged
Aiden up to make Richie feel better. He hadn't been a nice man.
But Richie carried his key ring around like a talisman. After
losing Honor, the absent Aiden could have assumed great
importance.

Eve shared her thoughts with Robin. 'I think I should talk to
Richie tomorrow.'

He put an arm around her. 'Want me to come with you?'

But Eve shook her head. 'He's still working at the Marbeck's
shop in town. I'll find him there. I won't be in danger.'

43

The following day, Eve went early to Marbeck's and caught Richie on the way in, half an hour before opening time. She didn't want to talk to him in front of an audience, but the sunny street was already busy. She'd stay within sight of the window.

He invited her in readily enough. He looked a million dollars in his dark suit and crisp white shirt. He fitted in to the store, with its glittering jewellery, plush display cases and dramatic lighting.

'Sorry to bother you. I was just passing. How are you coping? It must have been a terrible shock when Abby was found.'

He nodded. 'We weren't close – she hadn't been here long – but I liked her.' He offered to fetch Eve a coffee but she didn't want to muck up his routine.

'A friend's involved in a local history project, and she's given me some photos to review. I'm sorry – it might be emotional for you – but I found one that shows your dad. I thought you might like to see it.'

Richie looked dazed.

Eve found the photo and handed it to him. 'I can let you have the digital version if you'd like it.' She'd taken a copy. Their eyes met. 'Your mum told you he'd never have chosen to leave you, didn't she? And perhaps he didn't. Most people thought he'd gone by the time this was taken.' She watched him carefully. 'This was just a week before your mum died. Did you know he was still around then?'

Richie's eyes opened wider and then suddenly without warning they filled with tears. 'Please don't tell anyone. They'll think he did it! And he never would. I'm sure of it.'

But how could he be, when he'd hardly known him?

'I know Mum wasn't reliable,' he went on. 'They had their arguments.' He gave an unsteady sigh. 'I remember listening from upstairs. But I also remember Mum telling me he was a good man. And that he loved me. Those are two of my earliest memories. They're contradictory, but people are complicated, aren't they?'

Eve couldn't deny that.

'I knew Dad had been around for a bit,' Richie said. 'Granny Joyce told me she'd sent him away because people in the village had vicious tongues. She said they'd assume Dad had pushed Mum because she was "no better than she should be". She said that's why he never came back. That he wanted to visit, but he couldn't.'

That excuse didn't wash. Honor's death had been ruled an accident. He could have returned at that point. Eve hesitated. 'Do you think Cleo thought your dad might have killed your mum?'

'I don't know,' Richie said very quietly, his eyes not meeting Eve's.

Eve dropped in at Monty's on her way home. Viv dashed up to her, having rested a tray laden with cakes on the table of a surprised-looking couple who already had their order.

Eve gave her a stern look. 'I'm not telling you anything until you deliver those cakes to their rightful owners. How will Tilly and Emily learn if you set a bad example?'

Viv looked where Eve was pointing, seemed surprised to see the tray sitting there, picked it up and whisked it to a table near the window.

By the time she'd returned, Eve had taken stock of the customers. No one else needed attention.

She filled Viv in on what had happened the night before and on her conversation with Richie, then she googled Aiden Hamilton. 'Look, here he is, working in manufacturing in the north of England now. And here's another one of him at some kind of gala with a second wife and kids in tow.'

'I hate to say it,' Viv said, 'but I'd say he didn't care a jot about his mum or Richie.'

'I agree, but it's not what Richie thinks.'

'Do you really reckon he'd have lashed out at Cleo if she'd wanted his dad arrested for murder?'

Eve wondered. 'I'd say it's not impossible. He's had so much mixed messaging over the years. He was taught to revere his dad and despise his mum. And on top of that, the villagers blamed him for working with Cleo. By the day of the open gardens he must have been a mess. And he was on the spot when Max was pushed. Perhaps Abby discovered the truth and became another target. For all we know he has a key to The Briars. He was in and out when Cleo was alive.

'But Perry's still top of my list. He was hurling accusations at his dad at the pub, but his motive's there for every victim. Stevie's flashback could have convinced Cleo he'd pushed Honor. He'd have needed to silence her there and then.'

Eve was back at home, trying to order her notes, when Robin messaged the WhatsApp group.

Just finishing a gardening job on the Old Toll Road, but Greg's been in touch. There's more news about Abby's death. Shall we meet in an hour? Monty's garden again, down by the river?

44

By the time Eve had returned to Monty's, she'd finished reviewing her notes, paying attention to the tiniest details as well as those that leaped out as significant. She'd been itching to know what Robin would say, but forced herself to concentrate, not speculate. She needed to make every second count.

As she walked to the teashop, she kept the information playing in her mind, her thoughts floating to Cleo's character. She'd been a fascinating mix. She was underhand in business dealings for sure. Looked at objectively, her behaviour had been appalling, but from what her sister said she wouldn't have seen it that way. She'd probably thought of herself as deserving: organised and better informed than the people she'd ripped off. Tougher. Her father would have applauded every penny she made. It made Eve think of Richie's views on his dad again. Perspective was everything. One person's idol was another's villain. People could be extraordinarily ruthless if they invented a moral code to back their actions.

The sun sparkled on the River Sax at the bottom of Monty's garden as Eve walked down the gently sloping grass to join the others. Allie had come on duty. Eve watched her grimace and stride firmly towards Tilly as she sat down at one of the tables, the better to chat with the customers. Words would have to be said, but not now.

'So, what's the news?' Viv looked like a coiled spring as she turned to Robin, her hands clasped together.

He cocked his head. 'Greg's received the fire investigators' full report. The blaze was started by some curling tongs, plugged into a timer. It was a week-long one. The sort you can set to any hour, any time in the next seven days. There's not much left of any of it, the fire was so intense. When the appointed hour came, the tongs heated up. Whatever they were nestled amongst acted as very effective kindling, and there was an air brick close by, and those aerosols I mentioned.'

'All this was in the understairs cupboard?' Eve asked.

Robin nodded. 'There was a socket in there, so it was self-contained.'

Eve closed her eyes as she visualised the location. 'Abby opened the door to that cupboard when we met at The Briars to discuss the open-gardens event. It was very untidy. Is there any way of knowing when the booby trap was set?'

Robin shook his head. 'It could have been any time in the previous seven days. The guy who checked that room after Cleo's death claims he looked in the cupboard, but Greg's not sure he trusts him. Unless he removed every item, he could have missed it and you can see why he'd lie, given what's happened.'

'And why he might imagine the cupboard was unimportant at the time,' Simon said. 'After all, Cleo died outdoors, and the murder weapon was obvious.'

'Either way, it makes it harder to believe Abby was the intended target,' Eve said. 'Unless they set it up on Friday after her interview with Norah Campbell, there was no reason to suppose she'd be there.' The fact that she had been – and probably by coincidence – was heartbreaking.

'The poor, poor woman.' Daphne's head was in her hands.

Eve nodded. She couldn't bear to think of it: Abby's excitement at her new job, her keenness to read up on everything she needed to know. And then her settling down to sleep, with no idea her life was over. Thoughts of the brutal killer who'd robbed her of her future filled Eve's head. It made her so sad and angry she couldn't speak for a moment. Everyone else was silent too.

'So, do we need to revisit the theory that someone wanted to destroy something incriminating in Cleo's house?' Simon said at last.

Eve sighed. She still couldn't believe it. 'It's like I said before, it feels too risky. No one could bank on everything being destroyed. And The Briars has been empty for days. If someone was that worried about evidence, why not break in and search for it?'

Robin was nodding.

'So what then?' Stevie asked. Her eyes were slightly red.

Eve checked her reasoning before she spoke, but it seemed to hold together. 'I think it was attempted murder, and that Cleo was the intended victim.' It made much more sense. The fire had been timed to start well after any normal person would have been in bed.

Everyone started talking at once.

'Are we looking for one killer and one would-be killer?'

'Who could have got in?'

'Did they use the tunnel?'

Eve was thinking back to watching Abby inside The Briars. 'I'd guess someone used the tunnel for something recently. The false floor hiding the entrance had been left out of place. If someone escaped that way, they couldn't have replaced it unless they'd had an accomplice inside.'

'You'd think they'd have worried Cleo might notice,' Simon said.

But Eve shook her head. 'There wasn't much chance of that.

The entrance is hidden behind a false panel and that was in place. It was a good bet she'd never see the booby trap either, given how untidy the cupboard was.'

'You don't think it was Perry who used the tunnel to plant the necklace?' Robin asked.

Eve frowned. 'He claims not, but he could be lying. He might have planted it and set the booby trap at the same time. Maybe he wanted Cleo publicly shamed and then dead. He really hated her.'

'And then a third party finished her off before he got the satisfaction?' Sylvia said.

'Maybe. Or there was just one killer and they brought their plans forward. Either way, I think something happened that made Cleo's murder desperately urgent.'

'My flashback,' Stevie said.

Eve nodded. 'I'd guess so. All of this points to Max or Perry. They knew how to access the tunnel. It seems almost certain it was Max who moved Honor's body. He might have pretended to investigate her death to disguise his or Perry's guilt. Perry hates Max's guts, but Max seems to have developed late-stage protectiveness. I'm sure he coerced Abby into alibiing Perry.' Eve filled in the details.

'I can't believe the police didn't arrest Max after what Stevie remembered.' Daphne sipped her tea.

Robin sighed. 'Greg updated me. Max pointed out that Stevie could have nipped into his house any time while the building work was going on, and overlapped two memories – what she saw at The Briars and what she saw at his place. There's no way of proving the lipstick wasn't scrawled at The Briars. The fact that it was removed indicates someone was involved in Honor's death, but it doesn't prove it was Max.'

Eve wondered if Palmer had queried the memories of a four-year-old too. It was all so long ago. 'What about the tunnel entrance at Max's place? The police must have wondered why he'd covered it up.'

'I'm afraid he's been busy protecting himself. Maybe he realised someone had been there. Either way, he'd rearranged things by the time they looked. The tunnel entrance was still covered, but he'd made the layout more logical. He claims he's always had his stuff like that and that the unit over the entrance was left there by a former owner.'

It was so frustrating. Eve needed to think.

'I might go back to the hide,' she said, before the gang broke up.

'But not on your own.' Robin took her hand. 'Max knows you go there, don't forget, and I can't join you. I've got another gardening job.'

'I can come.' Viv stood up.

Eve opened her mouth to protest but she waved a hand. 'Monty's will be fine. The baking's all sorted and it's excellent training for Allie, marshalling the others. Think of her CV.'

Eve looked at Emily, who was swiping a plate from under a customer's nose the instant they took their final mouthful. They were still chewing! They'd have to give Allie a medal after this.

'What about you, Stevie?' Viv was saying. 'You should stay with someone.'

'I'll go with Simon to the stables.' She was keen on horses, an attitude which mystified Eve.

Once they'd made sure Allie was all right, Eve and Viv crossed the village green. They bumped into Lara on the way. She looked faintly stressed.

'How are you doing?' Eve asked.

'All right, thanks. But I've just taken a big step.' She took a deep breath. 'I'm selling up. I suddenly realised that I'd dug my heels in all these years because Cleo bullied me. But maybe it is time to move on. I've been trying to live in the past.'

'Where will you go?' Viv asked.

'I've not made up my mind yet. Somewhere less quiet – where the hustle and bustle will distract me. Help me move on.'

'Good luck,' Eve said.

Behind her, she could see Rose Hobson heading up Parson's Walk.

45

Eve and Viv walked up the boardwalk to reach the bird hide.

When they arrived at the top and found themselves alone, Viv looked eager. 'Talk to me!'

But Eve needed silence. She wanted to look out over the marshes and let her mind freewheel until her thoughts coalesced.

'Let's think first. We could give ourselves twenty minutes, then pool ideas.'

'Twenty? Oh, all right then. Your cast-iron will mystifies me sometimes.'

Gut instinct told Eve the booby trap which had killed Abby had been meant for Cleo. She could have had two killers after her, but it would be extreme. Assuming it was one, she guessed Stevie's flashback had made them bring the murder forward. They'd swapped a cold, calculated move for an urgent and desperate attack.

The flashback had told Cleo that Honor could have been killed at Max's place. That was bound to affect her thinking on who might be guilty. But it was more than that. The killer had acted so quickly, and with such force, that the flashback must have been enough to make their guilt indisputable.

Perhaps Cleo had been on to Perry or Max and Stevie's memory had been the last piece in the jigsaw. But as a kid, Perry and his friends had broken into The Briars. He could have killed Honor there just as easily as at his dad's. Why would the flashback confirm Cleo's thinking so decisively? Or if it was Max who was guilty, why hadn't he removed the booby trap when it was no longer needed? He had easy access to the tunnel. Leaving it in place made no sense. It just gave the police more clues.

Someone else would have found it harder to remove the device. They might have used the tunnel to plant it, breaking into Max's outhouse just as Robin had. It hadn't been hard, apparently. With a cheap combination lock like his, you could work the wheels one by one, feeling a slight give each time you got a number right. But if they'd dared to go back to try to remove the curling tongs, they'd have found the trapdoor blocked.

Eve imagined them weighing up the risk. The noise they'd make, dragging the furniture out of the way. Even re-entering the outhouse could have felt like a bridge too far. And leaving the booby trap in place wouldn't have seemed disastrous. The killer would have expected The Briars to be empty. Instead they had an extra murder added to their tally.

If Eve was right, it had to be someone who knew about the tunnel. That pointed her back towards the Bancrofts and the objections to their guilt she'd just listed. She stood up and turned to look over Parson's Walk, far below.

Wasn't that Max Bancroft? And who was he talking to?

Eve used her binoculars. Rose Hobson.

Of course, Rose had been friends with him and his wife.

'Thoughts so far?' Viv said brightly.

'There's still five minutes to go.'

'Spoilsport.'

Eve gave in and explained her ideas. 'What about you? Any fresh thoughts?'

Viv looked guilty.

'You weren't thinking about wedding-cake designs again, were you?'

The look of guilt intensified. 'I started off just worrying about the wedding. I can't bear it if all this is still hanging over us. The designs were the only way to take my mind off it.'

Eve sympathised really. She'd be in a heck of a state if her son's fiancée was a murder suspect.

'Let's focus again.' She took out her notebook and skimmed over the words, trying to immerse herself in everything she'd learned.

A moment later she broke the silence herself. 'You know, this business of Cleo approaching the villagers for saleable jewellery is odd.'

Viv frowned. 'In what way?'

'How would she know not to bother with your parents? Yet decide others were worth a visit?'

'Maybe she went to a selection of Saxfordites she'd seen with attractive baubles.'

'But one of the villagers said she'd kept the one Cleo bought in a drawer. It wasn't her style.'

'Oh.' Viv scuffed her Converse on the hide floor. 'Just good instinct on Cleo's part then?'

But the more Eve thought about it, the more she wondered if Cleo's approaches had been targeted. She took out her mobile and called the people she'd interviewed. After she'd rung off, her eyes met Viv's.

'Honor cleaned for both the women I spoke to. But also your parents, whom Cleo didn't approach. The question is, did she try to buy from anyone Honor didn't clean for, or were all her marks also Honor's clients?'

Viv's brow furrowed. 'Oh my goodness. You think Honor was

scouting for Cleo? Peering in people's bedside tables and jewellery cases?'

It made Eve sad. 'I do wonder. I've asked the two I spoke to to ask their friends. Perhaps that was the secret Cleo wanted Honor to keep. She could have been pressuring her to do it for extra money. Honor probably needed the cash, but it troubled her conscience. It would explain her upset. And it was certainly sensitive information. If it got out, people would have turned against Marbeck's. It would be shockingly intrusive and calculated. What Cleo did openly – buying cut price and selling at a big profit – was hard enough to swallow.'

'I think you're right. The idea of Honor going through Mum and Dad's things is horrible. A real violation.' Viv shuddered.

A text pinged in at that moment.

Viv raised an eyebrow.

'One of my interviewees reporting two more friends who had similar approaches, and Honor cleaned for them both. I should have smelled a rat earlier. The women I spoke to told Cleo they didn't have anything she'd be interested in. But instead of giving up, Cleo described what she was after, and they each found they had something that matched. That points to inside knowledge.'

And then Eve's mind shifted to Cleo's sister Beth, who'd been sent home after overhearing part of a row between Honor and Cleo. Was the argument about this? Eve flipped through the pages of her notebook to find Beth's words.

All I know is that Honor had fallen in love with someone and the upset was something to do with that. It sounded as though Cleo wanted her to betray him.

Eve thought of Max. Honor might have had a crush on him, but if so, she didn't believe Max had returned her feelings. And it didn't sound as though she'd visited his place to scout for jewellery – she'd hardly scrawl on the wall while she was at it. So perhaps she'd loved someone else. Aiden, her husband, had been a mistake, so Eve doubted it was him. Yet Honor had bigged him up to Richie, saying he'd never have chosen to leave him, which was a fantasy, according to Ella.

The way Richie treasured his father's key ring was striking. He'd been very young when Honor died, but her words about his dad had stuck with him. She must have said them with conviction and probably more than once. But why?

And then, suddenly, the faintest pinprick of memory flickered somewhere in the very back of Eve's mind.

'Wait...' She fumbled with her notepad, turning the pages back and back.

'What is it?' Viv was leaning forward.

There it was: details she'd scribbled down from the news report she'd found. It wasn't proof but it was a tiny link. Lara's brother Freddy had been driving a Mini when he was killed, and it was a Mini key ring that Honor had given Richie as a memento of his dad.

'Tell me!' Viv's blue eyes were wide.

'One second. I just need to...' Did it fit? Eve went through the other facts: the way Honor had left Richie home alone the day she died, relying on a friend's offer to babysit, without checking they'd arrived, which had been neglectful. Cleo's worries over Honor's ability to care for Richie properly. Honor might have adored him, but she'd been out of her depth. Depressed. And then there'd been Richie's 'bad luck' in business. The deadly booby trap under Cleo's stairs after she'd offered him the London role. The way she'd wanted to make him a junior version of herself, ruthless and calculating. And after Cleo's death, the attempt to scupper Richie's chances by sending Norah Campbell a message suggesting he wasn't up to the London job. It could have meant he'd stay in Saxford. Then on to Lara crying over her brother's photo. Her refusal to sell her house and her decision to move now. What was the betting she'd relocate to London?

The killing of Honor and the planned killing of Cleo all

made awful, horrific sense. But what had changed when Stevie had her flashback?

And then suddenly, Eve saw it.

'I know who the killer is, Viv. And why.'

But before she could explain, Viv's phone rang.

46

Viv answered her mobile. 'Simon! We've got news!'

Then she went silent. All colour drained from her face. 'What? How? Where did she—' Her hand went to her cheek. 'Oh no, oh no, oh no.'

Eve squeezed her arm and looked into her frightened eyes.

Viv looked back. 'Someone created a diversion with the horses. Opened a stable door and threw in an alarm that sent them crazy. While Simon's back was turned, Stevie disappeared.'

Her eyes were wide.

'Please, can I?' Eve took the phone from Viv. 'Simon, if someone's got her, they must think she's a danger to them.'

'*I know, I know. I'm so sorry. And no one saw who it was.*'

Eve took a deep breath. If ever they needed to think fast and calmly, it was now. 'Did anything significant happen after you left us, before she disappeared? Did Stevie talk to anyone? In particular, Lara Oxley?'

Simon's words stuttered in his throat. '*Lara? We passed her on Dark Lane.*'

'And did you speak?'

'*She smiled and said hello. Mentioned she'd put her house on the market.*'

'And Stevie?'

'*She was unusually quiet, now I come to think of it.*'

'Did she refer to it afterwards?'

'*I don't think so. But when we reached the stables, she looked puzzled and muttered something about "voices behind her in the passageway".*'

Eve went cold all over. The voices Stevie remembered hearing as a four-year-old, to the rear of Max's house when she'd found Honor's body.

'Lara killed Honor, Simon, I'm sure of it. I think Stevie was just coming to that conclusion too. Maybe Lara saw something in her eye as you talked and decided to come for her.'

'*Eve, I can't bear it. What can we do?*'

Eve took a quick breath. They had to be smart. 'You message the open-gardens WhatsApp group.' It had the biggest reach in the village. 'Ask everyone to search for Stevie and Lara and message the moment they spot them.' Lara might see the messages too, which could make her panic. A second message was essential. 'Then please send another message, to us and Lara. Tell Lara we know she's guilty and more violence will only make things worse.' Thank goodness she'd been added to the group when she volunteered to stand in for Abby. Eve wouldn't have had her number.

'*Right, right.*' Simon's voice was shaky. '*Got it.*'

'Viv and I will call Robin and the police and come and join you to search. We'll keep the group updated with anything we know.'

Eve handed the phone back to Viv, who wished Simon luck and rang off.

'You call Robin,' Eve said to her. 'Ask him to round up the villagers. Get search parties going. I'll call Greg.' She needed to be the one to do it. She had to convince him she was right about Lara. 'Let's run to the stables as we ring.'

Persuading Greg wasn't easy. No one had seen Lara chuck the alarm into the stables or abduct Stevie. Greg was a gem, but a level-headed one; he wanted more than hunches.

'I believe Stevie will have the evidence you need, when we find her. She heard Lara outside Max Bancroft's house when she found Honor's body.' Eve was pounding along the boardwalk, down from the hide.

'*But she told us she couldn't identify the voices. And Cleo swore she bumped into Lara along the river at the time when Honor was killed. You said yourself Cleo had no reason to lie for her. She can't have decided to cover up Honor's murder. She was busy searching for her killer.*'

'Yes, I know, but I got it wrong. Cleo thought Lara had to be innocent and she *did* have a reason to lie about where she was. Her affair with Max. The last thing she wanted was a witness saying they'd seen her near his place.

'Listen, I think Cleo bumped into Lara just after Lara left Max's house having killed Honor. I'd guess Cleo was planning to nip in to see Max. Their affair had already been going on for years. I suspect Lara had heard the rumours and guessed Cleo was about to enter the house. She must have been terrified. If Cleo went in, she'd have found Honor's body. Lara must have managed to deflect her. She could have said she'd seen Max's wife through a window or something like that, so Cleo changed her mind.

'Afterwards, I guess Cleo asked Lara to say they'd met by the river, not outside Max's house. She wanted an alibi for Honor's death, but not one which hinted at the affair. If I'm right, I imagine Lara made the favour seem like a big deal. She and Cleo weren't on good terms.' Eve wondered how on earth Cleo had begged the favour. 'But deep down Lara would have been pleased. And someone had moved Honor's body, which was tremendously helpful to her. But if it ever came out that Honor had died at Max's place, Lara had a cast-iron alibi, thanks to Cleo's guilty conscience. But of course, when Cleo realised where Honor had really died, she guessed the truth.'

Eve was gabbling, almost out of breath, and it wasn't enough. Just theories. But at that moment she was distracted by a WhatsApp message.

One of the youngest open-gardens volunteers had seen Stevie and Lara. She said Stevie had looked tearful, though she'd only seen them at a distance. She'd been walking stiffly, just in front of Lara.

Heck. The possible reasons for that didn't bear thinking about. A gun or knife to her back? With Lara's army connections, a gun didn't seem impossible. She read the rest of the message. The pair had been on Blind Eye Lane. The open-gardens volunteer wanted to know if she should go after them. But she was only sixteen. She could be in danger too.

Eve relayed the message to Greg as they dashed on.

'*All right, that's enough for me. We're on our way.*'

Thank goodness.

Robin had already responded by the time Eve rang off, telling the junior volunteer not to approach them, but asking everyone who was available to go in that direction en masse, keeping their distance. If Lara had a knife that was terrible for Stevie. If it was a gun, she could be a danger to anyone who got within range.

Eve messaged the group and Lara to say the police were on their way. If only Lara saw it... but it felt horribly unlikely. She'd be focused on Stevie.

'I can't bear it if Lara doesn't realise her secret's out.' Viv looked just as desperate as Eve felt. It was crucial to get the message through. Lara might not harm Stevie if she knew it was pointless.

Thoughts whirled in Eve's head. The appalling realisation

that Lara was probably making for cover. Somewhere where she could kill Stevie, hide her body, and get away.

'We need Lara to hear us, even if we can't find her. To know that we know.' As they reached the end of Blind Eye Road, Eve messaged the open-gardens WhatsApp group again.

Does anyone have a megaphone? Please bring it with you.

She followed up with:

Any fresh sightings?

But there was no reply.

Eve's breathing was ragged now and she and Viv were gasping as they fell in with other villagers: Toby and Matt from the pub and Jim Thackeray were there. Sylvia and Daphne appeared a moment later, and Moira drew up in her car.

When she got out, she was holding a megaphone. Moira smiled for just a moment at Eve's surprise. 'They don't call me the amateur dramatics props queen for nothing, Eve.'

'The question is, where do we broadcast our message?' Toby said.

Eve shivered. 'My bet is she'd make for somewhere like Watcher's Wood. It's a lot lonelier than Blind Eye Wood.'

There were tears in Viv's eyes.

They could drive there in Moira's car, but if Lara had taken Stevie across country, they'd end up away from the road. Better to continue on foot.

As they all surged forward, Eve realised Robin and Simon were ahead of them. But where were the police? It would take them longer to reach Saxford and Stevie and Lara were nowhere to be seen.

As they neared Watcher's Wood, Eve took Moira's megaphone and called out. 'Lara, we know you killed Honor, Cleo and Abby.' A rook flew up from a nearby tree in fright at her voice. 'It's time to stop now. Half the villagers are here, and the police are on their way.'

She passed the megaphone round then, so the others could call out too. The more voices there were, the more compelling the message would be. But could Lara even hear them? Apart from the birds, the wood was deathly quiet.

'I think I've got it wrong,' Eve said. 'I don't think they're here.'

Then a cry rang out. Simon.

'Look. There! Isn't that them?'

There was a boat, heading out to sea. Eve grabbed her binoculars from her bag. He was right. She could just make out Stevie, cowering, pressed against one end of the vessel. Lara was hunched at the other.

Robin took the megaphone and called at the top of his lungs, but Eve knew it would be no good. They were out of earshot.

47

Robin called Greg to let him know they'd need a sea rescue, but how long would that take? There were police with them on the shore now, and scores of villagers.

Lara must have taken the boat Eve had seen when she and Robin had picnicked here. Eve had her binoculars trained on it. It was pitching. Lara was doing something. She couldn't tell what, but she was closer to Stevie now. Eve felt sick as she handed Robin the binoculars.

He focused them. 'I don't like the look of that. The police won't be in time. We need to do something now.'

Viv was wringing her hands and Simon was wading into the sea, as though he could swim for it.

'We need another boat. Ella! Ella Tyndall!' She'd bought a new one with an outboard recently. 'I haven't seen her. She might be back in Saxford.'

Simon and Viv called out for her as Eve dialled her mobile.

There was no answer.

The landline. It had to be worth a try.

Ella picked up. Thank goodness, but there was almost no time.

In the quickest way possible, Eve explained.

Ella cursed. '*Sorry. I was marking. I'd left my mobile on silent. I'll call you back on my way to the boat.*'

The boat Lara was using was rocking like crazy. Stevie must be putting up a fight.

Eve's phone rang again.

'*I'm on board. I'll be in open water in just a moment.*'

Thank goodness Ella lived so close to the estuary. 'We need Lara to turn and see us. She won't kill Stevie if she knows she's got an audience.' Eve hoped to goodness she was right. 'Can you set off a distress flare that will catch her attention? Make her look round? If you head south, then when she turns she should see you and all of us.'

'*Got it!*'

Ella's boat was visible now. Eve willed Lara to look round at the sound of the engine, but it was probably drowned out by her own vessel, the wind and the waves.

There at last was the flare, shooting into the sky. Very high, very bright. Thank goodness the wind was blowing in the right direction.

'Everyone wave. Jump up and down. Lara needs to know she's being watched!' It was Robin who shouted the instruction. After that, he yelled to Lara through the megaphone again.

Eve was using her binoculars. The boat was still rocking, but now it was because Lara was standing up. The villagers were all yelling and jumping and at last, in the distance, Eve could see a police launch.

'What's happening?' Viv was waving for all she was worth. 'Oh no! The boat!'

Lara had jumped and the vessel tipped sideways. 'It's capsizing.'

Ella was motoring towards it now.

'Can you see Stevie?' Viv grasped Eve's arm.

The waves were choppy. For a moment, only the upturned

hull was visible. But then she saw a small round shape. A curly head of hair, bobbing in the water.

'She's there. She's all right.' She was clinging to the capsized vessel and Ella was close by now.

Lara was nowhere to be seen.

48

Eve was with Viv, Simon and Robin making for the cottage hospital when Jonah rang.

Viv and Eve's eyes met as his name flashed on her screen. Viv had wanted to call him, but only after they'd checked Stevie was really all right.

She picked up. 'Jonah. I was just about to ring.'

She went silent and looked more and more confused. Eve caught faint tinny snippets of what he said.

'*Going really well.*' '*Glad she's had a nice quiet week with…*' '*and the masterclass was amazing.*' '*… something to try at the wedding reception.*'

Viv answered mechanically. At last, she said, 'Stevie didn't tell you, did she?'

There was a pause, then Eve heard Jonah's faint voice again. '*Tell me what?*'

Poor Jonah. It was a lot to pass on to a very unsuspecting fiancé. By the time he rang off, Eve gathered he was catching the first flight back and coming straight to Saxford.

'I thought it was odd that he hadn't rushed home.' Viv still looked stunned. 'I can't believe Stevie lied to me.'

'I'd say fibbed,' Simon responded. 'You've got to admit it was brave of her.'

Eve nodded. 'She's tough. And she minds so much about Jonah. She didn't want him to miss the chance of a lifetime.'

Viv's smile went mushy. 'I know. I couldn't love her more, could you?'

Stevie *was* all right – shocked and very cold but uninjured. It was Ella who'd brought her back to shore. Lara had been picked up too, by the police launch. She was under arrest and being treated by doctors. When Stevie was allowed visitors, Viv asked if Eve could come in too, with Simon and Robin. The nurse looked askance at them but agreed in response to Simon's sweetest smile. He was nothing if not a charmer.

Viv hugged her future daughter-in-law. 'Jonah's on his way.'

Stevie blushed. 'I have a feeling he'll tell me off when he gets here. I'm sorry I pretended I'd told him.'

'It was brave of you to cope without his support, but he loves you to bits. He'd have wanted to know.' Viv gave her an extra squeeze. 'That sort of connection's precious.' She let her go.

'So you recognised Lara's voice?' Eve asked, eventually.

Stevie nodded. 'The moment I realised she'd been outside Max's house and not along the river, it changed everything.'

'Of course,' Eve said. 'Cleo had no idea Honor had died there when she was trying to work out who'd killed her. As far as she was concerned a chance encounter with Lara led to a handy alibi. Lara couldn't have been involved in the death, so that was fine. When the truth sank in, and she guessed the killer had smashed Honor's watch, she must have known the timing was looser, and there were multiple suspects in theory, including Lara, but I think Joyce's hatred of Honor blinded her to other possible killers at that stage. You remember Honor left Richie alone, the day she died?'

They nodded.

'Well, one person told me Joyce didn't go straight home to look after him when a neighbour let her know he'd been left unattended. If Cleo had heard that too, it's no wonder she was convinced Joyce was guilty. I'm sure Joyce must have gone looking for Honor in an utter fury. When she died though, and Cleo decided she'd been wrong, I imagine Lara was on her suspect list, just like the others. I'll explain, but I think she'd picked up on links we'd missed between her and Honor. I suspect she sneaked into her house while she was away to look for information.'

It tied together, though Eve still wanted to know how Cleo had got Lara to alibi her, given their poor relationship. Perhaps she'd hear more after the police interviews.

'It all makes sense.' Robin shook his head. 'If you're right, Lara would have been one suspect amongst several, and Abby's motive probably looked stronger, but everything changed when you had your flashback, Stevie. Cleo would have realised that Honor could have died at Max's and not only had Lara been on the spot, she'd also discouraged Cleo from entering the house. And then I guess she clicked.'

Eve nodded. 'It must have been sinking in while we were at The Briars, looking at her garden. Ironically, I think Lara dashing in, full of righteous indignation over the supposed theft of her mum's necklace, might have made Cleo less sure of her ground. Lara probably didn't hear about your flashback until after that. In which case, she had no idea of the danger she was in as she acted her part. I wonder if her obliviousness led Cleo to question the conclusions she was drawing. I imagine she wanted time to think it through and work out how to handle it, but she never got the chance.'

'Wait, wait,' Viv said. 'Rewind. Why did Lara kill Honor? And how did you know it was her, Eve? It's not like *you* heard her voice outside Max's place.'

'As I said, I think there were links between Lara and Honor that we didn't initially fathom. I was puzzling over the way Honor sang Richie's dad's praises, despite him being a louse, according to Ella Tyndall. Richie remembered Honor's words, even though he was small. It made me think she must have said them repeatedly, and with feeling. The more I thought about it, the odder it seemed.

'And then I remembered the key ring Honor gave Richie. She said it was his dad's and Richie had held on to that, along with the memory. Those thoughts finally triggered a recollection of my own. It was a Mini that Lara's brother Freddy drove into the Sax, and the key ring was for a Mini too. I noticed it because I've got one as well. I'm fond of them.'

'I would have put that down to coincidence,' Viv said.

'So would I, if it hadn't been for the way Honor spoke about "Richie's dad". As it was, it raised the faintest query. Was it possible that Aiden wasn't his father? And then I thought about Freddy's watch. Cleo knew about that. She went to Lara's mother just after he was killed and asked to buy it. I'd already concluded that Honor was scouting for Cleo – checking households where she cleaned for jewellery. But Lara told me Honor never worked for the Oxleys; they couldn't afford it. And Freddy rarely wore the watch, apparently. I started to wonder how Cleo had known about it. If it had been via Honor as usual, then how had Honor seen it? It was another hint that she and Freddy might have had a connection.

'It wasn't too much of a leap to imagine Honor sneaking into his family home because they were lovers. When Beth Marbeck heard Cleo asking Honor to betray someone she loved, I think she was talking about Freddy. He was dead by then, and Cleo wanted to know if he'd had anything worth selling. Telling would have felt like a betrayal, but Cleo probably pressured her, and Honor needed the money.'

'So you think Richie was Freddy's child?' Stevie said.

'Yes. And I believe Lara knew. Freddy or Honor must have told her. So Richie was very special to her – all that Lara had left of her beloved brother.'

'That's so sad.' Stevie wriggled to a more upright position against her bank of pillows. 'I suppose Lara hid the truth to protect Richie. Joyce would have made his life intolerable if she'd discovered he wasn't Aiden's. I wonder if Honor ever thought of leaving Aiden for Freddy.'

Eve had wondered too. 'It might have seemed too great a hurdle. Freddy wasn't around most of the time, thanks to his army career, and Lara didn't think much of Honor, any more than Joyce did. She wasn't assured of a warm welcome. But I think Lara adored Richie, albeit in a skewed unhealthy way.

'When I looked at Richie's failed business ventures, I came to the same conclusion as Cleo and Norah Campbell – they were bad luck. And oh boy, had he had a run of it. When I looked at my notes again, I realised he'd once lost out because Barnwell and Greene, a rival cookware firm, had spotted the same gap in the market he had. They set up just before him. That name rang a bell. Barnwell and Greene have a presence in Parker's. I noticed their concession when I went to talk to Abby there. What's more, Lara was chatting to a member of their staff. I can't help wondering if she meddled so Richie never got his chance. And the stationers Brown's – run by Lara's cousin – was the same stationers involved in Richie's "misfortune". They snapped up a premises from under his nose. I didn't make the connection at first because Brown is such a common name. Finally, Lara must have sent information to Norah Campbell in Canada, arguing Richie wasn't up to opening Marbeck's London store. My guess is that Lara couldn't bear him to move away. While he lived opposite, she still had a little bit of Freddy left in her life.'

'That's why she wouldn't sell up?' Viv said.

Eve nodded. 'I think so. Up until now. She was planning to kill Cleo because she'd offered Richie the London role. It combined two things she couldn't stomach: Cleo transforming her sweet, innocent nephew into a ruthless schemer, and Richie moving away. I wonder if she almost saw Richie as Freddy reincarnated. So she set up the device under Cleo's stairs.'

'Perhaps she thought she'd be able to remove it again, if her and Perry's plan to frame Cleo for theft worked out,' Robin said.

Eve had wondered the same. 'It's possible. If Marbeck's had gone under because of it, then Richie would have been safe in Lara's eyes. He could have stayed in Saxford, untainted by Cleo. But things never got to that stage. Your flashback led her to lash out, Stevie. So Cleo was dead and Lara couldn't remove the device easily because Max had got frightened. He hid the entrance to the tunnel he'd used all those years ago to move Honor's body.'

'So you think Lara used the tunnel to plant the device?' Stevie asked. 'But how did she know it existed?'

Eve should have made that link a lot earlier. 'It was you who gave me the answer, Viv.'

Viv looked confused.

'You told me family friends of the Oxleys lived in Cleo's house before she did. Lara probably explored the tunnel just like Perry and his friends. The adults might never have known it existed – the kids would keep it secret.'

'So Max found Honor with no idea who'd killed her?' Simon chipped in. 'Then moved her to avoid the scandal, coming back to clean the lipstick off the walls?'

'I think so.'

'So what did Honor write there? And why?' Simon said.

'I've had to rethink my theory on that. At first, I wondered if Cleo had asked Honor to scrawl something about her affair with Max, to break up his marriage. If Honor had had a crush on Max, then betraying him could account for the conversation Cleo's sister overheard. But now I'm sure the talk of betrayal referred to Freddy and his watch. Thinking about it, my original theory never did hold water. If Cleo wanted to up the ante, she could have just confronted Max's wife. I guess she wanted Max to make a move.

'I still suspect Honor went to Max's house to reveal the affair though. She and Cleo had been close for a long time, but her asking Honor to betray Freddy changed things. Cleo was practical – she couldn't see it. But I suspect Honor's guilt and misery ate away at her. Then after their row, that final day, she sneaked into Max's house, full of drink, to hit back at Cleo.'

'You don't think their row was over the way Honor was looking after Richie then?' Viv asked.

'Not only that, I'd guess.' Eve recalled the report she'd read. 'Cleo said: "So we're agreed then, you'll say nothing, do as I say, and work for me." I think she'd persuaded Honor to carry on spying for her, and Honor hated herself for it.'

'Poor thing.' Viv shook her head. 'And Max only cared about covering his own back.'

'Apparently.'

'I can't believe he covered it all up to protect himself.' Viv's fists were clenched. 'What a monster.'

'You said it.' Eve couldn't get past the way he'd treated his wife and son, let alone hushing up the murder. 'But it's possible he moved Honor to protect Perry. He might have thought he'd shoved her in a fury at what she was writing.

'Coming back to the present day, Lara must have been devastated when she heard Cleo's will meant Richie would still move away. She told Abby that Richie was way too young.'

'I remember you saying.' Viv's eyes were still wide. 'At the time, I thought she was just fighting Abby's corner.'

Eve nodded. 'I guess the will explains her decision to finally sell up. I imagine she intended to follow Richie to London.'

'What a horrendous mess,' said Simon. 'And what about the attempt on Max Bancroft's life?'

'Again, when I thought about it, Lara fitted. Max quizzed her recently about her and Cleo's whereabouts at the time of Honor's death. I think part of him still wondered if Cleo was guilty. But I'd guess Lara thought Max was on to her and panicked. I presume she managed to open the key safe at his rental place, then lay in wait for him. But pushing someone downstairs isn't a sure way to kill them. I doubt Lara set out to murder Honor – I think she was livid with her for leaving Richie alone, spotted her through Max's window perhaps, and decided to give her a piece of her mind.

'I guess she went in the back way, under the tarpaulin, and her anger spilled over when she challenged Honor. If she knew she'd been drinking with Cleo, who she hated, instead of looking after Freddy's child, that could have triggered it. And then it was all too late.'

There were tears in Stevie's eyes.

'Yet this most recent time, Lara acted deliberately, but Max survived,' Simon said.

Robin nodded. 'It makes sense. When Lara pushed Honor, she was fuelled by hot-blooded anger. The force would have been a lot greater than she could muster, going in cold.'

'So things were going awry,' Eve visualised Lara's panic, 'but she had two lucky breaks: Max didn't see her, and he confused things by assuming it was Perry who'd attacked him. Richie hanging around muddied the waters too. That must have upset Lara. In trying to protect herself, she'd put him in the frame. And then came poor Abby. I believe her death was pure accident.'

They were all quiet. It was desperately sad.

Lara confessed everything to the police. Greg said her emotions made it easier: she was still full of pent-up anger towards Honor and Cleo and intense grief for Freddy and Abby. It was Freddy who'd told her that Richie was his child. Lara hadn't believed him at first. How could he be sure? But she'd watched Richie grow and seen the likeness. When Freddy died, the thought of Richie had kept her going. She'd wished at that point that she could tell Joyce she was Freddy's aunt. She desperately wanted to be part of his life and her mother did too. But Freddy had sworn Lara to secrecy. She couldn't break her promise and she knew what Joyce was like. Telling would unleash her venom and ensure Richie suffered.

She'd made up her mind to try to befriend Honor instead, but it had gone disastrously wrong. She'd guessed it had been Honor who'd told Cleo about Freddy's watch. They were as thick as thieves. Then, on the day Lara had pushed Honor downstairs, she'd heard Richie crying inside the house and realised he was unattended. She said that, and finding Honor drunk and trespassing, left her furious. She'd grabbed her violently by the cardigan she was wearing, tearing it at the seams. Honor hadn't been wearing it when she was found. It was the violent tear which had told Max someone had attacked her. He'd removed the cardigan to hide the truth. It was horrific.

For Lara, it was Freddy's watch which was the final straw. When Lara challenged Honor, she'd burst into tears and confessed to telling Cleo. It was then that Lara had shoved her.

Lara had gone away for a few days before the open-gardens event, just as she'd told Abby, but she'd returned in time to give Perry her mum's necklace to plant at The Briars. She'd broken into Max's garden store and used the tunnel to set up her booby trap under the stairs too, taking time to remove the batteries from Cleo's smoke alarms. As they'd thought, the idea of trying to retrieve her improvised device had seemed too risky. Greg said she'd dug her nails into the palms of her hands as she'd talked about it, drawing blood. But it was too late for regrets now. Poor Abby.

When it came to the attack on Max, she'd been convinced he'd started to wonder if she was involved in Honor's death. She'd remembered the 1066 key-safe code and gone into the house ahead of him. Easy as pie. Except he'd survived.

Lara told Greg that Honor and Cleo only had themselves to blame, but she was devastated about Abby. She'd been one of Lara's few friends. It was grimly ironic. Lara had been isolated, just as Honor was.

Jonah had got to Saxford quickly and hadn't left Stevie's side. He'd made her promise never to hold out on him again. Viv said they'd spent the first day crying and talking about what had happened, but Stevie was seeing a counsellor and Viv was distracting them with final arrangements for the wedding. She'd settled on the cake design at last. It was just as well they'd decided against a recipe that needed to mature.

Richie had been talking to Norah Campbell in Canada. The plans for Marbeck's London expansion were on hold. He was going to take the reins in Suffolk instead with her input, then see how it went from there. Richie had sounded relieved when Eve spoke to him.

He and Lara had both taken a DNA test and it was true, they were very near relations. It must be a huge shock, but everyone said Freddy had been a dear who'd lit up the room. Richie never saw Aiden anyway and he hadn't liked Joyce. He was clutching Freddy's key ring when Eve saw him next.

As for Max, he'd admitted everything, from moving Honor's body to coercing Abby into alibiing his son. Abby had been reporting back when she'd called him from The Briars, the night she died. He was under arrest for perverting the course of justice.

'How serious is it for him?' Eve asked Robin.

'It depends on what happens at the trial. What he did was horrendous. It can carry a life sentence, but I doubt he'll get that.'

Perry's contract to write about Marbeck's had been terminated 'by mutual agreement' and he was going back to London.

Eve's one outstanding query had been answered during Lara's questioning. Cleo and Lara had met in the passageway at the back of Max's place – Eve got that – but given the bad blood between them, how had the alibi arrangement come about?

The background was clear now. Lara *had* become aware of Cleo and Max's affair. She'd seen Cleo starting to push her way through Max's hedge, just after she'd killed Honor. She'd stopped her going any further by claiming she'd just seen Max's wife through a window. When Honor's body was discovered at The Briars, the police wanted to interview Cleo because of the drunken row. Cleo was glad Lara could alibi her, but she'd asked her not to admit she'd seen her trying to enter Max's garden. There was no way she could make that look innocent. She'd begged her to do it for the sake of Max's wife and son. She might have been fed up with Max's inability to end his marriage, but when push came to shove, she hadn't wanted to reveal the truth herself.

Lara had seen an opportunity then – a way to protect herself if the true location of Honor's death was ever revealed. She'd told Cleo she was willing to claim they'd been walking up the river, nowhere near Max's house, but only for a price. Cleo must pay her mother the true value of Freddy's watch. It was cleverly done. If Lara had meekly agreed to Cleo's request, Cleo might eventually have wondered why.

At last, Eve finalised the opening to Cleo's obituary.

CLEO ANITA MARBECK

Entrepreneur and founder of Marbeck's, the renowned vintage jewellery stores

Cleo Marbeck has died in Suffolk at the age of fifty-five. A woman has been arrested for her murder.

It was Cleo's father who taught her the ways of business. She was a favourite of his and accompanied him on trips to buy and sell furniture from a young age. He had a tough approach. To him, it was simply making the most of his natural talent for wheeler-dealing. If he was better informed about an item's value, it wasn't his job to enlighten the person selling the goods. Cleo adopted his 'all's fair in love and war' philosophy. Guilt never seemed to trouble her when she paid a few pounds for jewellery worth thousands. In the early days, it seems likely that she sent spies into the homes of friends and neighbours to check for valuable goods. Armed with her secret knowledge, she approached the owners and quickly made her fortune.

As her business matured, so did she. Her practices

changed a little, though she was still renowned as exceptionally single-minded. She was also charismatic and approach-
able. People tended to say she was indefensible, then admit
that they liked her.

She suffered a lot because of local gossip. Though she
was innocent of the most heinous crimes she was accused of,
there can be no doubt she took advantage of people.

Nevertheless, she was fiercely loyal to those she valued,
such as Richie Hamilton, who will take over the running of
Marbeck's. Richie plans to clean up the business's opera-
tions. You can find his piece here in this magazine.

Robin appeared at her side. 'Ready?'

Eve felt a warm glow. It was character that counted, obviously, but he looked stunning in his dark-grey suit and dress
shoes.

Eve was wearing a cropped jacket and a calf-length fitted
rose-coloured dress, patterned with sprigs of flowers. She hadn't
bought it at Parker's. It was too sad to go back after what had
happened to Abby. She closed her eyes for a moment, then
Robin took her hand, squeezing it as though he knew exactly
what she was thinking.

'Let's go and watch the happy couple tie the knot.' As she
stood, he drew her close. 'I can't wait until it's us!'

When they returned, late that evening, Eve knew that her own
upcoming wedding would be the most perfect day, but that
Stevie and Jonah's would be up there with it. She'd rarely seen a
couple look so joyous. Stevie had all her colour back, and her
eyes had danced as she'd walked up the aisle, towards a highly
emotional Jonah who watched her over his shoulder, his eyes
glistening. Even Gus, who'd been allowed to attend, had looked

affected. Though it was possible Eve hadn't been able to focus properly – her own eyes had been a touch teary.

Robin had passed her a tissue as Jim Thackeray began the wedding vows.

It was time to take a deep breath, be grateful for current happiness and look to the future.

A LETTER FROM CLARE

Thank you so much for reading *Mystery on Meadowsweet Grove*. I do hope you had fun solving the clues! If you'd like to keep up to date with all my latest releases, you can sign up at the following link. Your email address will never be shared, and you can unsubscribe at any time. You'll also receive an exclusive short story, *Mystery at Monty's Teashop*. I hope you enjoy it!

www.bookouture.com/clare-chase

The idea for this book came to me thanks to a beautiful photograph of some snug cottages on a tiny country lane. The setting looked idyllic, but I started to wonder what it would be like, living in such an intimate setting. There must be tensions... And then I imagined amping those pressures up several notches and why such intense feelings might develop. Before long I had my story!

If you have time, I'd love it if you were able to write a review of *Mystery on Meadowsweet Grove*. Feedback is really valuable, and it also makes a huge difference in helping new readers discover my books. Alternatively, if you'd like to contact me personally, you can reach me via my website or social media. It's always great to hear from readers.

Again, thank you so much for deciding to spend some time reading *Mystery on Meadowsweet Grove*. I'm looking forward to sharing my next book with you very soon.

With all best wishes,

Clare x

www.clarechase.com

facebook.com/ClareChaseAuthor
x.com/ClareChase_
instagram.com/clarechaseauthor

ACKNOWLEDGEMENTS

Very much love and thanks for everything to Charlie, George and Ros!

And as ever, I'm more grateful than I can say to my fantastic editor Ruth Tross for her perceptive and inspiring input, which is so important to the final book. I'm also very grateful to Noelle Holten for her fabulous promo work and to Hannah Snetsinger, Fraser Crichton and Liz Hatherell for their expertise. Sending thanks too to Tash Webber for her wonderfully atmospheric cover designs, as well as to Peta Nightingale, Kim Nash and everyone involved in editing, book production and sales at Bookouture. It's a privilege to be published and promoted by such a skilled and friendly team.

Love and thanks also to Mum and Dad, Phil and Jenny, David and Pat, Warty, Andrea, Jen, the Westfield gang, Margaret, Shelly, Mark, my Andrewes relations and a whole bunch of family and friends.

Thanks also to the wonderful Bookouture authors and other writers for their friendship and support. And a huge, whole-hearted thank you to the generous book bloggers and reviewers who pass on their thoughts about my work. I appreciate it so much.

And finally, but importantly, thanks to you, the reader, for buying or borrowing this book!

PUBLISHING TEAM

Turning a manuscript into a book requires the efforts of many people. The publishing team at Bookouture would like to acknowledge everyone who contributed to this publication.

Audio
Alba Proko
Sinead O'Connor
Melissa Tran

Commercial
Lauren Morrissette
Jil Thielen
Imogen Allport

Cover design
Tash Webber

Data and analysis
Mark Alder
Mohamed Bussuri

Editorial
Ruth Tross
Melissa Tran